Chronicles of the Ilaroi
Book One

As Fire is to Gold

Mark McCabe

Serotine Press Australia
www.sereotinepress.com.au

ISBN: 978-0-6484918-0-4

Cover artwork and design by Jeff Brown Graphics
www.jeffbrowngraphics.com

Maps by Fictive Maps
www.facebook.com/fictivemaps/

Author website: https://markmccabeauthor.com

To my mother, Edith, who told me stories and imbued me with a love of books.

To Walter Bellin, who showed me the way to make it happen.

.

ACKNOWLEDGMENTS

Thank you to John Clark, Wayne Barlow and Michael West for all those war games and role-playing games that helped shape my love of fantasy worlds.

Thanks to Jeff Brown for his cover art and cover design. Jeff was a pleasure to deal with. He made the effort to listen to my thoughts and goals, and then wove his magic to reflect them in his work.

A big thank you to the Dunedin Speculative Fiction Group for their support and a special thank you to Kura Carpenter who kept asking the questions I hadn't considered.

And finally, thank you to all those who gave me feedback on the draft text and helped me to mould the story into its final shape.

ignis aurum probat, miseria fortes viros

"Fire is the test of gold; adversity, of brave men."

Seneca
4 BC to 65 AD
Roman philosopher and tutor to the Emperor Nero

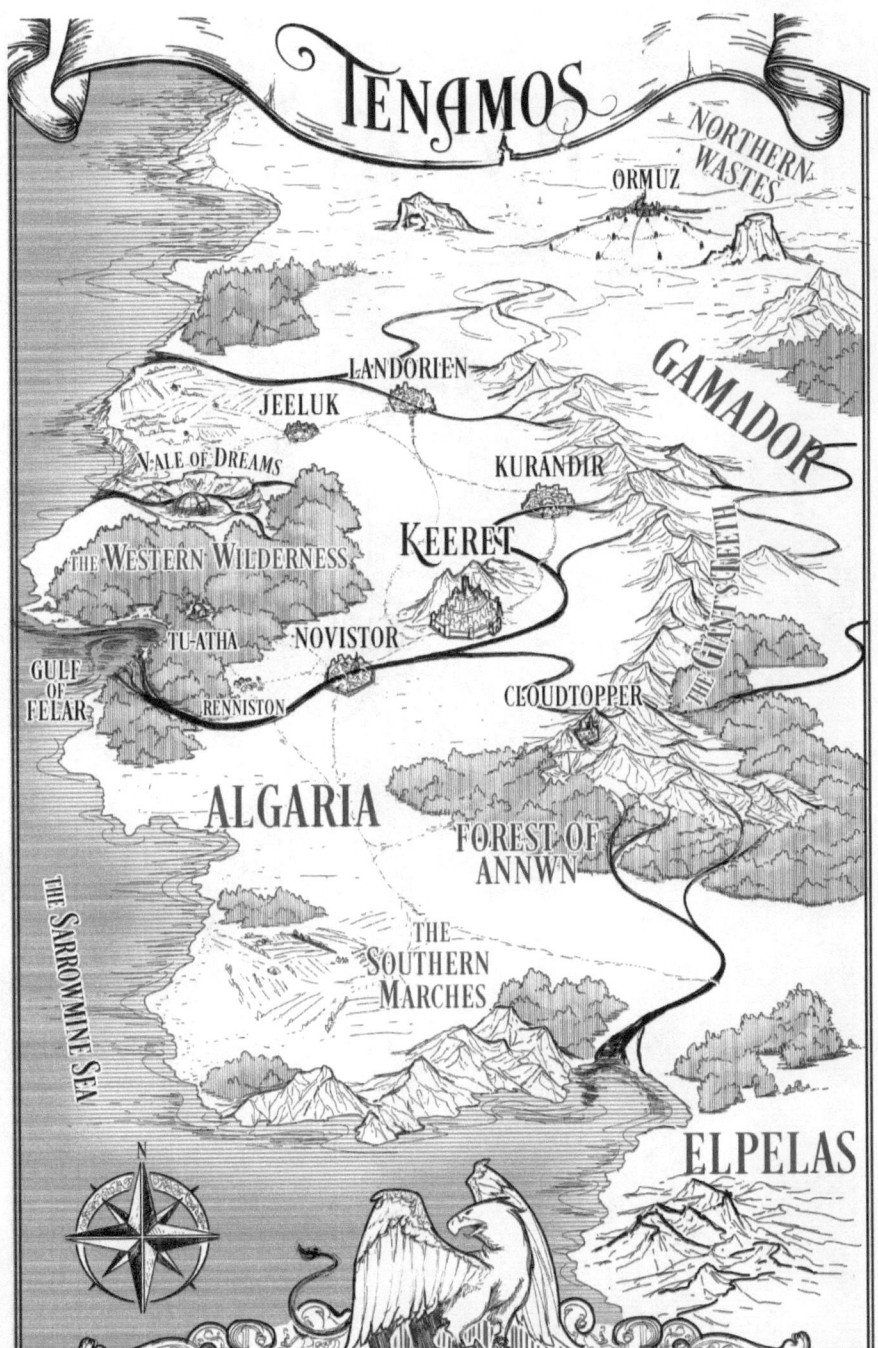

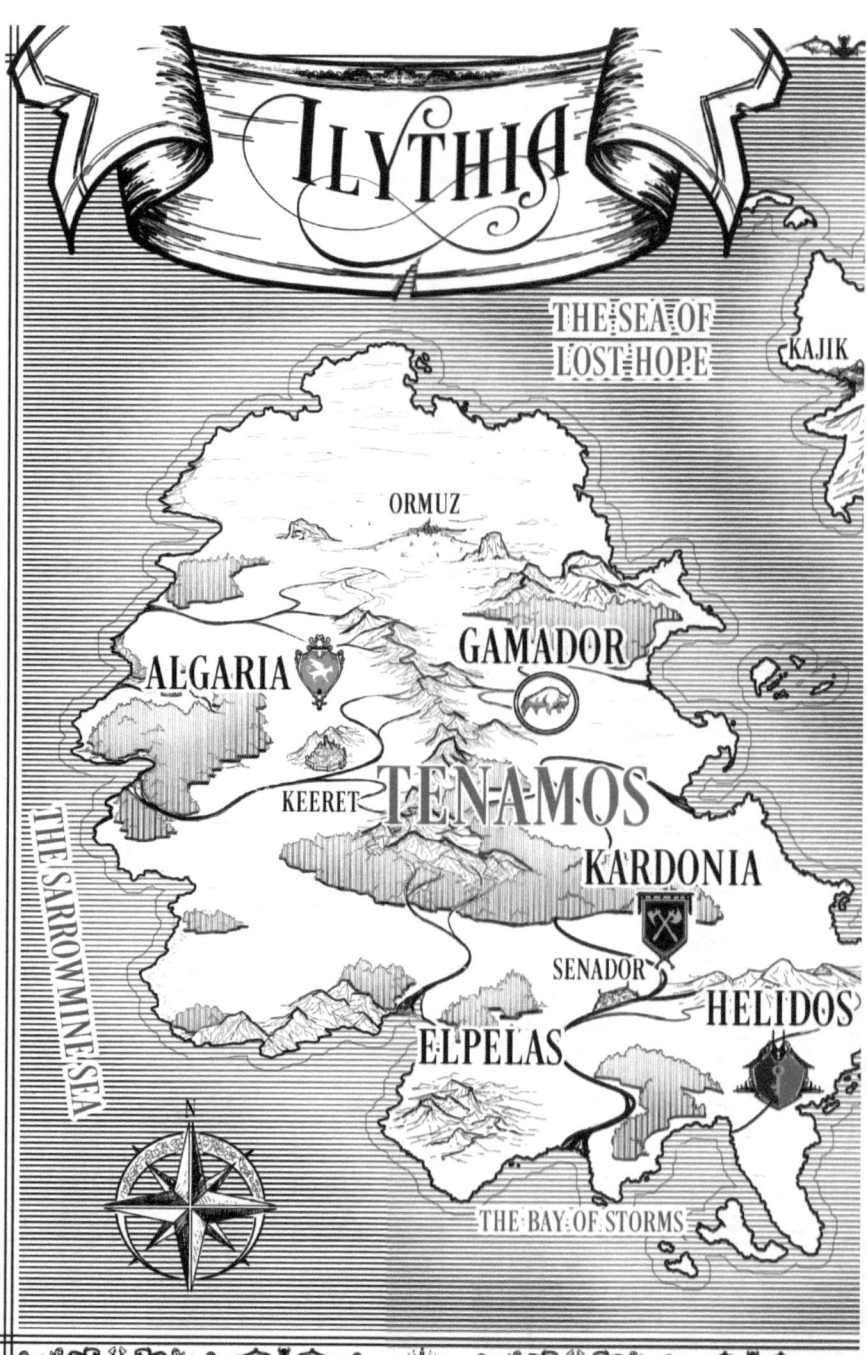

USONOR

F.INDAR

THE DARK WALL

KAJ

NARVONY

LIRICOR

TRINKOLAI

THE TOMB OF THE SUN

BEIRINYA

TALIR

THE BRIDGE
OF ROGAS

TREST

VERINOR

KADRINE

THE ENDLESS SEA

CHAPTER 1

Later, when she'd had time to reflect on what had followed, Sara wondered if the words she had uttered had been the link . . . a thread they had followed, purely by chance, that had led them to her. But that was later. Here, looking up into the seemingly infinite darkness, she had no idea there could be such consequences to something so innocently done. The words had just rolled off her tongue, as easy as the blinking of an eye.

"I wish, just for once," she had said, "that something extraordinary would happen to me."

She had spoken the words out loud . . . well, not 'loud' really; it had been more like a whisper. After all, she didn't want to wake her parents. It was nearly midnight.

Sara had sat up watching television for ages after she'd come home from the library. She found that to be the best form of therapy to balance such intense studying. 'Vegging out' she called it, and it always did the trick, stopping the incessant whirring of her brain cells, slowing everything right down and readying her for sleep.

And that's almost where she was now, about to cross that threshold, the one that takes you from dozing into a deep slumber. She was halfway through the door, almost there. Almost, but not quite.

Just as her fluttering eyelids were about to close for the last time, she heard a noise, a creak of the floorboards. Instinctively, she opened her eyes and turned her head in the direction the noise had come from, knowing as soon as she did so how pointless her reaction was. With the heavy drapes closed, and the light off, her room was blacker than the deepest hole. It would take a while for her eyes to accustom themselves once again to the darkness that enveloped her room. Still, the sound had startled her and she couldn't help but respond.

She lay as still as she could, listening intently in the darkness. The room was silent. All she could hear was her own breathing. She was just overtired. That had to be it. She remembered how, when she was much younger, she would be so scared in the dark sometimes that the slightest noise would startle her. Then she would creep off and slip into her parents' bed. Her dad would carry her back to her own room in the middle of the night and she would wake up the next morning blissfully oblivious to how she had got there.

But she was grown up now. Rational thought had replaced childhood fears. She would have heard if someone had opened the door, and there was certainly nowhere to hide in her room. Apart from her bed, the only pieces of furniture it contained were a chair, a cupboard, and her dressing table. She'd had the cupboard open putting her clothes away just before she went to bed so there couldn't have been someone hiding in there. Sara brought her line of thinking to a halt, wondering what she was doing entertaining such thoughts. It was just a creak of the floorboards after all. Their house always creaked as it cooled in the night air.

Then she heard it again. This time it definitely sounded like it had come from right next to her bed. Slowly, she turned her head, half opening her eyes again despite the improbability of seeing anything. Maybe it was just her mum or dad checking to see if she was all right. They'd been in bed when she got home but it was possible that one of them had got up to check on her. They always worried about her when she went out at night.

Before Sara could turn her head around, her heart jumped as a body pounced on her and a hand clamped over her mouth. More hands grabbed her as she began to fight back. After a brief and frenzied struggle, strong hands finally flipped her over on to her stomach. A knee in Sara's back pinned her in place as a cloth rag replaced the hand over her mouth. She felt someone tying it behind her head, quickly gagging her attempts to cry out for help. At the same time, her arms were roughly pulled up behind her back and twisted painfully towards her shoulder blades. She felt something, rope she assumed, being wound around her wrists, binding them together, pinching her skin as it was pulled tight. Within a matter of seconds, she'd been immobilised.

Sara was frantic. She tried to scream through the gag and desperately wriggled and struggled, but whoever they were, and she could tell that there were at least two of them, they were quick and strong, and they knew what they were doing.

If it hadn't been for the gag, her screams would have been heard a block away. Even as it was, her muffled cries had a clear and instant effect. Someone moved to straddle her waist, sitting astride her lower back. Her heart skipped a beat then as she felt her head yanked back. The person behind her had grabbed her ponytail so violently she arched up from the bed like a bow. Her hair felt like it was being wrenched right out of her scalp and she wondered if they intended to snap her neck. She knew it couldn't possibly stretch any further. Then she felt hot breath against the side of her face as a strange voice came out of the darkness.

"Stop struggling and be very quiet or I'll bleed you here and now little hu-maan. I'll slit that pretty throat of yours and let your blood pump out right here, trussed up like a pig for the Winterfest as you are." It was a male voice with a thick accent. He was whispering right in her ear, so close to her neck she could smell his breath. Indeterminate odours wafted across her face. As he spoke, she felt what must have been a knife, cold and hard, pressing against her throat.

Sara froze. Her heart was pounding and wild thoughts flashed through her mind. She was certain she was going to be killed, or worse. For the first time in her life, she knew genuine terror.

Her fears seemed to be confirmed when she felt a hand on the back of her legs just above her knee. It clearly belonged to someone other than the individual who sat astride her waist; *he* still had her head pulled back with his knife at her throat. For a moment the offending hand lingered, as if its owner was uncertain what to do, then she felt it slowly sliding down her leg towards her ankles, its touch against her skin making her want to heave with revulsion. The muscles of her legs tensed involuntarily, betraying her fear. Sara felt like her heart might burst through her chest. It was hammering so loud she could barely think.

"Be still or die right now," the voice at her ear whispered insistently.

Sara did as she was told. She didn't doubt for one moment she was in serious trouble. It didn't seem right. She was only eighteen; she was too young to die. For a moment, she felt her heart stop and she held her breath. She didn't want to die like this, senselessly, before she'd had a chance to taste life to its full. *No, please no*, she screamed inside her mind, fighting the urge to urinate as her fear, careering out of control, began to peak.

She began to struggle again, kicking her legs violently as she felt the sudden touch of a cord against her ankles. They were trying to bind her legs. For some reason, she determined not to let them. She started to twist and writhe, flailing with her legs and struggling at the same time to throw off the attacker astride her back.

"That's enough, Tug" the voice near her head hissed urgently to his companion. "She ain't getting away. She's already tied good and hard. It'll be easier if she can walk, anyway. He said to make it quick."

"By all the demons of Ergu, just cut the dog!" came the exasperated reply. "That'll keep her quiet." It was another male and he was at the other end of her bed, out of her view. His anger was obvious and he had the same strange accent as his companion.

As he spoke, Sara quickly stopped struggling. Somehow she sensed she'd had a minor victory. She didn't want to push her luck. As she did so, the one astride her waist leaned in close to her ear again and spoke, his voice angry, harsh and full of menace. "That was stupid. I nearly cut you then. You try anything like that again and it'll be the last thing you do." As he spoke he jerked her arm up towards her shoulder blades again, wringing a muffled gasp of pain from his victim.

Without further ado, he moved from his position astride her waist. As he rose, he pulled Sara up as well so that she stood beside the bed next to him, her legs trembling and barely able to support her, her bound wrists held firmly in one of his hands. Her eyes were becoming accustomed to the darkness and her state of semi-slumber had now well and truly fled. She could see the gleaming knife he held in the other hand. For the first time, she also was able to get a proper look at the two men who had somehow gained entry to her bedroom without her hearing a thing. She was more than confused by what she saw.

The man, or more accurately, the boy, who had touched her, was wearing some sort of costume. Sara could only assume it was a disguise, as absurd as that thought was. He looked like someone dressed up for a costume party, or Halloween. His garments, a pair of long trousers and a long-sleeved shirt with no collar, were made of leather, or some other sort of hide. The buttons on his shirt were of the hook and eye type and for a belt, he had a simple cord, knotted at the front. It was his face that really caught her eye, however.

His ears were slightly pointed at the top and his face was covered in a light down, almost like fur. Sara could only assume he was wearing a mask; one of those rubber masks you can buy in costume shops, the ones you pull right down over your whole head. This one was an elf-mask, or at least something like that. It was so realistic she could almost believe he really was an elf, the backwoods attire adding to its authenticity. Turning her head she saw that the person standing next to her was similarly dressed.

Sara thought it peculiar that someone would go to the trouble of such elaborate make-up for a break-in, or even an abduction. How in the hell a costume was going to help them if they tried to take her outside was beyond her. Her thoughts flitted back to the few words she had heard them speak. The one next to her had said something about a 'he', as if there was someone else waiting for them. It didn't make sense. Was there a whole gang of them somewhere, perhaps downstairs, waiting for these two to join them? What could they possibly want?

Whatever they were after, she decided she wasn't going anywhere without a struggle and as much noise as she could make. Once out in the corridor, she would make sure she made a hell of a racket no matter what the consequences.

For a moment it occurred to Sara she might be dreaming. What was happening to her was like something out of a movie, not real life. Before she could focus properly on the proposition, the one behind her yanked on her bonds, disrupting her line of thought. "Let's get going," he hissed as he took her elbow in a tight grip and started dragging her across the room.

Now she knew she was dreaming. They weren't heading for the door, or the window for that matter. In the corner, towards which she was being dragged, and where there should have been a chair with her dressing gown draped over it, there was some sort of opening. It looked completely surreal, a rough slit in the air from just above the floor to just below the ceiling, with light peeping through it. Sara shook her head, convinced it would disappear. But it didn't. It was still there. It looked like a movie screen with a film being projected onto it and a long rip in it, with light shining through from behind. To Sara's complete astonishment, before she could examine it more closely her captor stepped up to the slit, pulled it aside with one hand and stepped into the bright light, taking her with him. Sara felt herself pulled through.

I say *through* because that is what it felt like; as if she were pushing through a heavy curtain or some sort of similar barrier. Incredibly, it had no depth to speak off. She immediately moved from the darkness of her bedroom into an area of intense light. Now she could see nothing at all except herself, her abductor, and bright, sourceless light; sort of like being in a snowstorm, a whiteout she thought they called it. Wherever she was now, there were no apparent boundaries, no up or down, no sides. It seemed limitless.

Before she could make any sense of this new environment, she was pulled through yet another opening. The impossible scene she'd just experienced vanished as quickly as it had appeared. This time she found herself in a room again, though it was no room she had ever seen before, and certainly not one in her house. It had a wooden floor and the walls seemed to be made of large stone blocks. Sara swayed on her feet. She felt dizzy and slightly sick, like she had just got off a merry-go-round.

Although her heart was still hammering insistently against the walls of her chest, demanding to be let out, the turmoil in her mind took on a new form. Disabling fear receded to a corner of her awareness, allowing her senses a chance to absorb and analyse the new information that was flooding in. What was happening to her simply did not compute, however, and her mind struggled to make any sense of the bizarre situation she found herself in.

She had to be dreaming. That was the only explanation that made any sense at all. Only this was so weird. She had never had such a vivid dream in her life, or one where her sense of touch and smell had been so acute. She tended to *think* things were happening to her in her dreams, not to feel and smell them. But this didn't seem like a dream at all; on the contrary, it felt very real. At the same time, she knew the things that she was experiencing, that she was seeing, simply didn't happen in real life. Real people don't have pointed ears and you can't step through a rip in the air and go from your bedroom into some house you have never seen before. It had to be a dream. Her mind could find no other rational explanation.

More like a nightmare than a dream, she suddenly thought. Her arm hurt from where her captor was holding her. He still had her in a vice-like grip and the pinched skin stung like hell. She didn't like the way the other boy had touched her either, the way his hand had lingered on her leg.

Pushing those thoughts from her mind, Sara stared at the opening through which she had come. It looked much the same from this side as it had done from her room. She watched the second boy pulling it open and stepping through to join them. Behind him, she could see the same bright light she had experienced. Once he was through, the opening closed and the slit simply winked out of existence. If it weren't for her strange new surroundings, Sara would have been quite willing to believe it had never really been there in the first place. Its disappearance offered her no relief, however. Somehow Sara knew that getting back home had just become a lot harder.

Looking around, she slowly took in her new surroundings. Her eyes were immediately drawn to a young girl seated at a table a few paces from where she stood. Sara hadn't noticed her at first as she had been focusing on the strange means by which she had arrived in the room. Now that she saw they weren't alone, however, she took little comfort from the presence of another person. If anything, it only served to heighten her fears.

The girl, who looked very young, perhaps twelve or thirteen years of age, was seated upright at the table, but with her head slumped forward, as if she was asleep or unconscious. With a shock, Sara realised she was tied to the chair. Her young face looked unusually pale and her hair was wet, as if matted with sweat. A thin trickle of blood ran from her nose to her upper lip. Sara reeled in horror at the spectacle before her. This was no longer a simple abduction. Her situation had suddenly changed from the incredible to the macabre, her state of mind from one of apprehension and confusion to revulsion.

Looking around frantically, she could see that the room they were now in was nearly twice as big as her bedroom. Two thick rugs covered wooden floorboards, and the walls, which consisted of big rough blocks of stone, seemingly held together with some sort of mortar, were bare except for a map on one wall and a large tapestry depicting a hunting scene of some kind on another. A big open fireplace in the centre of one wall, a heavy wooden table almost covered in old books and sheets of paper, some of the latter rolled up like scrolls, a few chairs, a window set into a deep casement and a wooden door were the only other items of note.

Looking up, Sara saw that the ceiling was made of wooden beams, blackened on the side closest to the fire, which was blazing away strongly.

The thing she found most unusual, however, was the way everything appeared so roughly made, so old in some indefinable way. The room had none of the accoutrements Sara took for granted living in a modern city as she did. In fact, there were no signs of anything modern at all, no evidence of electricity, no appliances of any kind. Light was provided by the fire and a large wooden torch burning in a bracket on the wall beside the door.

The fire made the room quite warm, for which Sara was most thankful. All she had on was the nightshirt she had been sleeping in when the two strangers had grabbed her. She flushed in embarrassment as she suddenly realised how she must look.

Though there was much about her appearance she would like to change, Sara sensed that she was at least moderately attractive and was glad to have inherited her mother's tall, slender build. She'd seen the appreciate glances she drew from men when she worked out at the local gym, and she liked that attention, even if she still wasn't always quite sure of the best way to handle it. It was a welcome change from the feelings of inadequacy she'd endured through her early teens. Her form and looks had undergone some substantive changes over the last few years; she only had to look at her old school photos to see that.

Not that she was unhappy with the transformation. Slowly but surely her circle of companions was changing, from one dominated by members of her own sex to a much more evenly balanced mix. The increasing attention she was receiving from boys at college was helping her build a sense of self-confidence that would have been unthinkable to the shy girl she had been at school. Where she'd once dreaded being the centre of attention, now she felt much more relaxed . . . normally that is.

At the moment, her long black hair was pulled back into a ponytail for sleeping and she was dressed for bed, which meant a short nightshirt and nothing else. The attention of boys at college was one thing, but she desperately wanted to cover herself in front of these strangers.

With the arrival of the second boy, her captor turned her around. It was then she noticed the man seated in the armchair in the corner behind her. She'd had her back to him until then and hadn't noticed him, even when she had turned to review her surroundings. She got quite a shock when she turned around to see him there, realising he must have been watching them all of the time.

He was an older man, possibly in his forties or fifties, about her dad's age she guessed. Like the two boys she had already met, he also was strangely attired, wearing a long, richly embroidered, maroon robe, belted at the waist with a broad black sash. His hair was jet black, as was the goatee beard and moustache he sported. The latter gave him a swash-buckling sort of look, very debonair and all that sort of thing, although something about him made him seem more menacing than dashing to Sara; the way he looked at her perhaps, running his eyes over her body, his gaze lingering in a way that made her feel decidedly uncomfortable. The armchair he was seated in was like one of those big ones she'd seen in some rich person's study in a movie, very masculine and very comfortable looking, with big, curved, padded arms.

Paradoxically, despite a real sense of presence about him, he didn't look very well to Sara. Like the young girl at the table, he was quite pale and had hardly moved in the time she was looking at him. He just stared at her in an intense, unnerving sort of way. At least he wasn't wearing a mask. He looked very human.

Sara watched as he lifted himself up from the chair and, with a sense of great fatigue, began to approach her.

~~~

Golkar's mind was drifting. He was struggling to keep focus. He wanted so much to sleep, to let the growing blackness envelop him, to let it wash over and embrace him. It seemed so desirable, so enticing, so right to want to succumb. He wanted to rest. If he could sleep there would be no need to struggle anymore, no need for the pain to continue. He could just slip down into the darkness. It would be so easy.

But no. Something was not right about that path. Something deep inside him rang out a warning. The darkness offered false respite. It was the harbinger of doom, a siren's call, not a welcoming note. If he gave in to that enticement he would be lost, perhaps forever. That was it. That was the very thing he must not do. He remembered that much at least. He must keep fighting it. He must not give in. He had to resist. He knew that he had to find his way back, wherever back was, no matter how tired he felt, no matter how hard it seemed.

He tried to focus on the light at the periphery of his vision. That would help, he was sure. And it did. It felt right. Slowly, like climbing a long ladder with a sack full of rocks slung across his shoulders, Golkar willed himself back, back from the abyss. Time passed. He could not tell how long. Minutes? Hours? Days? Who could tell? He felt clammy. He could feel the sweat running down his back, dripping from his brow. This was his greatest challenge, his greatest test. Never before had he felt that he was losing control, that he might not even *want* to return, let alone be able. The void was something to be tapped, not a destination, he had always known that before, never been tempted to join it.

The light, which had been a blur at first, was like a beacon now. Something to steer by. A marker. Yes. Another memory. He had embedded that thought before he began, use the light as a marker to guide his return if he was in danger of losing contact. He struggled towards it with all of his might now, concentrating, fighting the blackness which even yet gripped him, clinging to him like quicksand.

And then it was done. With a final wrench of his mind, and his body, he awoke, like someone suddenly freed from a terrifying nightmare. His flailing arm struck the candle beside him, knocking it aside and scattering wax across the papers strewn in front of him. He had made it; he'd survived. The sense of relief was so strong, so liberating. But what of the spell?

Lifting his head, the first thing he saw was the girl seated across from him, dead now, just a husk. He remembered. He had used her essence, her life force, every drop of it, to weave his spell. That was a first. He had never sucked someone completely dry like that before, never needed to. He remembered how exhilarating that had felt. How he had felt the build-up of power within him as he delved to the very depths of her soul, seeking out the very last vestiges of her spirit. How she had cried out in the end, begging for release, pleading for mercy. How the last dregs of her essence had slipped from her, leaving her empty, skin and bones, blood and flesh, but nothing else, lifeless, a shell. There was nothing to compare with that, thought Golkar, nothing in this world. But what of the spell? Had it worked?

Golkar's eyes searched the room, quickly finding what he sought, shimmering in the corner of the room. Leaning back in his chair, he raised his clenched fists above his head in exultation. He had done it. He had achieved what had been done before by only one other, by Tanis himself.

There, in the corner of his study, the portal hung, a tear in the fabric of space and time, the radiance of the void beyond peeping through the opening as he had expected it would. He had achieved the unthinkable; nay, the seemingly unattainable. He had created a bridge to another world and another time.

A further quick scan of the room revealed no sight of Ruz or Tug. They must have gone through, as he had told them to do if he succeeded. Now all that they had to do was bring back what he needed. Doubt flickered momentarily across his thoughts. If it was there. If the spell had correctly targeted what he sought. Surely he couldn't fail now, he tried to assure himself, not after having come so far. Everything hinged on this venture's success, nothing could be more important.

Important. What a small word for something that would change the fate of the world.

The fate of Ilythia . . . in *his* hands! How right that felt. How could he doubt it? They would succeed. He had done the hard part, the rest would be easy now, even for Ruz and Tug. Tanis' diary had been quite clear on how to do it, *and* on what it could deliver. The question had always been whether he could summon the mana required, and he had, even though it had taken him to the very brink.

The Spell of Portal had been the most difficult he had ever attempted, by a very large degree. Its execution had almost been his undoing, it had nearly killed him. It certainly had killed the young peasant who had lent her essence to the enterprise. He was sure that the other Guardians had no idea it could even be done, assuming they would be willing to try it themselves, which he doubted. That, of course, was the best part of his plan. They wouldn't know how he had done it.

What a plan he had forged, so simple in conception, so daring in execution; to bring into this world something outside of the balance established by the Ilaroi, a life force from another place and time. A small thing in so many ways and yet it would be enough, enough to upset the balance.

As it was, the Guardians were equally matched. No one could overthrow another, let alone the combined powers of the remaining two. But to introduce an alien element, something from another world, that was the stroke of genius that Golkar knew only he could have devised. Certainly, finding Tanis' diary had helped, but no one else had even thought to look for it. Golkar knew that the spells he could weave with the blood of such a creature would outdo even this one, unparalleled as it was. Then he would make them rue the day they underestimated him, Kell, Tarak, even the pitiful Algarians. He would watch them all bend their knees to him. That and so much more.

His mind wandered on for some time in this fashion, re-examining each of the elements of his plan, like a jeweller admiring the intricacies of a many-faceted gem. His weariness finally brought him back. The spell had sapped his energy like none before it and he knew he would need rest before he went on.

Straightening himself in the chair, Golkar rose wearily from the table. Reaching over he righted the candle. With his remaining strength, he dragged himself from the table to the armchair in the corner of the room, turned, and slumped into it. And there he sat, settling in to wait for the return of his minions.

It hadn't taken long; a matter of minutes at most. Of course, he realised, it might have taken much longer for them. He couldn't be sure; time may have moved differently where they had been. He watched silently, exultantly, as Ruz stepped through with the young girl, bound and gagged as they had planned. A smile of satisfaction crossed his face as he saw that the spell had worked just as Tanis' notes had indicated it would.

Golkar's gaze roamed greedily over the otherworld creature before him. Innocent blood. She will do nicely, he thought to himself, very nicely. Any life force would have done, but an innocent, all the better. And beautiful to boot. His anger flared momentarily as he wondered if Ruz or Tug had tampered with his prize. He would flay them alive if they had. She was not for the likes of them. She was destined for something much more than that.

From the corner of his eye, he saw Tug step through and the portal close behind him. Golkar felt a sense of relief with it sealed. With the three of them safely through the portal, he watched Ruz look around for his master, turning the girl to face him when he spied the wizard seated in the armchair behind them.

He was pleased with the startled look that crossed her face as she turned. She hadn't noticed him until then. How perfect, he thought. She was scared, and rightly so, like a trapped animal with nowhere to run. He was definitely going to enjoy this.

Now that he had a clearer view of her, Golkar drank in her loveliness, this prize beyond all prizes, watching her squirm under his gaze. She was a rare beauty, he thought, tall, and slim, an innocent young girl on the verge of womanhood. Golkar couldn't contain his excitement. He had to touch this treasure, to have one last drink of the cup of attainment before he rested. He could already smell her fear. He wanted to feel it as well, to feel her tremble at his touch.

Wearily he raised himself from the chair and approached his two servants, and the bound girl trembling at Ruz' side. The power, which had swelled to a crescendo within him when he had summoned the Spell of Portal, was slowly subsiding. As it did so it seemed to drain him of energy.

"You have done well, Ruz, and you too, Tug," he said as he approached them. "You will be rewarded for this. Was there any trouble?"

"It was as easy as bagging a bantuk," replied Ruz, smirking. "She never had a chance. It was just as you said it would be."

"And what is your name, my lovely?" asked Golkar, turning to the girl. Motioning for Ruz to undo her gag, he waited the few moments it took for his command to be accomplished.

He knew that she would have no difficulty understanding him. Undoubtedly his words would be in a language the girl couldn't possibly have any experience of. But that didn't matter. One of the beauties of the portal was the cunningly wrought Spell of Translation embedded within it. It affected anyone travelling through the portal, no matter which direction they travelled in. Because of its effect they understood whatever language was spoken to them in the world they had entered, and they, probably without even realising it, in turn, would speak in the language of whoever they encountered in that world. Just as Ruz and Tug would have been able to understand and be understood by Sara in her world, the reverse was true for her now that she had entered Ilythia.

"Sara," the girl replied, interrupting his thoughts and looking up at him with wide eyes once the cloth was removed from her mouth. "What's this all about?" she asked breathlessly. "Wh . . . why have you brought me here?"

"Never mind that," he replied. "Sara. A strange name. But then I guess you're finding all of this a bit strange." As he spoke he raised his hand to the girl's face, lightly brushing his fingertips across her cheek as she flinched from his touch.

Golkar felt the tingle and crackle of power as his skin touched hers, but too late to stop it. Desperately, realising the danger, he tried to pull back, but it was useless. It took only the merest fraction of a second for the energy to course up through her body, across the contact point where his skin touched hers, along his arm and throughout his frame. Suddenly, and unexpectedly, the energy from two worlds combined chaotically in Golkar's body, welling up, out of control, hers drawn to his all the quicker by the spell's residue within him.

With a scream, Golkar was flung back across the room, his body thudding into the wall behind him. His carcass slumped to the floor like a broken doll. Ruz and Tug both stood there, mouths agape in astonishment. Sara's cheek tingled where he had touched her. She had felt nothing more than that.

CHAPTER 2

Ruz bent down and placed his head against Golkar's chest.

"He lives," he announced, standing up. His sideways glance at Sara showed a deal more respect than he had been prepared to grant her previously. "I think he's unconscious, but he lives. What was that? It was incredible. I actually saw it arc across his arm toward her and then jolt back throughout his body. I don't understand. We've both touched her and nuthin happened to us."

"I know," replied Tug. "I've never seen it like that before, with me eyes I mean, just what he could do with it."

As Tug spoke, Golkar groaned. The wizard's arm twitched slightly as he reached out and grabbed hold of Ruz, like a drowning man, desperately searching for something to cling to. His eyes fluttered and a series of tremors rippled across his prostrate form.

"Get the hu-maan locked away . . . quickly," commanded Ruz, as he knelt to help his master. His voice betrayed his concern. "Then come back here and help me."

Before Tug could move to obey, Sara made her move. She'd stood silently while her captors had attended to their master, realising this might be her chance to escape. Wrenching herself away from Tug, who had not had as firm a grip on her as Ruz had had, she darted for the door, only to realise that with her hands tied behind her back there was no way she could open it. Spinning around to look for other options, she found herself slammed into the door by a charging Tug. Quickly grabbing her as she thudded against the door, he twisted her wrist with one hand and gave her a stinging slap across the face with the other.

"Don't try anything like that again dog or you'll really know what pain is," he snarled, his face inches from hers. As he spoke, he opened the door and pushed her out into the corridor.

Sara grunted as she stumbled and fell heavily against the wall opposite. Her shoulder scraped across the stone as she fell to the floor. With her arms tied, there was nothing she could do to break her fall. Her head thumped sickeningly against the floorboards. She had barely hit the floor when Tug was on her again, pulling her roughly to her feet and dragging her down the corridor, away from the room she'd arrived in. Sara stumbled uncertainly after him.

Torchlight flickered across the floor as she shuffled along in his wake, half in a daze and with little awareness anymore of where she was. Her head rang and tears blotted her eyes. Unable to wipe her face, and with her vision blurring, she could barely see her feet in front of her. Searing pain radiated across her cheek from where she'd been slapped. Her shoulder felt like it was broken. Tug was cruelly twisting her wrists as he dragged her along behind him and the rope was burning her skin despite her attempts to move with him.

Sara was dimly aware of steps down and a turn, followed by more steps and more turns. Before she could regain any real sense of direction, Tug opened a door at the end of a corridor and pushed her through it. Once more she stumbled and fell. As she lay there slumped on the floor, too dazed to move, she felt Tug kneel behind her and undo the bonds at her wrists. To her relief, he went no further, seemingly satisfied that he could expect no more trouble from her for a while at least. A moment later she heard a key turn and click and realised he'd left.

Rolling over, Sara dry retched with her face inches from the dusty floor. She felt shivers running through her body as she eased herself to the floor, curling up as she fought the urge to vomit again.

She lay there shivering for some time. After what seemed like hours, but was probably much less, she slowly began to regain her composure. She felt like she had been to hell and back. Her mouth tasted of bile and it seemed that whichever way she moved she hurt. Rubbing her wrists, she dragged herself to a sitting position, wiping the tears from her eyes as she did so.

Looking about, Sara surveyed the small room to which she had been consigned. From the sound of the lock turning when Tug had left, she guessed that she'd been put somewhere 'safe' and out of the way. Her instant appraisal was that this was indeed the case. Her current accommodation looked, and felt, distinctly like a cell.

For one thing, the room's one door bore a metal plate, a little bit like a letterbox slot, at about head height, no doubt for looking and passing things through. If any further confirmation was needed, it could be found in the room's sparse furnishings. Functionality and not comfort had clearly been the primary goal. The only items of furniture were a bed, a small table, and a wooden box. A porcelain basin sat on the table. This was not a room anyone would choose to spend much time in, assuming they had a choice.

The wooden framed bed stood beside her. On top of a lumpy, hessian covered mattress lay a pillow and two blankets. The blankets were neatly folded and positioned at one end. At the opposite end, equally tidily placed, lay what appeared to be a set of clothes. It seemed to constitute a shirt and a pair of trousers. The latter brought a small but welcome glimmer of hope. If only they would fit her. She felt very exposed in her nightclothes.

Sara remained where she was for a few minutes, then pulled herself up and explored more thoroughly, shuffling painfully around the room. The door was locked, as she had expected, and the grate couldn't be opened from her side. The box turned out to be a primitive toilet of sorts. The lid was hinged and had a hole you could sit over with a metal bucket inside which could obviously be taken out and emptied. The porcelain basin contained water, whether for cleaning or drinking she was not sure, but she did both, cupping her hands to drink first and then washing her face and hands.

A lantern hanging from a hook near the door provided light. There was no window. Though a small grate with bars, very high up on one wall, appeared to let in fresh air, the room had a musty smell. Clearly, the ventilation was inadequate. Other than that, it was reasonably clean, though the mattress had seen better days. It was stained and gave off a rather earthy smell. She thought it might be filled with straw or something similar. Sara continued to shiver as she quickly changed into the clothes provided. They were a surprisingly close fit for her. A welcome find of a pair of moccasin shoes completed the outfit.

Adequately dressed for the first time since her ordeal had begun, Sara sat on the edge of the bed. Now she was alone, the enormity of what had happened to her began to sink in. She'd been abducted from her house in the middle of the night and taken to a strange place where everything looked like it belonged in a museum. Of the four people she had encountered, one, a girl, had been bound and badly hurt and two of them looked like elves. And then there was her bizarre encounter with that man.

To add to all of this, she had been slapped, shoved and pawed almost continuously from the moment her ordeal had begun. She knew her body would be a mass of bruises within hours. Finally, she had been locked in a room that could only be described as a cell. God only knew what they planned for her next. It didn't even bear thinking about.

Sara slumped to the floor again, leaning back against the edge of the bed and pulling her knees up to her chest as she did so. Dragging a blanket around her shoulders and wrapping her arms around her knees, she soon found herself sobbing uncontrollably. She could no longer hold back. *I want to go home*, she thought. *Please, just let me go home.*

Sara's eyes flew open as she heard the click of her alarm clock, that telltale sound it always made just seconds before it rang. She was home. It had all been a dream after all, a horrible dream, but just a dream. She felt a smile creeping out from the corners of her mouth. She had never been so happy to greet a new day in her life, even if it was a weekday. Sunlight glinting off the mirror on her bedside table momentarily blinded her as she rolled over, still groggy with sleep, to switch off the alarm before it could ring. At that same moment, she heard her bedroom door opening.

Shading her eyes with one hand, Sara looked up at the shape in the doorway. Her stomach churned as she recognised her visitor.

It was Tug. The dread creature stood there for a moment, leering at her, with a tray in his hands, then stepped into the room. Her smile withered in an instant. The sound she had heard had been the click of the lock as he had opened it. Sunlight bouncing off the lantern on the wall was the source of the warm beam on to her face.

It was morning, that much was right, but this was not her bedroom. She was still in her cell. The lumpy mattress, the stale smells, Tug; they all made her wonder how she could have been fooled. This nightmare wasn't over yet, no matter how much she might wish it.

Snapping back to reality, Sara frantically scrambled to the back of the bed, crouching against the wall with the blanket pulled up around her body with one hand and her other arm defensively shielding her face. She grimaced as she felt the stabbing pain in her shoulder, remembering Tug's rough treatment of her the night before. It all came flooding back to her, in a rush, as if a tap had been suddenly turned. "P-please don't hurt me," she stammered. Her heart was thumping and her eyes swam as unbidden tears began to flow.

The terror of the previous night flashed through her mind. She'd been distraught by the time Tug had locked her in the cell and she had sat on the floor crying and sobbing hysterically for what must have been hours. She had no idea how long she had stayed there but remembered climbing up onto the bed at one stage and pulling the blanket over her. The floor had been cold and the bed had offered warmth, if not comfort. Thankfully, once she had finally gotten off to sleep, she had slept right through the night.

And now she had awoken to another confrontation with the creature that had assaulted her the night before. 'Creature' was the only word she could apply. She didn't know what else to call him. He clearly wasn't human.

To Sara's relief, her fear of Tug was unfounded this time. She'd been convinced that when she saw him or Ruz next they would be coming to take her away to do something ghastly to her, like whatever it was they had done to the girl she had seen. Tug made no attempt to approach her, however, and the tray he was carrying appeared to bear food, for her it would seem. Her instant thought was of death-row prisoners, waiting for their sentence to be executed. Maybe this was to be her last meal.

Tug simply laughed at her as she cowered on the bed. "Don't worry, me pretty," he sneered. "You're safe for the moment. The boss is laid up for a while so you'll be our . . . 'guest' till he's better. I've brought you some lovely grub. I ain't a bad cook when I put me hand to it." The last was said with a surprising sense of pride. With that he turned and left, locking the door behind him as he went. Sara hadn't missed seeing the dagger sheathed at his waist as he had turned.

As the lock clicked back into place, she felt the tears begin to run down her cheeks once again. She had hoped she would wake up back in her own bed and realise it had all been a horrible dream, and for a few brief moments when she had woken she had convinced herself that was the case. But it wasn't to be. Here she was, right back in the middle of her nightmare.

Realising she was still cringing against the wall, she tried to relax a little, consciously easing the tension in her body. It was then that she realised how much her shoulder ached. Just to move it was painful. Moving carefully to the edge of the bed, she gingerly undid her shirt, easing one sleeve down so she could examine her neck and arm more closely. As she had suspected, a massive bruise covered most of her left shoulder and a large part of her upper arm. Twisting, she was aware that her hip also hurt. Standing and easing her trousers down on one side, she quickly found more bruising. She must have landed there when she fell.

Sitting down and wiping her eyes, Sara turned her attention to the tray Tug had left for her, finding a bowl of warm soup, some rough chunks of bread and a mug of hot liquid that might have been tea or something similar. At least it was clear they didn't intend to starve her. Tentatively, she tried some of the soup.

Once again, she was surprised. Tug's boast regarding his cooking hadn't been too far off the mark. The soup was very tasty and within a few minutes it was all gone, along with the bread, wolfed down with little regard for the manners Sara had been taught by her parents.

Her hunger satiated, she leaned back cautiously against the wall, careful not to aggravate any sore spots. She stayed there like that for some time, sipping her drink, which smelt, incredibly, of cloves and honey, and wondering with an increasing feeling of despair what was going to happen to her next. Her reverie was rudely interrupted a short while later when Tug returned for her plates.

At his appearance, Sara scurried across the bed again, huddling with her back to the corner as he opened the door, her heart pounding. To her great relief, once again he made no attempt to harm her or touch her. "Ate it all up, did we?" he exclaimed smugly when he saw the empty bowls. He took the tray away then, locking the door behind him again as he left.

She was left alone for the rest of that day. Although in many ways it was a relief not to have to face them again, after a while she almost wished someone would come and talk to her. Just sitting there waiting only gave her more time to worry and to think of dread things they might have planned for her. Try as she could to avoid thinking about it, grim and

wouldn't take kindly to an attempt at escape. If she didn't succeed, she could end up much worse off than if she did nothing at all.

Then she realised that wasn't possible. How could she be worse off? They had killed the girl she had seen. She had to risk something or that would be her fate as well. It was no use waiting until she could think of the perfect plan. She knew if she didn't act soon Golkar would come for her and that would be it. Game over, as they say.

There was in the end then, no real choice. The plan she had settled on was the best she could come up with and it would have to do. At least its greatest virtue was its simplicity. She knew it would have to be executed flawlessly, though, and she went over it again and again in her mind, trying not to think about the fact that, no matter how well she performed, luck would have to be on her side if she was to have even the slightest chance of success.

That night, when she went to bed, Sara said a final prayer. "Please God," she whispered in the darkness. "If you are there, if there even is a God, please help me. I know I haven't always been the best person, but I don't think I've been so bad as to deserve this. Please help me get out of here."

After that she went through the plan again, going over the weak points. There were many. What if they didn't do what she expected? What if they changed their routine? What if she froze up and couldn't do it? And then the big ones. What if there were other people in the house she didn't know about? There might be many of these draghar. And if she did get away, would she be able to find her way out of the building she was in? Would she run into Golkar? And what would she do if she did get out? Where is out and where would she go?

Slowly, and methodically, Sara went through her answers to each of these problems. First up, she knew her plan had flaws but she had already established she had to try something. If they didn't do as she hoped they would, she would just have to improvise. Her coach had said she was good at that, 'a good tactical thinker, quick-witted and inspirational' he had once written on her report card at school. If Ruz and Tug changed their routine she might just have to wait till another day. As to her freezing up, that was simply not an option. She would do what she had to. She had no choice.

She knew there was a possibility that Ruz and Tug weren't the only ones in the house other than Golkar. In all of her time there she had not seen anyone else, however, and all of her attempts to find out more on the subject had been either deflected or ignored. As to finding her way out, she was just going to have to trust to instinct and luck. Sure, she had no idea what would happen when she got out, or even where in the hell she was. One thing was for sure though, out had to be better than in.

It was some time before she could get off to sleep. She knew that the next day she would be either out of there or in even deeper trouble than she was now.

Sara sat nervously on the edge of the bed, waiting for Tug to arrive with her breakfast. She had woken early, anticipation of the day better than any alarm clock. Quickly preparing as morning light filtered through the grate, she had then had to sit and wait, tense and apprehensive, going over her plan and psyching herself up as she did for a big basketball game. She was as ready now as she would ever be. As she leaned back, trying to appear calm and relaxed despite her anxiety, her right arm firmly grasped the wooden strut she had prised loose from the end of her bed. She felt her heart rate increase as Tug's footsteps approached the door. She held her breath as she heard his key turn in the lock.

Tug gave Sara no more than the casual glance she usually got as he swung open the door. Stepping into the room, he moved to place the tray of food on the table beside her bed, exactly as she had expected. As he turned and bent, Sara sprang into action, adrenaline fuelling her effort. In a flash she was up off the bed, swinging the club down towards his head.

Quick though she was, Tug was even quicker. Somehow sensing the unexpected movement behind him, he quickly turned, spying the lump of wood in her hand and ducking under it in one deft movement. Grabbing Sara's arm and spinning her around with ease, he twisted her wrist painfully up behind her back, wrenching the makeshift club from her hand as he did so.

Sara struggled futilely as Tug wrestled her towards the bed. It had all gone wrong. She couldn't believe she had been thwarted so abruptly. With her arm twisted painfully behind her and frustration fuelling her anger, she desperately tried to kick out at Tug with her legs, succeeding only in catching the food tray and scattering its contents against the wall and onto the floor of her cell.

"Ya filthy little grink," Tug snarled from behind her as he brought her other arm up, holding them both behind her. "I told ya I'd make ya pay if ya tried anythin like that again." As he spoke, he lifted her twisting body off the floor and pushed her from him across the bed.

Sara lashed out at him with her flailing legs as she fell, but once again Tug was too agile for her. Laughing, he dodged her foot with a quick jump in the air, shoving her away from him as he did so.

Not quite as clever as he thought though. As his feet came down, one skidded out from under him, catching the angled edge of an upturned bowl instead of the firm floor. With his other foot still in the air, there was nothing he could do to regain his footing. With a shock, Tug found himself reeling backwards, unable to stop his fall. His arms, which had released the struggling girl as he had flung her across the bed, desperately reached out for something to grab onto as he went down.

Sara heard a loud crack from behind her as she hit the bed. Turning around quickly to defend herself from the onslaught she expected from her enraged captor, she could, at first, see no sign of Tug. Then, peering down over the edge of the bed, she was amazed to see his prostrate form flat on his back on the floor. His eyes were closed and he lay there unmoving. The remnants of her breakfast were scattered about him. It was then that Sara noticed the smear of blood on the edge of the table. Tug must have cracked his head on it as he went down. Sara's pulse raced as she realised that he was unconscious.

Quickly jumping up from the bed, Sara bent over the body, gingerly removing the knife from the sheath at his belt with her trembling hands. At any moment she expected him to open his eyes and reach up and grab her.

As Sara stood up, with the knife secure in her hands, she wondered if there was indeed a God. She had thought her plan doomed before it had even begun. Then, as quickly as it had turned against her, the pendulum of luck had swung back her way. She still had a chance. It was as she had expected though, she thought grimly, it was all or nothing now. Tug would certainly make her pay for this if he ever got the chance.

Stepping over his body, Sara peered out into the corridor, noticing the keys to the cell still dangling in the lock beside her. Seeing no sign of Ruz, she stepped out of the cell. Quickly, but silently, she pulled the door closed behind her.

Her cell was at the end of a short corridor. Only a few paces away, at the other end of the corridor, was another door. There was no choice now. She had to open that door and hope that Ruz was not there waiting for her.

Sara took a deep breath and tried to quell her trembling limbs. Pushing herself into action again, she crept up to the door as stealthily as she could, bending and putting her ear to the wood as she reached it. Though she couldn't hear a thing, she wondered if the door was simply too thick to hear through it.

Seeing there was no lock on the door, Sara ever so slowly twisted the handle and eased it open a fraction, just enough to peek through. Still nothing but silence from the space beyond. Unfortunately, she couldn't see much either. It was a room of some kind, that much was clear, but she wouldn't be able to see much more unless she opened the door right up.

Sara felt her muscles tightening, locking up. Her mouth felt dry. She had to make a conscious effort of will to keep going, to override the fear that threatened to immobilise her. As slowly as she could, she eased the door open. She held the knife ready in her shaking hand. She was as scared as she had ever been in her life. Maybe Ruz wouldn't be there. Maybe he had gone out for a while. Maybe, and maybe not.

Sara heaved a sigh of relief as she saw that the room was empty. It looked to her like some kind of guardroom. In the centre was a table and four chairs. The one closest to her was pushed back, like someone had gotten up to go somewhere and was coming back soon, she thought. On the table, a big saucepan with a ladle beside it looked like the source of more soup. A mug of steaming liquid sat beside it. In the far corner of the room, she could see a pot-bellied stove with a flue disappearing into the ceiling. Beside it sat a dozen or so faggots of wood, neatly stacked. A metal jug with cloth wrapped around its handle sat on top of the stove. Two more doors, one opposite the one she stood at and another on the wall to her left, led out of the room. As Sara stepped inside she wondered which one led out and which one led to Golkar or Ruz.

Once again, she moved quickly to each door, listening for any sounds that might indicate what lay beyond them. Like the door that she had entered by, neither of these appeared lockable. Simple handles were the only mechanism that she could see from her side.

Before Sara could commence a more detailed inspection of the room, she was startled by the sound of a door closing. It had come from somewhere beyond the door opposite the one leading to her cell. She realised it might be Ruz coming her way. Like a fool, she had been too busy checking out the room to prepare for this eventuality. In a panic, she rushed over to stand behind the door, thinking she might catch whoever it was off-guard as he entered. Her mind raced. She knew that wouldn't do. She had to have the element of surprise or she would have no chance at all. As she repositioned herself against the wall on the opening side of the door, a flash of inspiration came to her.

Sara dashed across to the table and grabbed the mug of steaming liquid. A moment later, she had resumed her position, flattened against the wall with the mug in one hand and Tug's knife in the other. She took some deep breaths to calm herself again. A few moments passed and she was beginning to wonder if it was a false alarm when she suddenly heard the sound of approaching footsteps, not far from the door.

Sara held her breath as the door opened and Ruz stepped into the doorway. Once more, she was quick off the mark. In the instant that Ruz turned his head towards her, she brought up her arm with the mug of steaming liquid, flinging it directly at the surprised look on his face. Although Ruz instinctively raised his arm in protection, she was too quick. The scalding liquid caught him full in the face. With a cry of agony, he flung his head back, his hands coming up in a belated attempt to cover his scorched skin.

His face had caught the hot tea full on. Although his eyes closed reflexively, the scorching liquid splashed across his cheeks and forehead. Then, even as his hands were still coming up to his face, Sara swung round with her other arm. The knife that she wielded caught Ruz in the centre of his exposed stomach, burying deep within him as she swung at him with all of her strength.

In horror, Sara released the knife and stepped back. As she did so, Ruz slid to his knees, his hands now scrabbling for the weapon buried within his vitals. Removing the bloodied knife from his stomach, he desperately attempted to crawl towards her, one hand clutching at the gaping wound, the other blindly groping for her in his agony. "Kill you . . . you . . . now," he grunted through his pain as he shuffled towards her on his hands and knees.

Backing away and looking around frantically for something to defend herself with, Sara found herself up against the table. Her hand grabbed the back of a chair for support. "Get away from me, you animal," she hissed as she grabbed the chair beside her and, in a final moment of rage, brought it crashing down on his head. Ruz slumped to the floor with the shattered remnants of the chair littered about him, one bloodied hand stretched out towards her, the other twisted awkwardly beneath his prone body.

Sara scrambled away from his body, unable to believe what she had done. Although she couldn't take her eyes from it, she wanted to put as much distance between them as she could. An air of unreality hung over the scene before her. She had stabbed him. Just like a cold-blooded murderer. Just like them.

Somehow she willed herself to get a grip. Although she could feel the emotion seething within her, she knew that she couldn't cry now. There might be time enough for that later. But not now. This wasn't over yet.

Tearing her eyes away from Ruz' body, Sara picked up the bloodied knife and thrust it under her belt. Moving to the open doorway, she peered out. Surely she had made enough noise to bring the whole house down on her by now.

The door opened on to yet another corridor. Taking a deep breath, Sara inched her way as silently as she could, down the corridor and away from Ruz, away from the horror she had just undergone. A left-hand turn brought her to yet another door. Once again she paused to listen, with her ear plastered to the door.

Easing this door open, just as she had done with the previous one, she was relieved to find yet another empty room. This one seemed to be part of the living quarters. It was a large room with a big open fireplace, around which sat two big lounges and some smaller chairs. On one side a wide staircase swept up and out of sight to another level. More doors to who knows where were a worry to Sara. More importantly, however, a window beside the fireplace provided a glimpse of trees and the sky.

Quickly rushing over to it, Sara could see a path leading away from the house through a small clearing and disappearing into the woods beyond. The house looked as if it was surrounded by forest. Fir trees clustered thickly not far from the house. The path, which was wide enough for a car, if they had such things here, led in a sweeping arc past the entrance to the house and looped back onto itself. It was rutted on each side, not unlike the old country roads Sara had seen back home.

Without a further thought, Sara rushed to the door and opened it, beaming with delight when she realised she was free. As she raised her foot to step out into the open air, she suddenly felt her feet pulled out from under her.

Crashing to the floor, she looked back in horror to see Tug with his arms clutched at her ankles as he struggled to pull her back across the threshold. Sara screamed. He had fallen to the floor himself but his bloodied hands had her legs in a strong grip. He was moving, uncertainly and slowly but nonetheless relentlessly, pulling her back towards him, one handgrip at a time. He had a large gash on his forehead and she could see blood matted through his hair and streaming down his face.

Grunting unintelligibly in her fear, Sara fumbled for the knife she had slipped under her belt. Desperately she slashed at his wrists and hands, producing a groan as he loosened his grip. In a flash, Sara struggled clear of him and was up and running. Out the door and down the pathway she flew, a momentary glance across her shoulder showing no sign of pursuit. That didn't slow her a bit, though. Sara ran. She ran as if her life depended on it.

CHAPTER 3

The surface of the mirror hanging on the wall of the wizard's study rippled as Golkar emerged, feet and hands first followed by his tall, lean frame. It was as if he had stepped through a wall of mist into clear air. Golkar quite enjoyed the sensation he felt at that moment of transition and wondered idly if Tanis had savoured it as much as he did.

He now knew Tanis had mastered a variety of exotic means of transit. The Spell of Portal might have been his *piéce de resistance*, but mastery of mirrors was a little gem in itself. He could see why the mage had succumbed to the predilection. With it as his passport, it was anyone's guess how many worlds away he would be after all these years. Not that this concerned Golkar. Tanis' departure had after all created the opportunity he was now so busily exploiting.

Still, he did find it curious that the mage had left his diary behind. He'd worked so hard to tidy up all the other loose ends, training the Guardians, establishing the Council, and so on. It was very unlike him to have neglected something as important as his diary, particularly given the wealth of information it had contained. Although Golkar had puzzled over this for some time, he was no nearer an answer now than he'd been in the past. He could see no point in continuing to dwell on it.

Looking around his study, Golkar satisfied himself he had all that he needed. Having completed arrangements with Grartok, the slig leader, he was ready to act. It had taken him some time to recover from his strange encounter with the otherworld creature, but he was ready now for the final phase of his plan. The weeks he'd spent propped up in bed had given him the time to conclude the arrangements. He'd kept his two minions busy running errands and attending to business he couldn't deal with himself and had taken advantage of the time available to review Tanis' notes, finally deducing what had happened between him and Sara.

Strangely enough, it was turning out even better than he'd planned. Although the latent power that he now knew resided in the girl staggered him, the opportunities it presented were enormous. To the girl it was useless, but to him it was priceless. Unfortunately, he'd not initially guessed its true strength, or how easily it could be brought forth. He would need to be careful, to be sure, but now he was alert to the danger it should prove easy to harness. The most important thing would be to not drain her too quickly. He'd need to keep her alive as long as possible. Golkar suspected that Tug would be happy about that.

Anxious to get on with it now that he was ready, Golkar made his way down from his tower to the living chambers below. He decided he would have Ruz bring the girl to him once he had washed the smell of slig from his limbs and he'd changed into fresh clothes. Idly he noted that once he had done with his meddlesome colleagues one of his first acts should be to find bigger quarters . . . and more suitable staff. Tu-atha was adequate for the moment, but soon he would require something more aptly befitting his station. Perhaps Elissa's palace would be more appropriate, or something altogether new, something grand and imposing.

Ambling down the staircase with his head filled with visions of grand mansions and delegations that prostrated themselves at his feet, he was surprised to meet Tug, on his way up to him. Golkar instantly sensed that something was wrong, very wrong. The moment he saw the bloodied bandage that was wrapped around the draghar's scalp he sensed his plans had gone awry. The bandage on Tug's right hand only heightened his foreboding.

"Tell me she's not dead, Tug, tell me she's not dead," he roared as his face darkened. If the draghar gave the wrong answer he would die right where he stood.

Tug's reply was almost a whisper. "She got away, Master." As he spoke he slowly backed down the staircase away from Golkar, his feet groping blindly for the stairs behind him. He dared not take his eyes off the wizard.

"Ruz is badly wounded," he mumbled. "He may die."

"I don't care about Ruz," screeched the wizard, reaching up to his full height and glaring down at the pathetic creature cowering on the steps below him. "Find her, and quickly. Get some of those scum you deal with from the village and find her. And if you want to live to see another moon, bring her back here, unharmed, and untouched, you filthy scum."

"Y-yes, Sir." Tug scrambled back down the stairs and out of sight without a moment's further hesitation.

Golkar grasped the railing to steady himself as Tug disappeared from sight round the bend in the staircase. A few moments later he heard the front door slam shut. Tu-atha lay silent. The only noise Golkar could hear was his own laboured breathing. His plans lay in ruins and he cursed himself for staying away so long.

Grartok had invited him to meet with his hunt leaders and he had thought it a necessary though distasteful chore to comply with the barbarian's request. As far as he was concerned the sligs were foul-smelling, bloodthirsty and treacherous, and those were some of their more acceptable traits. Not that any of that mattered to Golkar, of course. They were pliable and they treated him with the respect and the awe he deserved. He would let them rape, pillage and plunder till they held all of Tenamos in their sway. Liricor would fall to them quickly enough after that. Then, while they ruled Ilythia, he would rule them.

His plans for the sligs didn't end there. At the moment they saw him as a benefactor. Their leader Grartok was no fool, though. He would use Golkar to get what he wanted and then try to throw off the yoke. They would then find, however, that they had got more than they bargained for. While Kell and Tarak were distracted by the slig threat, Golkar would be able to deal with his colleagues at his leisure.

Enhancing his own power, through Sara at first, and then through others of her kind, he intended to destroy each of them, Kell first, and then Tarak. Then he'd bring Grartok to heel. The slig leader and his bloodthirsty rabble had no idea what they were dealing with. Grartok was too engrossed in his own power plays to see that he was playing with fire. Once he saw Golkar's full power revealed, he would have no choice but to grovel at the wizard's feet along with the rest of the sligs. Why, thought Golkar, they might even make him a god.

But now, with only the first steps of his plans put into action, he had miscued. Those fool draghar had failed him. At least, he reassured himself, the girl couldn't have gotten far. Although he had been gone most of the day, he knew she wouldn't be able to get far in the forest on foot.

Continuing quickly down the stairs to his living quarters, Golkar crossed the room and opened a cabinet. Picking up a slender porcelain jug, he slowly filled a small goblet with wine, spilling a little as his thoughts raced. He needed to calm himself, to think. All was not lost. The girl couldn't have gone far and he'd put enough of a scare into Tug to ensure he'd slit his mother's throat if he thought it would secure her return.

Where could she go, anyway? Tu-atha was far from the major towns, way out on the western edge of the wilderness. She wouldn't find help easily anywhere nearby. Tug's cronies, though ruffians, were competent enough and they knew how to hunt down prey. They'd proven that to Golkar before. He was sure it wouldn't take them long to find her.

Golkar breathed easier. Sipping his wine, he realised that what had seemed a disaster might be only a setback, perhaps just an annoying delay. Of course, he realised, the concern mounting within him once more, there was one possibility that could have appalling consequences. If the girl should somehow come to the attention of Tarak or Kell, as unlikely as that was, then the tables might be turned. He couldn't allow that to happen. He'd rather kill the girl himself than let a weapon like her fall into their hands.

Golkar took another sip of wine before he rose from his chair. He would need Grartok's help to ensure she didn't get that far. He would have to move now, and quickly.

~~~

Sunlight filtered through the trees and onto the trail in front of Rayne as his horse carefully picked its way through the rotting branches and twigs that littered the path. It was clear no animal had used the track for some time. While this in itself wasn't unusual, Rayne felt the hairs on the back of his neck rising. He hadn't seen a single living creature in the valley since he'd entered it that morning. Turning his head, he looked over his shoulder for the umpteenth time. In direct contradiction to the apparent solitude, Rayne had the constant feeling he was being watched. With a shiver and a shake, he urged his horse forward. "Let's go, girl," he whispered in encouragement, leaning forward to duck under an overhanging branch as he did so.

Rayne was certain he'd turned the wrong way when he'd entered the valley. It was that fork in the little stream that led him here that had thrown him. He'd been following the watercourse for some time and hadn't expected it to branch. Although he and his father had worked much of the broader wilderness extensively over the years, this particular area wasn't one they'd often frequented.

Rayne was following directions he'd got from the blacksmith in the small settlement he'd passed through two days previously. The smith had given him very specific advice of a trail he claimed to know of from both personal and recent experience. Either Rayne hadn't listened closely enough or the man had erred. No matter, he thought, he could easily cut back to the right and get himself back on course once he crossed the next ridge.

His thoughts drifted back over the past few weeks. Yet again he wondered if he was doing the right thing. He could have stayed on after his father's accident; the Southern Marches was a vast area and had plenty to offer a young man with enterprise. Their trapping business was still a going concern and he could have managed it easily enough on his own, his father had done so for years before Rayne had been old enough to join him. There was also still more than enough game if you knew where to look, and plenty that would pay for the pelts.

It wasn't a matter of the coin then; it simply wasn't very interesting. Nor were any of the other jobs he could have picked up on the Marches. Rayne wanted something more. He wanted a life of adventure, as his father had had when he was young. The Marches couldn't offer that.

Rayne doubted if there was a single story his father had told him of his earlier life that wasn't etched in his memory. For many years he had led what seemed to Rayne about as exciting and adventurous a life as one could hope for as a mercenary in the eastern realms of Tenamos, travelling extensively through Kardonia and Algaria and right up to the edge of the Northern Wastes. Then he'd given it all up for the life of a trapper on the southern fringes of the Western Wilderness, as far away as he could get from his earlier life.

He'd had two cherished mementos of that life, Rayne knew. One was his sword, the very one that Rayne had taken as his own after his father's death. His father took great care of it and taught Rayne to do the same for with own weapons.

He told Rayne not to be fooled by the sword's appearance. Though there was nothing fancy about it to look at, it was incredibly well-balanced. He said that it was as fine a sword as you could ask for. He and it had shared many adventures and he wouldn't swap it for another no matter how much anyone offered him to do so.

He took the view that if you were going to bear arms, then you needed to know how to use them. To reinforce that, he and Rayne practiced dueling together almost every day. He also taught Rayne how to use a bow, how to care for it and the arrows, how to hold the bow right, how to judge the distance to a target and whether there was any wind that had to be allowed for, and a myriad of other seemingly small but important things you needed to know if you were going to use a bow with accuracy. As a result, although, like his father, the sword was his preferred weapon, Rayne also knew that he could use a bow and arrow with some accuracy when he needed to.

His father's other memento was a small silver brooch, in the shape of a small wheel with spokes radiating out from a central hub, into which was set a deep-blue gemstone. The brooch was kept locked away with their most valuable possessions most of the time and Rayne had only seen it the once while his father was alive.

When questioned about it, his father had simply smiled and looked off into the distance, as if cherishing a memory. He said that it was a 'little trinket' he had acquired many years ago in Trest. "It's only a little thing," he had said after a few moments, "but it changed my life." Trest, Rayne knew, was the principal city of Helidos.

That was the kind of life that Rayne hungered for, then, that of a sword for hire, someone who had adventures that he would remember all of his life, someone who would be respected. He had wanted it ever since he had been old enough to swing a blade. If he didn't try to fulfil the dream now he probably never would.

Their friend, Terrin, had sensed his unrest and had offered him work helping out on his smallholding. Rayne knew it wouldn't have lasted, though. Terrin wouldn't have been able to afford an extra mouth to feed for long, he could barely feed himself and his wife as it was. He was just feeling guilty about Rayne's father. It wasn't Terrin's fault though. It wasn't anyone's fault. Terrin had helped his father many times; it was natural for him to ask for aid in return. Felling the big firs was a dangerous business. The accident was just one of those things. At least it had been quick.

With a sigh, Rayne chose to skirt the more painful memories. The future was what mattered now. He had left the day after Candlemas. It seemed to him an appropriate time for new beginnings. Just as the Feast of Renewal celebrated the end of winter and the first signs of regrowth, so Rayne saw his venture as a fresh start, a chance to carve out a new life and throw aside the old one, like an old bear casting off his winter coat to make way for the new.

A month or so and he'd be in Keerêt, signing on with the Algarian Rangers. He'd heard of the trouble the sligs were making and he knew the Algarians were looking for men who could handle themselves. Those years of weapons practice with his father at the end of the day would pay off for him now. The ex-mercenary had tried to impart what skills he could and Rayne had lapped it up, his thirst to emulate his father's competence a constant driver. Now the adventure he'd longed for was there for the taking and he meant to grab it with both hands.

His father had always said he'd never regretted his earlier days; he claimed it was just that he'd tired of that life and had wanted to settle down somewhere quiet with Rayne's mother. But Rayne knew that he wasn't born to the land any more than his father had been. It just didn't run in their blood. Maybe he would return to it one day, like his father had done, but first, he wanted a taste of real life.

Rayne's thoughts were interrupted by a rustling sound from the trees up ahead. As the noise continued, his attention was drawn to a copse of trees to the left and ahead of him. Quickly stringing his bow, he notched an arrow. It seemed from the snapping of branches and twigs he could hear that dinner was heading his way. His stomach rumbled at the thought of herbed venison roasting slowly over an open fire.

To Rayne's surprise, instead of the doe he'd expected, a young girl burst through the undergrowth, running as hard as she could, her wild eyes reflecting her panic. She was running from something, that much was clear from the glance over her shoulder, and she was frightened, scared out of her wits by the look of it. Her face was bleeding from small scratches, no doubt from the brambles and bushes she'd been bashing through, and she was dressed in the buckskins that were typical here in the west.

As the girl emerged from the trees, almost stumbling as she cleared a fallen branch, she suddenly caught sight of Rayne. She screamed as she came to an abrupt halt, only a dozen or so strides away from him.

"It's okay, I mean you no harm," said Rayne as he drew on his rein. It was clear the girl was distraught. Dropping his bow he quickly jumped down and moved towards her with his right hand outstretched in a gesture of friendship. "Let me help you. What are you running from?"

The girl backed away from him. Dropping to a half-crouching position, she slipped a knife from her belt. Rayne could see it was bloodied. Her eyes were wide and her body was tensed and ready to spring. Rayne saw tears running down her cheek as she spoke. "Leave me alone," she pleaded. "Please. Just let me go." Though her blade looked sharp enough, the girl wielding it didn't seem quite as menacing. The bloodied knife seemed strangely out of place in her hands.

Rayne halted, holding his arms wide to indicate he meant her no harm. "Just calm down. I don't know who is after you but I'm not one of them, I promise you. If you're in trouble perhaps I can help you." As he spoke, her trembling limbs gave way and she slumped to her knees, sobbing. Rayne cautiously approached.

"What's your name?"

"Sara."

"What's wrong Sara? Why are you running? What's happened?"

~~~

Sara looked up at the stranger, wondering at her fortune in running into someone out here in the middle of what seemed to be endless forest. Perhaps she wasn't as far away from civilisation as she had feared.

The lad before her was older than her, by a few years, she guessed. He was tall with long, thick, sandy hair, bound into a short ponytail at the back. He was human, and that was a relief, and his face was a friendly one, with a look of concern that comforted and reassured her. She slowly lowered the knife she'd been holding so uncertainly in front of her.

"Some people . . . they kidnapped me . . . they killed another girl . . . I escaped . . . they'll come after me," she sobbed.

"Well, let's get you out of here then, as fast as we can." With a quick look around, he helped Sara to her feet and led her back to his horse. "My name is Rayne. You can ride in front of me," he said, cupping his hand to help her to mount.

Sara didn't hesitate. It was a choice between continuing to run aimlessly through the forest in the middle of she knew not where, or taking her chances with this stranger who offered her help and a friendly face. The opportunity to put distance between her and this valley was too good a one to refuse.

Once she was mounted, Rayne climbed up behind her, putting a hand on her waist as he righted himself in the saddle. Sara flinched involuntarily at his touch, remembering Tug. She felt her muscles tensing as she suddenly questioned the wisdom of so hastily accepting his offer. He was a total stranger. Why had he been so quick to offer her help?

A gentle voice came from over her shoulder as they started to move. "Sorry, I didn't mean to startle you, I'm not used to riding with someone." After her experience with Tug, Rayne's consideration both surprised and relieved her. What real choice did she have, anyway? She'd have to rely on her instincts, and at the moment they said to trust the lad.

Sara tried to calm herself as Rayne urged the horse forward. Her heart was racing and her chest still heaved from the exertion of the last few minutes. She'd no idea how far she had run or whether she'd been chased. Fear had driven her blindly into the forest and away from the road and she hadn't been game to stop until she'd stumbled on Rayne.

Remembering her sports training, Sara sucked in deep breaths, quenching the oxygen debt in her lungs and slowing her pulse at the same time. As she began to recover, Rayne started to talk to her, questioning her about what had brought her to such a state in the middle of nowhere. His gentle voice and apparent concern helped to calm her even further. Once she could breathe more evenly, she responded, telling her story from the beginning, glad to finally be able to tell someone what she'd been through.

As her tale unfolded, she could tell that he was astounded at what had befallen her. Surprised as he was, he seemed to accept the bulk of her story, though his scepticism regarding her origins was patently clear. When she explained to him something that Tug had told her about the portal she came through having the effect of allowing her to speak and to understand the language used here in Ilythia, he was quite surprised though. He didn't seem to have considered that if she had been brought here from another world she might not be able to understand or speak the local language. Again and again, he would come back to the beginning, seeking to know more about where she had come from and who she was. The part about Golkar seemed to interest him most of all.

Rayne kept them moving at a good pace as they talked. He said he was concerned at the prospect of pursuit and although he told her he hadn't seen any sign of the house or the road she'd described, he urged his horse on. He suggested that if there were people after her then the sooner they got as far away from that valley as possible the better off they would be.

Despite this precaution, he told her he thought pursuit was unlikely. "Once," he told her, "when I was fishing with my father, I let a big salmon get out of our net, just as we were ready to pull it into our skiff. When I cried my father said, 'Don't worry, his brother or sister'll do just as nicely.' I think they're more likely to go and look for another victim than for someone who bites back like you did."

When he started to tell her about himself she knew he was trying to comfort her and help her to focus on something other than what she'd just been through. The names and places meant nothing to her but it did help. He sounded like a normal sort of person and although she had no idea what to do next, Sara finally began to hope she might be free of her captors for good. With a shudder, she remembered the image of Ruz with Tug's knife in his belly. He was dead, she was sure. Tug wasn't though, although he must be badly injured. And what of Golkar? She hadn't seen him again since that first night. Would he come after her? She hoped he would go looking for easier prey and leave her alone as Rayne had suggested.

Sara plied Rayne with questions, seeking the information she'd been unable to get from Ruz or Tug. She found him much more forthcoming. She learnt that the world she was in was called Ilythia. Rayne's knowledge of its geography was limited, but he knew that there were at least two large landmasses, Tenamos and Liricor, joined by a narrow neck of land. The region they were travelling through was part of Tenamos. If his knowledge of the extent of Tenamos was limited, he knew virtually nothing of Liricor or whatever else there may be beyond its shores.

The forest they were travelling through was part of what was known as the Western Wilderness. Rayne's home had been in a fairly isolated area to the south of where they were now. The Southern Marches he called it. From what Sara could gather it constituted a loose confederation of independent provinces which had a long history of resisting central rule and which had, to date, through a combination of various geographical factors and the locals' willingness to unite sufficiently to resist takeover, been able to resist any attempt to absorb them into either of the neighbouring kingdoms, Algaria or Kardonia. Rayne was on his way to a town called Keerêt, the capital of Algaria, to join the Algarian militia.

Apparently, he was an orphan. His mother had died from pneumonia when he was only four and his father had been killed in an accident on their neighbour's farm only three weeks ago. In many ways, Sara felt some affinity with his plight. Her loved ones were certainly far from her now too, possibly beyond all reach.

As they talked on, Sara slowly augmented her knowledge of Ilythia, of its people and their lives. Technologically it was as she'd thought, they had no knowledge of electricity or of modern machines. Rayne didn't even understand those words. From what he told her, it seemed a fairly primitive society. He talked of a nobility, of merchants and of peasants, most of the latter tied to the land. She'd learnt terms for that at school, 'pre-industrial' and 'feudal' were words that came to mind.

The most stunning difference from the world she knew, though, was the use of magic, even if it was only practised by a select few. Although it amazed her, it helped her to make sense of Golkar and what had happened to her. Her ready acceptance of all that she heard brought home to her how inured she'd become to the strange circumstances that had befallen her since she'd entered this enigmatic and frightening world.

Eventually, they tired of talk and for a while they were silent. By the position of the sun, Sara guessed it was early afternoon. They had been riding for some hours without a break, chattering incessantly and swapping stories about their backgrounds, both delighting, though for different reasons, in the unexpected company. Sara felt more heartened then she'd been for a long time. In the few short hours since they'd met, she'd begun to find hope. At the very least, she'd been able to dispel the notion that this was a world peopled entirely by demons, cutthroats and evil wizards. Rayne's experience was clearly very far from that.

"Can I come with you?" she pleaded suddenly, breaking the silence and making every effort to keep her voice steady and natural. It was a question she'd been wanting to ask for some time, fear of the answer suppressing it till she could no longer restrain herself. She liked Rayne. He was kind and considerate and she'd hit it off with him right from the start. He had a quaint sort of rustic charm to him and seemed both open and honest. Her intuition told her he was someone to trust, not that she had others to choose from.

"I've nowhere to go and I don't know what to do," she rushed on. "Perhaps if I could get to a town there would be someone who could help me get home. Keerêt sounds like that sort of place. If Golkar could bring me here, someone must be able to send me home."

"There you go with that name again," said Rayne with a touch of exasperation in his voice. "I don't think you can have heard it right. Golkar is one of the Guardians. They don't go around kidnapping people. Everyone reveres them and they've protected us for centuries. It must have just been a name that sounded like that. It couldn't have been Golkar."

Anger and frustration boiled up within Sara, fuelled by an awareness that Rayne had completely ignored her plea. "It was Golkar," she said indignantly. "They said it a number of times and I know what I heard. Don't call me a liar. I'm not an idiot. I heard what you said about him. Maybe he's been fooling everyone. How many wizards are there, anyway?"

"Only three. Everyone in Ilythia knows of them although only the highest deal with them, and certainly not the likes of you or me. Golkar, Tarak and Kell are their names. We even measure the passing of time in honour of them. This is the Year of the 712th Summer of the New Age, though most folk just call it 712. That's 712 years since the three guardians assumed their roles."

"Well," said Sara smugly. "Doesn't seem like there are any other wizards with a name like Golkar then."

Rayne said nothing at first in reply. Then, after a few moments, he responded. "Okay. You can come with me. What did you think? That I'd just leave you here?" He couldn't see the broad grin that spread across Sara's face.

CHAPTER 4

The smell of roasting meat drifted up from the crackling fire. Sara had never eaten rabbit before but relished the thought of doing so now. She was starving. But for some dried meat and nuts from his pack and a handful of berries garnered from bushes beside the trail, she and Rayne had barely eaten all day. Their dinner would be a well-earned one. They'd pushed on through the day till they were both completely exhausted.

Most of the afternoon she'd spent seated behind Rayne. They'd quickly found that arrangement had the twin virtues of being both far more comfortable for her and infinitely more practical for Rayne than trying to crane his neck around or over her shoulder to get a proper view of the trail ahead. It had felt nice wrapping her arms around his waist to hang on when they'd been picking their way over uneven ground. She'd also enjoyed watching the way his muscular back moved as he twisted and turned in the saddle. She'd fallen asleep like that at one point with her head resting between his shoulder blades, getting very embarrassed when she'd woken up just in time to save herself from falling off.

They'd left the valley long behind now and were camped in a small glen for the night, protected from sight as far as was possible. She hadn't liked being left alone when Rayne had gone off with his bow to search for food after tending to his horse. He hadn't been gone long though and had obviously enjoyed the fuss she'd made when he'd returned with two rabbits. She'd been even more surprised when he showed her the wild marjoram that he'd collected as well. The rabbits were slowly roasting on stakes before them now, the fat from their flesh hissing and sizzling as it dripped into the fire.

As Sara sat watching the flames, fighting the drowsiness she felt creeping over her, she knew she'd be sore on the morrow. Thankfully she wasn't a total stranger to riding. She and her friend Gemma sometimes went riding together at home, on a farm on the outskirts of their town. Unfortunately, the frequency of those trips had dropped away since she'd gone on to college. She remembered now how much she had always enjoyed the bond that developed between rider and horse, she could see it reflected here in Rayne's attention to Nell.

That was the horse's name. Sara thought it cute, if not strange for a horse, there was a girl at her college back home called Nell. The mare wasn't a large beast, a little over fifteen hands, she guessed, but her markings were striking. Her coat was dappled with speckles of black, like someone had taken a brush and flicked a fine spray of paint over her natural grey. Her tail and mane were darker than the rest. In contrast to her coat, the darker colour dominated there with fine streaks of grey flecked through the black. Rayne was obviously quite attached to the animal and had spent considerable time brushing her down and tending to her needs after he'd finally picked a campsite for the night.

"Will you show me how to use the bow tomorrow?" Sara asked, looking up at Rayne who, though he quickly averted his gaze, couldn't hide the blush that spread across his cheeks. She studiously suppressed the smile that threatened to crease her own face as she realised she'd caught him staring at her.

After a moment, Rayne looked back at her again with his face a studied mask of composure. "If you want," he said. "But it's not an easy weapon to learn. My dad used to say a bow could sing for the right person, but in the wrong hands it'd howl like a mangy dog."

"Well," replied Sara, wrinkling her nose at the comparison, "I have used one before. We did archery at school for a term. Only the bows we used were more complicated than yours. We had the latest sporting models at our school, and special gloves like they use in the Olympics."

"I'm sure I don't know what that is, but this is a fine bow, you'll not find many better in all of Ilythia. It was my father's and he said it's as good as you'll get."

"I'm sorry. I didn't mean to offend you. Really." Her constant references to how much better things were where she came from were obviously wearing thin. Sara resolved to resist such comparisons in the future. "I'd really like to learn. I'd like to be able to help in some way."

Rayne's tone softened. "It's okay. I'm sorry I'm so touchy. I know you've been through a lot and I can't begin to guess what it must be like having no way home. I know what it's like to have no home, but to have one and not be able to get there must be very hard."

Sara nodded, thinking of her friends and her family so far away. She could feel the moisture pooling in the corners of her eyes. Turning her head, she wiped her face with her sleeve.

Rayne quickly fumbled for his kerchief. "Damn it. Don't mind me. I'm just a clumsy oaf. Let's talk about something else. Do you know any songs?"

"Lots," said Sara, laughing as she sniffled and gratefully accepted the proffered kerchief. "But I can't sing."

"Oh, c'mon," responded Rayne, smiling broadly. "Your voice sounds lovely, even when you're talking."

Now it was her turn to blush. "I'll feel silly," she replied after a brief pause. "You start. If you sing something, I will." Sara felt she was on safe ground with that.

"Well, I definitely can't sing," said Rayne, appearing a little disappointed. "How about some riddles? Do you know any?"

"I don't know." Sara was uncertain what Rayne meant by the term.

"How about I start, then you see what you can do? The idea is that I describe it, then you have to guess what it is."

"Okay, I'll give it a go."

"I'll give you an easy one to start with." Clearing his throat and sitting up straight, Rayne gave Sara the first riddle:

"Four-legged hunter, wriggling prey,
One of them chases, the other runs away,
One of them bites, and feels a little pain,
Not really fighting, it's all just a game."

Sara thought about the words for only a short while before she shouted out excitedly, "I've got it. I've got it. It's a kitten chasing its tail."

She had a cat at home, a Burmese called Inca, and although he was older now and tended to sleep most of the time, she remembered when they'd first brought him home how he would chase his tail round and round, never seeming to tire of the game. She'd always wondered whether he really thought his tail was a snake or a monster or whether he knew it was his all along.

"Yes, very good. Your go now."

Sara thought for a while then recited the following. She knew it was easy, as everyone she knew had heard it, but it was all she could think of:

"Brothers and sisters I have none,
But that man there, is my father's son."

Rayne frowned as he looked back at Sara. He was obviously turning the words over in his mind. When he hadn't answered after some time Sara began to think that she might have stumped him.

"Do you give in?" she asked him, as soon as he looked up at her.

"What does that mean?"

"Do you give up?" The frown on Rayne's face made it plain that he still didn't understand. "Have you had enough time to guess it?"

Rayne was clearly perplexed. "Yes. I can't see it. I'm afraid I'm not good at working these out. I've heard lots and can usually get them because I know them, but I've never heard that one before."

"It's a man looking at himself in the mirror," said Sara, feeling very smug that she had stumped him first go.

Rayne thought about what Sara had said for a few moments and then looked up at her with a grin. "Of course, that's very clever."

"Your turn," said Sara. Thoughts of either home or her troubles were now far from her mind.

"Right," said Rayne. "Try this one:

"Down in the meadow, watching the sheep,
The old man stands, wanting to weep,
The stream rushes by, he waits and thinks,
And reaches right down, and silently drinks."

Sara thought about this for a while, thinking of sheep in a meadow with trees swaying in the breeze as a cool stream runs by. All of a sudden it came to her.

"Old man willow," she cried out, her face beaming as she spoke.

"We call him Grandfather Willow," said Rayne, "but that's right."

Sara was beginning to enjoy herself immensely. She was also gaining in confidence. "I've got a cute little poem I could sing for you," she blurted out excitedly, the riddles quickly forgotten.

"I'd like that," Rayne replied, his eyes twinkling with suppressed mirth.

"Okay. But don't laugh. I'm not a very good singer."

Sara sat up straight, then began to sing, slowly at first, then more strongly as she went on.

"One day one day
While in the woods
I met a bear
A great big bear

One day, one day, while in the woods
I met a bear, a great big bear

He looked at me
I looked at him
He sized up me
I sized up him

He looked at me, I looked at him
He sized up me, I sized up him

He said to me
Why don't you run?
I see you ain't
Got any gun

He said to me, why don't you run?
I see you ain't got any gun

And so I ran

Away from there
But right behind
Me was that bear

And so I ran away from there
But right behind me was that bear

Then up ahead
I spied a tree
A great big tree
O lordy me

Then up ahead I spied a tree
A great big tree, O lordy me

The nearest branch
Was ten feet up
I'd have to jump
And trust to luck

The nearest branch was ten feet up
I'd have to jump and trust to luck

And so I jumped
Into the air
But I missed that branch
Away up there

And so I jumped into the air
But I missed that branch away up there

Now don't you fret
Now don't you frown
Cause I caught that branch
On my way down

Now don't you fret, now don't you frown

Cause I caught that branch on my way down

The moral of
This story is
Don't talk to bears
While in the woods

The moral of this story is
Don't talk to bears while in the woods

That's all, that's all
There ain't no more
Unless you meet
A dinosaur

That's all, that's all, there ain't no more
Unless you meet a dinosaur."

Sara gave a mock bow, giggling as Rayne clapped his hands.

"That was great," said Rayne, laughing with delight. "What's a dinosaw?"

They made good progress over the next two days, slowly but surely lengthening the distance between themselves and the valley where Rayne had found Sara. On their third day together, they were taking a brief rest while Nell drank her fill from a small stream when Rayne suggested they needed a good break, both for them and for Nell.

"Let's light a fire and I'll stew up that coney I've been keeping, and those greens I brought with me. If they don't get cooked soon they'll go off."

Sara took little convincing. She'd found that riding for such long periods was tiring business and she quickly agreed to his suggestion, volunteering to help in case he thought better of the idea. Under Rayne's supervision, she then prepared and lit a small fire.

Sara knew she was a quick learner and she delighted in impressing Rayne as she lit the fire at her first attempt. The small twigs and dried leaves quickly burned and provided the necessary heat for the larger pieces of wood to catch alight. She saw no reason to tell him that, although she hadn't done this before herself, she'd often watched her father light their barbecue at home.

Once the fire was started, Rayne produced an ingenious assortment of metal stakes and cooking equipment from his seemingly bottomless saddlebags. Within moments he had a cooking pot with some oil in the bottom slowly heating over the fire. To this, he added some wild onions, shortly followed by all of the vegetables and roots, as well as the herbs he'd collected over the past few days whenever the chance arose. With a final flourish, he threw in some of the salted coney he'd been keeping. After all this had been thoroughly mixed, he added some water from the stream. It all began to look very inviting to Sara and the aroma alerted her taste buds that this would be a meal worth waiting for.

While Rayne continued to busy himself with the stew, Sara began to explore the small stream and the surrounding area. She quickly found a waterhole just below where they had camped. It was neither large, being perhaps several paces in length, nor very deep, and its sandy bottom, strewn with river rocks, could easily be seen through the clear water.

Looking at the waterhole, Sara thought of how much she longed for a bath. In her cell, she had been able to wash herself down from the basin of water provided, usually doing so late at night with the lantern out while Ruz and Tug were asleep. It wasn't the same as a proper bath, though. Even if she couldn't wash properly, she knew that just to be able to fully immerse herself in water would be pure delight. She also knew it wasn't just her body that needed a good wash, she was still wearing the same clothes she'd been given that first night. Although she'd become accustomed to the odour, she knew they must stink. She dreaded to think what Rayne must think of her smell.

To her relief, he readily agreed when she asked if they could stop long enough for a swim and a chance to clean up. He suggested she have a wash and a swim while the stew was cooking, saying it would take some time before it was done. Sara decided to push her luck a little further.

"I'd dearly love to wash out my clothes," she said forlornly. "There are a couple of large rocks I could dry them on in the sun and I'm sure they'd dry quickly but . . . I've nothing to put on while they dry." The last was said with a shy look towards her feet.

"Oh. I'm sorry," replied Rayne, suddenly very concerned. "I didn't think of that. I've got some spare clothes. I can lend you some to wear. Not just while your clothes are drying. I mean as a spare set. You'll probably have to roll the sleeves and trousers up a bit and pull in the belt, but they should do."

"Why, thank you, Rayne. That's very kind of you." Sara almost felt guilty for having manoeuvered him into the offer. Of all the people to run into here in Ilythia, she wondered if she could have happened on a kinder spirit.

For not the first time, Sara felt herself admiring his qualities. *The girls back home would crawl over hot coals for a guy like him*, she thought, especially when you added his looks to all his other attributes. As she watched him, he rose from what he was doing and proceeded to remove a rolled up cotton shirt and a pair of linen trousers from his saddlebags. Both had been dyed the pale green colour which matched that of the shirt he was wearing.

"Here. You might find these useful as well," said Rayne, passing Sara a small cake of purple soap, a wooden comb and a small glass flask with a cork stopper.

"Soap . . . and a comb!" squealed Sara. "Oh, you're wonderful. What's in the bottle?"

"Terrin's wife gave it to me as a parting gift. She told me to save it for when . . . for a special occasion. I think she meant for me to use it, not to give it to someone else, but you're welcome to use it. It's apple scented oil for your hair."

"Oh, Rayne." Impetuously Sara reached up and gave him a quick kiss on the cheek. "Thank you. You are such a treasure."

As Rayne flushed in embarrassment, Sara felt the blood rushing to her own cheeks. *What in the world did she think she was doing?* Taking the proffered items and quickly turning, she headed for the waterhole. It was downstream a short distance and discreetly obscured from their campsite by the intervening trees. *How embarrassing*, thought Sara, not daring to look back as she rapidly made her way off through the trees.

A few minutes later Sara was squatting naked over the rocks on the downstream side of the waterhole, merrily scrubbing her buckskins with the soap Rayne had provided. She felt strange being naked, right out in the open like that, but she knew it made good sense. She had to wash her clothes first so they would have time to dry and she didn't want to put on the clean ones until she'd bathed. Besides, there was no one else around except Rayne and he didn't seem the type to be a peeping tom. Once she'd scrubbed the grime and the stains of a few weeks wear from her clothes, she laid them out to dry on the large boulders beside the stream, with her fresh clothes nearby. She then slipped into the water herself.

The icy water made her gasp at first but nothing was going to deter her from this chance for a bath. Within a few moments. she was totally immersed, seated on an underwater rock while she washed her hair with the sweet smelling oil.

Determined though she was to be clean of the smell of her cell, she was careful to conserve both the soap, which smelled strongly of lavender, and the oil, not knowing how precious Rayne's supply of either might be. By the time she'd thought to ask, she'd been too embarrassed to go back and do so.

After a luxuriating wash and a small paddle, Sara climbed out of the pool and lay down on the grassy bank in the sun. She still felt a bit self-conscious, the only time that she had ever skinny-dipped before was with two girlfriends late one night in the local pool. She tried to relax though, telling herself she would soon dry off enough to don the new clothes Rayne had so generously provided.

As she lay there, soaking up the warm sun that beat down on her pale skin, she couldn't help but think of her plight. Although she felt wonderful lying in the sun, having just bathed and washed her hair, she knew reality still lurked close by, waiting to be dealt with.

Like Rayne, she felt that she'd left Ruz and Tug far behind. Her problem now was where could she go, and what could she do? Rayne would take her to Keerêt, but what then? From what she had learnt and seen, it was obvious that she'd been brought to Ilythia by magic, as wild as that might seem. Taking the thought further, that meant there were only three people who would have the power to return her home, the so-called Guardians that Rayne had told her of. Clearly, Golkar was out, so that left the other two. The only plan that seemed to make sense was to somehow convince one of them to help her to get home.

The problem was, she didn't have the first idea how she might do that. Rayne had said they only dealt with those at the top. That must mean the nobles. He'd also told her there was a queen in Keerêt, Queen Elissa he called her. Once Sara got there, she would have to find a way to approach her, if that was possible for an ordinary person, and see what happened then. Anything beyond that was too vague at this point.

Sara knew that all of this might prove futile, that there might, in fact, be no way back home. Golkar was clearly not what Rayne had believed. Far from being a protector, he was evil. It wasn't just what he'd done or planned to do to her either. She'd seen the dead girl in his study. Protectors didn't kill people. It was quite possible the other two wizards were equally untrustworthy. And even if they wanted to help her, would they be able to? Sara didn't want to pursue that line of thinking too far. The thought of being stranded forever in this world wasn't something she wanted to deal with unless and until she had to, it was just too frightening.

Sara's thoughts were interrupted by the sound of her name being called. It was Rayne, shouting from upstream.

"Yes?" she shouted back, quickly hopping up and beginning to dress.

"I was concerned about you," came Rayne's voice from beyond the bushes, in the direction of their campsite.

"I'm okay. I'm dry now. I'll be there in a minute."

Quickly dressing, Sara found she did need to roll up the sleeves and the trouser legs on the clothes that Rayne had lent her. Nonetheless, though the shirt was a bit loose and quite long, the clothes fitted her well. She still had the leather moccasins she'd been given that first night and she put them back on. They'd served her well thus far and she saw no need to discard them. The clothes she'd washed were still damp so she left them where they were for the moment, turning them over to assist the drying process.

Returning to the camp, she found Rayne checking the stew with a ladle. He stood up as she arrived and took the soap and oil she held in her outstretched hand.

"Thank you, Rayne," she said with a smile. "I needed that badly." As she spoke, she took the comb from her pocket and passed it to him as well.

"You're welcome," replied Rayne with a grin as he walked past her, heading in the direction that she'd come from. "It's my turn now. I can't ride with you like this now that you smell so lovely."

Nell stepped slowly and cautiously down the steep and rocky trail as it snaked its way through the towering beech trees that lined the cool mountain stream. They were almost down to the rock ledge and the roar of the waterfall was much louder now. Rayne had known there were falls somewhere near their trail and had managed to find the spot without much difficulty. They'd caught glimpses of the valley below as they'd come over a ridge an hour or so earlier. They'd made good progress over the last few days but were still deep within the Western Wilderness.

The path disappeared as it opened on to a wide granite ledge, devoid of trees. Before them lay a wide expanse of rock, worn smooth over the years and littered with boulders of varying sizes. The bubbling stream that flowed out from the trees sparkled in the sun, spilling over the rocks beside them and plunging out into the void some thirty to forty paces away from where they had halted. The roar from the valley below rushed back at them, muffling the sounds of the forest. Ahead of them, beyond the cliff's edge, stretched countless acres of woodland, a carpet of green, speckled with silver, that undulated in the gentle breeze, dotted here and there with the contrasting colour of a foreign species struggling to gain a foothold in the sea of beech. The scene was both breathtaking and exhilarating to the two weary travellers.

Rayne jumped down from Nell and helped Sara alight. "I know this is out of the way," he said, half apologising. "We'll have to backtrack to get down, but I thought you might like this."

"It's beautiful," cried Sara, skipping nimbly over the warm granite surface, keen for a closer view.

Rayne led Nell a few strides away from the trail and tethered her in the shade of a tree. Grabbing his bow he hurried after his young companion.

"What's that for?" shouted Sara over the roar of the falls, as he joined her at the cliff's edge. The stream plunged over the rocks beside them, falling some fifty metres to a large pool below before it ran on, rippling over rapids and around rocks. A bend in the distance took it from sight, the endless trees swallowing it up, disgorging it for a brief glimpse again further on as it twisted once more. The pool below them, its inner edge concealed by the overhanging rocks, broiled from the force of the water cascading down from above. As Rayne had expected, a person could climb down with some difficulty, but a mounted traveller would have to take the long way around.

He leaned over closer to Sara, raising his voice so she could hear him. "I was hoping there might be some game down below. Certainly later in the day, this would be an ideal spot to find deer." They could see no sign of prey on the mossy banks of the glistening pool far below them.

As Rayne turned, looking along the escarpment for the most likely path down, an arrow whizzed by his right ear. Spinning around he spotted its source quickly. A swarthy looking man, bow in hand, sat astride a horse, at the very spot where Rayne and Sara had emerged from the trees. As the man reached over his shoulder for another arrow, an elvish looking male was dismounting beside him. The elf was gesticulating as he shouted something at the man who had fired, but there was no way that Rayne could hear what he was saying. The din of the falls was blanketing all other noise. Two more mounted figures could be seen lurking behind them.

All this Rayne took in in an instant, dimly aware of Sara's scream from beside him. As their two assailants remonstrated with each other, Rayne quickly raised his own bow and fired. His aim was true, the man falling from his horse an instant later with Rayne's arrow buried deep within his chest. Instinctively Rayne reached for a fresh arrow, darting for the cover of a boulder as he did so. He was grateful for Sara's alertness as she scrabbled across the rocks behind him. His blood pounded in his ears. He'd never shot a man before.

Peering out from their cover, he felt Sara's trembling hand gripping his leather jerkin tightly as she huddled closely behind him. Somehow her fear calmed him. Her life, his life, was in his hands. Any doubts of her story evaporated instantly. These men were clearly in league with her kidnappers. The elf, more likely draghar as she'd said, may be one of the very ones that she'd talked of.

He watched as their attackers spread out. There were three of them now, the one that he'd shot hadn't moved from where he had fallen. All three had bows. He also noticed swords sheathed at their waists as they moved. Loosing an arrow and drawing another he realised the futility of their situation. Their attackers were alert now, moving from cover to cover as they spread out. He had to do something quickly. Within moments they'd be able to pick him off. There was nowhere near enough cover to conceal them from all three of their attackers at the one time.

Rayne knew what he had to do. Throwing down the bow, he grabbed Sara's arm, shouting into her ear. "We've got to jump. They'll surround us. We have no chance here. Don't let go of my hand."

She nodded in reply, still trembling with fear. There was clearly no time to debate the matter.

With a nod from Rayne, they both rose and dashed for the edge, leaping out into the void as another arrow whistled between them. As they plunged downwards, Rayne realised he hadn't asked Sara if she could swim.

Moments later their bodies sliced into the icy waters, spearing down into the darkness. Rayne held Sara's hand firmly in his, his lungs bursting as they descended. When their downward momentum finally halted, he kicked with his legs, up towards the light far above them. To his relief, Sara kicked too. Above him, he could see the light of the sky and the boiling area where the falls breached the surface. He headed for the darker, stiller water behind that cauldron.

A few moments later, they burst through the surface, both gasping for air. Rayne quickly paddled to the rocks behind the falls, grasping hold of their slippery surface while he pulled Sara out beside him. Allowing only a few moments for her to get her breath back, he started to move across the tumble of rocks at the foot of the wet cliff face, motioning for Sara to follow him as he did so. They both knew that speech was pointless in the deafening roar that surrounded them.

Slipping and falling over the rocks in the constant spray of the falls, they slowly made their way around the cliff face at the back of the pool. Emerging from behind the curtain of water and cautiously peering up, Rayne realised that he would need to move further, away from the tumbling sheet of water beside him. Moving along, a bit further away from the spray of the falls, he satisfied himself that he still couldn't be seen from above and then started to scale the wet cliff.

Looking behind him, through a mist of fine spray, Rayne saw that Sara had made no move to follow. She still stood, drenched and bedraggled, at the bottom of the cliff, looking up at him with a frown on her face and shouting something that was impossible to hear so close to the falls. Rayne knew they had no time for debate, time was of the essence. Waving vigorously for her to follow him, he continued to climb, moving cautiously up the slippery surface, carefully picking each foothold and handhold as he went. When, after a few moments, he looked behind again, he was gratified to see that Sara was now following him. *The girl sure has pluck*, he thought to himself.

As Rayne climbed, he hoped he hadn't sealed their doom through his actions. His plan depended on a number of things, successfully negotiating the slippery cliff face being the least of their difficulties. The ruse was one his father had once used. Rayne had thought of it, remembering his father's story and not thinking how soon he might use it when they had looked over and seen the pool disappearing out of sight below them behind the overhang of the rocks.

He had to hope their attackers would be taking the longer way, rushing to get their horses down so they could cut off escape from below. He also had to hope they'd left no one behind. He and Sara could be picked off easily on the cliff face once they came into view. The clincher was that they had to be up and out of sight from below before their attackers could get down. Rayne had no idea how long it would take them to get down with their horses, but he knew it was critical that he and Sara beat them. It would set the men a pretty puzzle and give him and Sara at least some start before they backtracked and worked out what had happened.

Looking down again, Rayne saw that Sara had moved up behind him. She was a better climber than he was, despite the slippery surface. Slowly but surely they moved on. The cliff face, though steep, was not sheer and abounded with spots to gain purchase. The fine spray of water that covered the rocks, however, made the surface treacherous and ensured they pressed on with agonising slowness.

About halfway up the face, disaster befell them as Rayne's feet slipped from under him. A granite outcropping that he was using as a ledge for both feet flaked loose, leaving him hanging perilously by one hand. The other had been reaching up for a fresh hold. He heard Sara's squeak from below as the loosened rock caught her on the shoulder as it fell. Rayne's feet flailed in the air as he frantically sought for support. Realising that his fingers were slipping and could hold him for only a few seconds longer, he shouted down to Sara.

"I'm going to fall. We both will as I'm right above you. Cling close to the face and I'll push out from the wall so that I fall into the pool and not onto you or the rocks."

As he prepared to launch himself out from the rock wall, he miraculously found the support he'd been desperately groping for. It was Sara's hand. Looking down, he could see the girl straining to push him up, supporting his boot with her outstretched palm. "Hurry up," she grunted. "I can't do this all day."

With Sara's help, he managed to find a rocky outcropping for one foot and in moments had secured himself once more to the cliff face. It had been a close call. He'd been only seconds away from jumping to avoid crashing down onto Sara. After a few moments' rest, he moved on, glad to be away from that section of the precipice.

After what seemed an eternity, they finally neared the top. Rayne slowed, alert to the prospect of attack from above. Although he still had his knife in his belt and had noticed that Sara had hers, he didn't relish the idea of needing to use them. Rayne had no delusions; these men were killers. He knew he'd been lucky to bring down one of them so quickly and doubted they'd be so lax a second time.

Still seeing no sign of their attackers above him, and aware of the pressing need to get off the cliff face before they appeared below, Rayne levered himself up over the final rock. There was no one in sight. After a furtive look around the immediate area, he reached back and helped Sara to climb up beside him, quickly moving them both away from the edge as she joined him.

With a sigh of relief, he saw that his plan had worked perfectly. In their haste to be after them, their attackers hadn't bothered with anything here at the top of the falls. Nell still stood tethered where he had left her and his bow lay right where he'd dropped it. He'd lost most of his arrows from the quiver on his back but had more in his saddlebags. Silently, he gathered his bow and motioned for Sara to follow him.

They were both wet and uncomfortable and he could see that she was exhausted from the fall and the climb that had followed. He pressed on, however, knowing there'd be time for them both to recover once they were mounted and gone. Untethering Nell, Rayne helped Sara to mount. As he led the horse toward the body of the man he had shot, Sara leaned down and placed a tired hand on his shoulder.

"That was pretty impressive. Thank you."

Rayne grinned back in silent reply, basking in her admiration. He saw no need to explain where his idea had come from.

The smile left his face as he looked down at the stranger he'd killed. Stopping for a moment, he gathered the dead man's bow and removed the quiver of arrows strapped to his back, passing them up to Sara who averted her gaze from the body beside him. Fighting to conceal his own emotions, Rayne realised that this was the third dead person she'd seen in what must have been for her a terrifying few weeks. Knowing there was no time to comfort her now, he climbed up behind her.

As he turned Nell onto the path that led back along the stream, he was startled to see another and more unexpected windfall ahead of them, just a short distance away. The dead man's horse stood between the trail and the stream, peacefully cropping some tufts of grass that had sprouted out from between the rocks. Dismounting quickly, he cautiously approached the horse.

"This gives us a chance," he called out excitedly to Sara, as he grabbed its reins and quickly slipped into the saddle. "Follow me," he said unnecessarily, as he kicked the horse into a gallop, back along the trail that had led them to the falls.

CHAPTER 5

Cool fingers of chill night air crept over the collar of Hrothgar's heavy cloak and slipped under his padded vest to glide icily across the gnarled skin below. The slig warrior shuddered as he made his way through the camp, wondering if anything could keep out the infernal cold that seemed able to penetrate the thickest of clothing. Arriving at his own tent and pushing aside the hides that concealed the opening, he stepped inside, immediately relishing the warm, smoky air that enveloped him.

As Hrothgar entered, he threw off his cloak, absently casting it in the direction of a pile of garments that lay to one side of the entrance. Turning to the large wooden barrel that flanked the opposite side of the opening, he pushed back its cover, revealing the fluid within. Lifting the ladle that hung from its side, Hrothgar took a long draught of the clear mountain water.

The tent, made from the hides of three or four brugon, the large, horned beasts that roamed the plains to the east in great numbers and provided the sligs with so much that they needed, was a sizeable one, as befitted the Second Warrior of the Sagath tribe. Its floor was covered in furs of varying sizes and types, strewn haphazardly around a central hearth, while the top, with its slight opening to provide venting for smoke and other smells, was supported by three long poles, each propped against the other in a triangular configuration.

Although Hrothgar found it warm and inviting after the chill of the night air, the stifling interior presented an assault on the senses from which anyone other than a slig would have recoiled in disgust. The thick air stank of the brugon dung the sligs used as fuel for their fires, the smell even quenching the stench from the two mangy camp dogs that lay huddled, unwashed and flea-ridden, to the rear of the tent. The rotting meat that hung from the pole was now on the bad side of rancid, but no one had bothered to discard it, nor probably would for some time. The small vent in the roof of the tent did little to alleviate any of this stink, its purpose being only to allow the smoke from the fire to escape, which it did adequately if not efficiently. And yet none of these observations would have occurred to Hrothgar. For now, this was home, and it was warm.

"What did he want this time?" came the sleepy voice of his tent-woman, Mardur, from beneath one of the furs.

"It seems that the wizard needs my brother's help sooner than he'd expected, curse his fetid bones," spat Hrothgar. Despite his disgust for the stink the human exuded, he'd maintained a calm and attentive look as Grartok and Golkar had spoken. Hrothgar was impressed by his brother's apparent ease in the presence of the wizard. Although he had striven to emulate it, he saw no need to maintain the façade here in his own tent.

"I'll be leaving first thing in the morning," the warrior grumbled, warming himself beside the still glowing fire. "Another errand to run for the great Grartok."

Mardur rolled over, careful not to disturb the baby that nursed at her breast and keeping as much of her body under the warm furs as possible. "He is the First Warrior. No use getting upset over it. Don't worry, your chance will come, he won't rule forever and he has no sons."

"Hmmmph," muttered Hrothgar grumpily in reply, sliding his weapon from his belt and carefully placing the double-handed axe beside the wooden barrel to one side of the spacious enclosure. He knew Mardur was trying to soothe his anger. She knew only too well what to expect when he was in such a mood. She hadn't rolled over to find a more comfortable position. She was simply protecting the child should he lash out with boot or stick, as he quite often did after a session with First Warrior Grartok.

Amused by her fear, Hrothgar let her lie there, not knowing what might come next. Although he knew such cruelty would probably dissipate the malice he felt for his brother, he wasn't in the mood for such pleasures tonight. Besides, he wouldn't do anything to endanger his son, it was Mardur that would take the brunt of his anger when he was ready to vent it.

With another grunt and a half-whispered curse that made even Mardur blanche, Hrothgar slipped under one of the big furs, turning his face to the smouldering embers of the fire. He watched Mardur's tight form relax as she sensed the danger had passed. I might be Second Warrior, thought Hrothgar, but she is the Second Warrior's tent-woman. Every dog has its place.

Hrothgar, however, had no intention of keeping his current position in the hierarchy for much longer. Before returning to his tent from what had been an unexpected second meeting with Golkar that day, he had paid a quick visit to his cousin, Norvig. By now, Norvig would be on his way with yet another message for Kell. Norvig was under strict instructions. The price for this information would be much higher than ever before. Hrothgar knew it was worth it.

The gold crowns the wizard would pay would be safe with Norvig; it wasn't wealth he hungered for. Hrothgar understood his cousin's fascination with pain, its use as a tool was after all deeply embedded in slig culture. For Norvig, however, it had become an obsession, one that Hrothgar was only too happy to indulge. As Second Warrior, his access to prisoners gave him the means to satisfy Norvig's needs. In return, Norvig had become a willing and loyal confidante. It was at times such as these Hrothgar was glad he had fostered that relationship.

Grartok wasn't the only slig who intrigued for a chance at more power. While his brother angled for the Sagath to replace the Ghorant as First Tribe, a move that would make Grartok overlord of all of the sligs, Hrothgar was busy with his own schemes. Selling information to Kell was just one of the stratagems by which he was rapidly accumulating the gold he would need to buy loyalty from the other Sagath chieftains. Dealing with the old wizard had the dual benefit of ensuring that Grartok's tactics didn't advance the Sagath too quickly.

Hrothgar knew that with Golkar's acquiescence the Sagath would soon overrun much of the Algarian western frontier. It would be a stunning victory and one which would enhance Grartok's reputation mightily among all sligs. Should the campaign falter, however, then Hrothgar would be ready and waiting. The Sagath didn't endure defeat well. In the recriminations that would surely follow such an outcome, heads might roll. Hrothgar intended that his brother's would be one of them.

His thoughts turned to the so-called 'mission' his brother had entrusted him with. He and twenty of his warriors would leave at first light, to capture a human girl child. Hrothgar felt his anger returning. He, Second Warrior of the Sagath, was being sent to capture a human child. He had almost called for *Shüglac* right there, in front of Golkar and the other warriors. He had only restrained himself by thinking of the plans that he'd laid and how much he would enjoy seeing the hunt leaders calling for his brother's head. He would see it on the end of his spear yet.

Having accepted Grartok's orders, Hrothgar determined to make the most of them. The gold Norvig would extract from Kell would be useful, but just a start. The girl was important to Golkar, that much was clear, and Hrothgar had no intention of meekly handing her over to Grartok, or to Golkar for that matter, once he found her. He intended to put a price on her head, a very large one. His cousin should have caught up with them by then. Rather than return her to Grartok, he would offer the girl directly to Golkar. If the wizard wouldn't pay, then Norvig could have some fun while they bartered.

Hrothgar knew the line he walked was a dangerous one. While no one would blame him for plotting the downfall of his leader, that was after all the stuff that slig politics was made of, his treachery to the Sagath would not be so easily forgiven. Should that come to light, there would be no one who would side with him. He would count himself lucky if his death was both swift and painless. For the sake of security, it would be best that he silence his cousin before much longer. As Hrothgar's father used to say to him and his brother, "a dead slig will never betray you."

The Second Warrior knew sleep would not come quickly. He would amuse himself for some time planning a particularly exquisite death for little Norvig. Not an accident this time, he thought, he wanted his cousin to know it was him. Something slow and deliberate would be best. Hrothgar knew how satisfying it could be when his victim begged, either for life or for death, it didn't matter; the result would be the same, regardless.

When Hrothgar finished with his plans for Norvig he moved on to those for his brother. As he finally drifted off to sleep some time later, his last thought was of his brother's bloody head, grinning down at him from the end of his spear. It was a pleasant thought and one that helped him to sleep.

~~~

Grartok smiled as he watched his brother ride off, he and his twenty companions quickly disappearing into the morning mist. *Hrothgar is a fool*, thought Grartok. *He will never be First Warrior, no matter how much he schemes.*

Grartok was well aware that his brother was selling information to Kell, and that he had been doing so for some time. Far from being angry when Norvig had first come to him, Grartok had immediately seen the advantage for himself. He had long known of his brother's desire to replace him as First Warrior. Hrothgar had never been good at concealing it. He was, nonetheless, just a little impressed at his enterprise in this more recent move, his attempt to undermine both Grartok and Golkar by selling information to Kell, impressed but unconcerned.

As long as Norvig continued to keep him informed of everything Kell was told of, Grartok was happy to lend his brother as much rope as he needed. All the more fun he would have when he reeled him back in. Grartok certainly intended to make that a memorable day. Humiliating his brother in front of the rest of the Sagath would be both fitting and amusing. He had promised Norvig the honour of inflicting the ritual dismemberment all would support once Hrothgar's treachery was revealed in assembly.

Turning back to the camp, Grartok strode purposefully through the tents, watching the other slig warriors that had risen with the dawn. Here and there, groups of warriors sat around fires, sharpening and repairing their weapons, preparing their morning meals, eating and chatting as all warriors do. The sligs were customary early risers, often attacking an enemy just before dawn, favouring the dim early light that preceded the rising sun.

Grartok knew the Sagath were a formidable foe. Standing taller than either elf or human, their scaly skin daubed with paint and bared from the waist up when ready for battle, their mere appearance was enough to daunt any but the hardiest of opponents. Wielding double-handed axes, they would charge into battle en masse, screaming blood-curdling oaths and striking terror into any who dared to withstand them.

In the next few days, now that Golkar had agreed, they would sweep down from their mountain camps in great numbers to strike at the ill-prepared Algarians on the plains below. The Giant's Teeth made for cold camps, but the high mountain passes were a perfect staging ground for the war they waited to wage. Assembling here in the last few weeks of winter had ensured their preparations had gone unnoticed. With the snowline receding, it was time to launch the assault. The hammer blow the Sagath would now deliver would send the under-trained Algarians reeling back in retreat. Then, when they rallied, as they inevitably would, Grartok's old friend, Third Warrior Nargal, would bring the remaining Sagath down from the northern passes, opening a second front that would seal the Algarians' doom.

Grartok was satisfied he had overlooked nothing. What he intended could only be achieved by one of the two largest of the slig tribes, the Sagath or the Ghorant, or by a number of the smaller tribes acting together. The latter had never been done. The sligs were no nation, merely a collection of tribes.

He, First Warrior Grartok of the Sagath, would change that. With victory over the Algarians, all would acknowledge the right of the Sagath to be First Tribe; the Ghorant would have no choice but to acquiesce. Once that was achieved, Grartok intended to weld all of the tribes into one mighty force, a force that would sweep over the whole of Tenamos. With the Algarians out of the way, there would be no one with the power to withstand them. Golkar would ensure that the Guardians were silenced. Any other resistance would be buried under an avalanche of slig warriors. Tenamos would burn from one end to the other. Grartok would be the greatest leader the sligs had ever seen.

It was a mighty dream, but one Grartok intended to make a reality. Beside it, his brother's petty jealousies were like the bites of a marsh-gnat, annoying but easily dealt with.

But not just yet. He would wait till Hrothgar had outlived his usefulness. Grartok knew a day of reckoning would come between himself and Golkar. Hrothgar's collusion with Kell would forestall that day and allow Grartok time to achieve his own goals first. Then he would see what could be done with the wizard. In the meantime, if Golkar got wind of Hrothgar's intrigues with Kell, then he'd simply feign ignorance and offer his bother's head by way of recompense.

Grartok had no illusions. He knew Golkar's magic was strong. If the price to be paid in the end was to be obeisance to Golkar, then it was a price he would be prepared to pay. Grartok would bend the knee to Golkar as long as all of the sligs bent their knee to him. And if some other opportunity arose, then he would take that just as readily.

Meanwhile, Golkar's aid was essential. It was his acquiescence which would make what had hitherto been an impossibility possible. The wizards were powerful. The magic they wielded had kept all but the foolish in their places for centuries. Grartok himself had seen Golkar destroy a band of Ghorant warriors with a mere pass of his hand and a few mumbled words. He had felt the dry air crackle with energy and then watched in horror as the Ghorant warriors' clothing had burst into flames. The sligs had fallen from their horses, screeching in agony. Some had run off screaming as the flames had enveloped them, others had writhed on the ground, desperately trying to beat out the flames that quickly spread to their hair and their skin. It had been an edifying sight, watching mighty warriors felled so easily, with no more than a gesture and some words.

But now, not only had Golkar agreed not to hinder the Sagath invasion of Algaria, he had also undertaken to deal with his fellow Guardians. Before they could act to forestall the slig advance, he intended to destroy the other two wizards. He'd told Grartok that he had gained access to magical power from another world. By tapping the power residing in its inhabitants, he would be able to overcome his two colleagues, leaving the sligs with unfettered opportunity to sweep all before them as never before.

Grartok now knew that the first of these otherworld creatures, a human girl child, had escaped from Golkar. Although she should be easily recaptured, the possibility of her gaining help from either of the other two Guardians had to be eliminated. Such an outcome could be fatal to both Golkar's and Grartok's plans. Grartok had readily agreed to assist and had chosen his brother to lead a small force that would plunge deep into Algarian territory. Hrothgar's warriors would split into two bands. One group would intercept any attempt to reach Tarak; the other would block any move towards Kell. Both groups would close in, intercepting the girl should she avoid Golkar's own men.

Grartok was well aware of the further danger that Kell would pose once he received the message Norvig would deliver from Hrothgar. Although it was useful for Kell to know of the growing threat to the unity of the Guardians, Grartok needed to ensure the wizard could only delay Golkar, not actually thwart him. The flow of information had to be closely controlled to maintain that delicate balance. Grartok had seen to that. Norvig would certainly tell Kell of the human and the danger she presented, but Kell would not learn that she had escaped. That piece of information would be kept from him for the moment.

Should Hrothgar find the girl, he would return her to Grartok. It wouldn't pay for Golkar to flex his muscles just yet. As long as he was sure the girl couldn't fall into the hands of his opponents he would eventually obtain another victim. In the meantime, the girl might be an interesting bargaining chip should the right opportunity present itself.

Plots and counterplots, and plots within plots, Grartok's prowess at such machinations had got him where he was. It was the way of the sligs that those best at such things quickly rose above the rest. Grartok was a master at it and he knew it. But right now he had other needs to attend to.

Having arrived at his destination, Grartok stooped as he slipped into the tent. Inside, Mardur sat beside the fire, nursing his brother's child. It pained Grartok to see the infant. While his brother had sired a son, he remained childless. Grartok meant to correct that with Mardur. His brother's child could live . . . until then.

~~~

The brief gust of brisk mountain air that slipped in as Grartok left chilled Mardur, inducing a shiver. *Now that the beast has rutted he can go on about his business*, she thought bitterly. Mardur could not give what had just occurred a more dignified name. It wasn't something she looked forward to. It was simply something she had to do if she was to survive.

Now that he was gone, Mardur leaned over and picked up her baby. He had cried from the moment Grartok had arrived and was still crying now. As she lifted the babe to her swollen breast, feeling the sucking lips quickly establish a familiar rhythm as the child found what it sought, Mardur could not help but wonder what its future might hold.

Grartok's hatred for his brother's son was barely concealed. Mardur knew the source of his loathing for the infant and it wasn't just because it was his brother's spawn. The child reminded him too much of his one and only shortcoming, his failure to procreate. Grartok was a mighty warrior, perhaps one of the mightiest the Sagath had ever produced. He was also a great leader, First Warrior of the Sagath tribe, second only to Nâgrat, First Warrior of the Ghorant. The only blemish his enemies could point to was his failure to impregnate a woman. Mardur knew that gnawed at him. It weakened him as nothing else could, wounding his pride and casting doubt over his manhood.

At first, Mardur had been proud of what she had achieved. She was not only tent-woman to the Second Warrior, but she had borne him a male heir, in very short time. She wallowed in the envy she saw in the faces of the other slig women. The deference paid her was both gratifying and useful; always receiving the best cuts of meat, the best places always reserved for her and none other; no other tent-woman dared to offend her. She had swelled with pride at the status she was accorded. Then Grartok had begun to visit her when Hrothgar was away from the camp.

Grartok's own tent-woman had disappeared. No one had seen her for months. She was the third he had taken in the last two fighting seasons, the previous two both dying unfortunate deaths. The first had choked, on a bone, it was said. The second had been inexplicably trampled in the horse enclosure late one night. Her bruised and battered body was found the next morning.

None of the tent-women ever spoke of these things, but Mardur suspected that all knew these were not accidents. Grartok hungered for offspring and both of the women had failed him. They had paid for their failure with death.

And now he had taken to visiting her. Mardur knew only too well why she had been chosen. Although she was sure he delighted in cuckolding his brother, it was a child he wanted, and Mardur had shown she could produce one. Now all she had to do was give him the male child he longed for.

It was clear to Mardur her future would be a bleak one, no matter what happened. If Hrothgar learnt of her adultery, his wrath wouldn't be reserved for his brother alone. Mardur would be tainted and he would most likely kill her to appease his shame. Knowing Hrothgar, Mardur was certain it would be neither a pleasant nor a quick death. If Hrothgar remained ignorant, Grartok's visits would continue. Should she not soon become pregnant he might simply desist, but she thought that unlikely. More likely he would deal with her first. No woman who had failed him still lived. Grartok did not like to be reminded of his failings. If she did produce the child he wanted, he would certainly claim it, male or female, as proof of his virility. Mardur's survival would then depend on the outcome of the *Shüglac* Hrothgar would undoubtedly call for.

Mardur could not see much hope for the child now asleep at her breast in any of these scenarios. Almost every eventuality would see the death of Hrothgar's child at the hands of the slig leader, whether openly or by 'accident'. The child would stay alive only until Mardur produced an heir for the First Warrior. Its only real hope was if Hrothgar slew his brother, either before or as a result of that occurring, and that was not likely. Mardur knew the two brothers well. Hrothgar dreamed of greatness, but he was no match for his brother.

What should she do? If she allowed the current situation to continue, her own chances of survival were good. As long as it wasn't, in fact, Grartok's own fault that none of his women had conceived, she would lose Hrothgar's child but gain Grartok's. And she would become the First Warrior's tent-woman. While Grartok was ruthless and cared little for her needs, he wasn't cruel like his brother. On the other hand, if she told Hrothgar of his brother's 'visits', her child might live but she would certainly die, undoubtedly slowly and painfully. The only other viable choice was to leave, with the child, and take her chances on her own. She was still young, and she knew how to give the slig warriors what they wanted. If luck went her way, she would find another tribe, another warrior, and she would survive, and so would her child.

The choices were grim. For the moment she would wait. She would first see what the new moon brought forth and then she would decide, hopefully choosing right, both for herself and for her child.

~~~

Norvig was enjoying himself. As he pushed on through the forest, bound for Kell's mountain fastness, he was amusing himself with thoughts of the Sagath leader's denunciation of Hrothgar's treachery and the role he, Norvig, would play as that tableau unfolded. The other chieftains would certainly vote for *Hlath-sha*. He could picture Hrothgar now, looking down at the twelve boar's teeth, knowing his doom was upon him. Then he, little Norvig, mistreated Norvig, always overlooked Norvig, humiliated Norvig, he would step forward to claim his revenge.

He wondered if Hrothgar would remember, as Norvig stood there before him with his glistening blade in his hand. Would he remember the time he had mocked Norvig for his size in front of the other children, or when he had told all the others how Norvig had puked when he had seen the elven prisoners beheaded by the warriors, or any of the other countless humiliations Norvig had endured at his hands? Norvig hoped he would remember.

Norvig certainly would. He had never forgotten. On that very day when Hrothgar had laughingly told their friends how he had thrown up until his belly ached, Norvig resolved. He would never forget, and he would never again be seen to be squeamish. From that day on he had steeled himself to the endless slaughter. As soon as he was old enough, he had joined in, pushing himself always, further than the rest, until finally, he longed for it, until eventually, he became renowned for it.

All this because of Hrothgar. Norvig leaned over in the saddle and spat as he thought of the Second Warrior and his pathetic little schemes. *Well, every dog has his day*, thought Norvig. Soon, he would be given the chance that he'd dreamed of, the chance to use his well-honed skills on Hrothgar himself, to show the Second Warrior what he was responsible for, what he had engendered, and how much Norvig had learnt. Yes, Norvig hoped that Hrothgar would remember. Norvig certainly would.

Looking up as he rode, Norvig could see the mountains rising up behind the trees ahead of him. The forest was thinning out now. He was into the foothills and would soon reach the trail that led up to Kell's lair, to Cloudtopper itself.

That's another high and mighty one, thought Norvig. He didn't like the wizard and he knew that the wizard didn't like him. He was on his fourth visit to the Guardian and didn't care if it was his last. All of the wizards made him uneasy. Golkar was the same, although he had seen him only the once. They had a haughtiness about them, as if they were looking down their noses at everyone. It didn't matter if it was Norvig or if it was Grartok, they were just the same. Grartok chose to ignore it, and he had advised Norvig to do the same. He said that it didn't pay to offend wizards, he had seen it done and the response had been a salutary lesson.

Norvig thought it good advice. Let them put on their airs. As long as they left him alone, he didn't mind. It did mean, however, that the task he had been given would not be an easy one. Hrothgar wanted gold in exchange for information and he said that Kell would be willing to pay. Although he was undoubtedly right, Norvig wondered how the wizard would react to the price hike, particularly as the message had been filtered by Grartok of its most valuable components. As Norvig began to negotiate the foothills, he practised in his mind the words he would use, thinking of possible responses from the wizard and how he, in turn, might respond himself. Bartering was not something he excelled at; his skills had always been more 'anatomical' in nature. He was more suited to the extraction of information than to its sale.

An hour or so later, having rehearsed the encounter innumerable times in his mind, Norvig found himself being led by Kell's quickling attendant, Nim, down a long hall inside Cloudtopper. The quickling had greeted him tersely and then left him waiting on the doorstep while he had sought his master's instructions. Although that had irritated Norvig, he was used to it, he had been treated much the same way on each of his three earlier visits, and in some ways he understood it. If Norvig had been in Kell's place he wouldn't have allowed a slig warrior to wander around his abode unaccompanied. Then again, he wouldn't have a quickling in his service either. He trusted them even less than he did humans, which was not at all.

The quicklings were an unusual race. In terms of stature, they were of medium height, adult males ranging from five to five and a half feet tall. They tended to be quite slender, with short torsos and long spindly legs, and their faces were narrow and elongated, resembling in some ways the snout of a hound. Although little was known of their ways, they were known to be highly intelligent and were quick learners. What few that there were in Tenamos tended to keep to themselves, rarely mixing with the other racial groups, though they were known to have some dealings with the elves of the south.

Although they were reputed to be exceptionally fleet of foot, being able to keep up with a horse and its mount over long distances, they were primarily noted for the brevity of their lives. Quicklings tended to mature early, reaching adulthood after only five or six years. They then led robust lives through to around twenty years of age, at which point they would quickly wither and die, often deteriorating from a mature and healthy adult through an accelerated ageing process in less than three cycles of the moon. Only a few quicklings had ever reached a quarter of a century in age.

Norvig thought it interesting that a creature with such a short lifespan would want to spend those years in service to another, even if it was to one of the Guardians. Maybe it was down to their belief that once they passed their spirit would be reborn, that it would enter the body of the next quickling child to be born.

Be that as it may, thought Norvig, if he were Nim, he would be ensuring that he packed as much activity into his few short years as he could. The quickling, however, gave no indication that the life he led was in any way unsatisfying or unfulfilling. As Norvig watched him, he strode through the wizard's residence as if he were almost as important as Kell himself.

Reaching the end of the corridor, the quickling pushed open the double doors that led into the sitting room with a flourish and then stood to one side, bowing ever so slightly as Norvig stepped past him and into the presence of the wizard. The old man was seated, exactly where he had been on each of the previous occasions, in a worn, suede-covered chair that tilted backwards alarmingly, defying gravity in some extravagant way that Norvig couldn't fathom. Norvig heard the doors close behind him. As usual, Nim had left him alone with the wizard.

Although he was seated, the wizard still showed all of the authority that Norvig had come to expect. His piercing eyes gleamed out from his lined face as he started to speak. "Greetings Norvig, what brings you here so unexpectedly? A message from Hrothgar, I gather. How fares the Second Warrior?"

Kell, with his few unanticipated words, threw Norvig's planned opening speech into complete disarray. Exchanging pleasantries with a wizard in his formal sitting room was not something that Norvig could imagine any slig, even Grartok, handling with comfort. He could see that this conversation was going to go no better than his previous ones. His left hand moved nervously towards the axe blade that protruded from his belt. Gaining reassurance from its cool touch, he sought for the right words to reply, unsure which question to answer.

"I . . . ummm . . . he is well."

"I'm sure he is. But let's get straight to the point. What word does he send?"

The wizard's smiling response only served to confirm Norvig's distaste for his manner. Silently he cursed Kell, knowing he was one of the few inhabitants of Tenamos who would dare to treat an armed slig warrior so disdainfully.

"He sends me with news that he's sure you'll find useful. Very useful."

"Yes?" The wizard looked back at Norvig, his stony face masking the interest that Norvig felt sure was now there.

"By useful I mean . . . valuable . . . very valuable." Norvig felt he was doing much better now.

"Oh . . . yes, of course, the money. Yes, I understand that this news isn't free. When is it ever? Go on, tell me what you have to say and I'll make sure that Hrothgar is adequately compensated."

Norvig found the last word insulting, it wasn't a matter of throwing scraps to the sligs. He decided to ignore the jibe. "Well . . . Hrothgar feels that you will find this piece of news very interesting. News like this doesn't come cheap. Hrothgar has put himself at great risk in this matter. This news is more expensive than normal."

"Oh? How expensive?"

"Two hundred gold crowns."

"What?" The wizard was visibly surprised. Norvig knew that his interest was also definitely piqued. Perhaps Norvig was better at this than he thought. He pushed on. "Hrothgar says it's worth it and that you won't be disappointed. Two hundred gold crowns is the price."

"By Mishra, I'd better not be. Two hundred it is. But if I'm not satisfied I'll go elsewhere in future. I won't be extorted. You can tell Hrothgar . . . no, better still, if I'm not satisfied with this transaction, I'll tell him myself. He'll rue the day if he tries to make a fool out of me."

Norvig was glad the wizard had changed his mind. There was no way he would be passing a threat like that back to Hrothgar himself. Until Grartok dealt with the Second Warrior, his temper was something best avoided.

Clearing his throat, Norvig recited the message he had brought for the wizard. "Hrothgar says that the Guardian Golkar has gained access to another world. He has brought a creature from that world into this one and intends to use it against his enemies." Norvig was glad that the words had come out as he had rehearsed them. He knew there was more to this news than what he had told, but he had carefully followed Grartok's instructions that he not pass on all that Hrothgar had wanted him to.

The wizard, whose left eyebrow had arched up as Norvig had spoken, sat in silence for some time before he responded. "What kind of creature?" he eventually asked.

"A human."

Kell nodded ever so slightly as he took that in. "And how does he intend to use this human against his enemies?"

"Hrothgar doesn't know." Norvig felt comfortable with this lie. There wasn't much that he was concealing. All that he knew was that it involved the use of magical powers in some way. No doubt Kell would guess that much anyway.

"What enemies does he intend to use this human against?" The wizard leaned forward as he spoke. Norvig could see that Kell hung on his reply.

"Hrothgar doesn't know." Norvig swore to himself as he uttered the lie. Kell had watched him very closely as he had responded to the question.

"I think he does," said Kell in a raised voice, standing up so that he could meet Norvig eye to eye as he spoke. "Who are these enemies?"

Norvig repeated his answer in as flat a voice as he could manage. "Hrothgar doesn't know."

The wizard stared back at him, allowing the silence to add to the pressure he was already under. Although Norvig would not admit it, even to himself, he was just a little bit intimidated. He would face anything or anyone in battle, that was something he understood; there was nothing to fear in combat, it was a fitting way for a slig warrior to die if Zar so willed it. But Norvig had heard the stories of the power of the wizards and the ways they fought. That was no way for a warrior to die.

The wizard repeated his question, glaring at Norvig as he did so. "I want to know who these enemies are."

"I . . . Hrothgar doesn't know," Norvig repeated, unable to hide his nervousness. The wizard stared back at him, saying nothing, examining the slig with an intensity that rattled him. Norvig avoided his direct gaze, using a trick that Grartok taught him and staring at the wizard's nose.

"Very well," Kell finally responded, as Norvig maintained his silence. "Tell Hrothgar I will pay him more for the answers to those last two questions, five hundred gold crowns, in fact. I want to know how Golkar intends to use the human and against whom. Have you got that?"

"Yes."

"Begone then," said the wizard dismissively, turning his back to Norvig and busying himself with some papers on his desk. "Oh," he said as an afterthought, barely glancing in the slig's direction as he spoke, "Tell Nim that I said he should give you your two hundred crowns."

Recovering quickly from his discomfort now the exchange was concluded, Norvig felt his anger rising rapidly. Wizard or not, he had no right to treat a slig warrior in such a manner. To turn one's back on a slig was not only foolhardy but an insult of the highest order. Commonsense deserted Norvig as his innate pride took over. Without a conscious decision having been made, his hand started to slide the axe shaft from his belt.

"Don't be a fool, Norvig."

Kell's response startled him. The wizard still fussed over his desk with his back to him. He couldn't possibly see what Norvig was doing.

"You'd be dead before you could even begin to swing it," the wizard continued quite casually. He made no move to stop what he was doing or to turn to face Norvig.

With some difficulty, Norvig eased his hand away from the axe handle. With even greater difficulty, he reined in his seething anger and turned and opened the door. Once out in the corridor, he steadied himself then headed for the exit, knowing that Nim would be close at hand. He was relieved to be out of the room and to be done with the task. His next one should be more to his liking.

As the doors closed behind the slig warrior, Kell moved from his desk to the chair beside it, turning to gaze out at the forest below as he sat. He had no interest in the papers he'd been handling, all that had been for Norvig's benefit. His slight had been quite intended and it had evoked just the response he had wanted.

Kell felt that it helped to keep the slig on the back foot when he dealt with him. Although he would rather have nothing to do with the foul-smelling cutthroats, they had proved to be an invaluable source of information. Without them, Golkar would have had free reign and Kell would not have had the slightest idea what was going on until it was too late, if it wasn't that already. Dealing with the sligs was a tricky business.

In Norvig's case, Kell always made sure the slig was kept off balance. He clearly rehearsed what he said but tended to get flustered and say more than he had intended when Kell ruffled him. Hrothgar was more difficult to handle and tended to clam up if he felt he was not being paid the respect he felt he deserved. He was, however, quite susceptible to flattery. In many ways, thought Kell, it was just a matter of finding the right pressure points. The trick was to not let them know they were being manipulated.

Kell was sure Norvig had no idea the wizard had been baiting him intentionally. As far as he could see, Norvig was hardly the brightest member of his race. He wondered if the slig had even the slightest awareness of how important the news that he bore really was.

The news was, quite simply, devastating. Things were much worse than Kell had thought. Although he could not be certain how Golkar had done what he had, or how dire the consequences might be, he felt sure that the enemies the slig had referred to were none other than himself and Tarak. As to his having 'gained access to another world', it seemed inconceivable that such a thing could have been done.

Although, thinking of it, Kell did remember Tanis once saying that there were worlds beyond this one, 'parallel worlds' he had called them, some similar, some dissimilar, all as real to their inhabitants as this one was to its. Apparently, that's where the mysterious Ilaroi had come from.

The Ilaroi. Now that's a name he hadn't heard in a very long time. According to Tanis, Mishra was the last of the Ilaroi, but who they were and exactly where they had come from, he either didn't know or was unwilling to say.

Assuming for the moment that all this was so, however, and that somehow Golkar had managed to gain access to one of these other 'worlds', something he thought that Tanis had said could not, or was it should not, be done, then what could Golkar possibly hope to achieve by so doing?

This creature that he had summoned, what was it? A demon? Presumably not. Norvig had said it was human. Another wizard then, to aid Golkar, or some powerful warrior immune to their spells? And why would it aid Golkar? Kell could only guess at the answers to these most critical of questions.

The one thing that he was certain of was that he had to assume the information that Norvig had brought him was accurate. He couldn't afford to treat it in any other way. If Hrothgar was lying, he would deal with him later, but if Golkar *had* actually brought some being into this world to use against his fellow Guardians, then Kell knew that both he and Tarak might be hard-pressed to resist him.

The wizard drummed his fingers absently on the arm of his chair as he sorted through his thoughts. His worst fears were being realised. He and Tarak may soon be fighting for their very survival. Hrothgar had said some months back he believed there was more going on then just support for the Sagath. It seemed now that he had been right.

To Kell that just went to show how far Golkar had fallen, when a slig could anticipate his motives more accurately than his fellow Guardians could. Although Kell had been expecting the worst, somehow a part of him had been hoping he was wrong. Unfortunately, this latest piece of information dashed those hopes. He feared now that Golkar's megalomania might just prove to be the undoing of them all.

A knock at the door broke into his thoughts. "Enter," he responded, knowing it would be Nim returning from seeing Norvig on his way.

As the quickling opened the door, Kell motioned for his companion to join him, indicating the chair opposite his. "Did Norvig count out his money, like he usually does?" he asked as Nim eased into the seat beside him.

"Of course," Nim answered with a laugh. "Only he had to start again a number of times. I don't think he's used to counting that high. I don't know what you did to upset him. He was as nervous as a long-tailed cat in a room full of rocking chairs."

Kell couldn't help but smile, albeit briefly, despite the seriousness of the situation. The frown that quickly displaced it, however, was a clear harbinger of the concerns he needed to share with his companion. "I'm afraid he brought grim news, my friend. It seems Golkar has indeed moved against us and I'm not sure we'll be able to resist him."

Nim's mirth quickly left him as the wizard went on, revealing the message Norvig had borne and the fears it confirmed. Once again, Kell was grateful for the opportunity to share his burdens. This responsibility was too much to bear by himself.

He had always found that sharing his concerns with others helped him to regain the clarity of thought he needed to find the right answers to his problems. And it was not surprising that it was to Nim he often turned in his need. The quickling was, after all, his closest confidante. Kell trusted him more than anyone else in the world. Even Tarak, his fellow Guardian, knew less of him than did Nim.

Kell knew that the loyalty he received in return was founded both in the genuine regard they shared for each other and in their mutual concern for their world and its peoples. He and Nim had spoken at length of the danger that an aberrant Golkar could present, not only to the Guardians but to all of Ilythia. Nim shared both his concern and his commitment to averting such a disaster. Unfortunately, despite all their efforts, they had achieved little. It was only Norvig's most recent news that had finally confirmed what till now had simply been a growing suspicion.

The wizard knew that for Nim it was now, in many ways, a moot point. Soon, like all quicklings, his time would come. He had but a few years to live. It was a measure of his commitment, both to Kell and to their cause, that he hadn't relinquished his work and returned to spend his remaining days among his own kind.

For his part, Kell had undertaken years of research, delving for ways to avert the senseless early demise his friend faced. His search had been fruitless. For all his efforts, he was still no closer to solving the riddle of the quicklings' mysterious and sudden decline. And now his work would have to be abandoned. Neither of their lives would ever be the same again from this day on. The danger from Golkar was now of paramount importance.

"I must leave Cloudtopper, as soon as I can," he said to his friend. "I may no longer be safe here." The time for thinking was done. Kell was anxious to be on with it.

"Shall I go to Tarak, as we'd planned?" said Nim as they both stood.

"Yes. I see no reason to do other than that. For the moment we have some small advantage, as Golkar doesn't know we're aware he has moved against us. At the same time, we don't know when or where to expect his first blow. He would want to strike at either Tarak or myself before we could combine. I think, therefore, that he, or this human who aids him, will move quickly. They will either come here to Cloudtopper, or they'll go to the Vale. Failing that, they'll look for us somewhere between the two."

"Yes," said Nim. "They would certainly want to deal with the both of you first. At least we must assume that, in any event. I think I'll need to be careful I don't run into either of them myself."

"Do that, Nim. Be very careful. Speed will be important, I think. The sooner you can get the message to Tarak, the sooner you can be out of harm's way." Kell was concerned for the quickling but knew that the plans they had laid for just this eventuality had been thoroughly considered. What they had to do now was to act, quickly and decisively.

"Don't worry," said Nim, helping the wizard to sort through the mess on his table and gather the few books and other items he intended taking with him. "I just hope that Tarak sees the sense in joining you in Annwn."

"He will. He said he'd be with me if my fears proved right. He'll see that we must act together." Kell hoped he was right. He and Nim had prepared a small hut buried deep within the Forest of Annwn for the need that was upon them. It would give the two wizards somewhere to base themselves while they worked out how best to resist Golkar. For a while, at least, it would be a safe haven. His concern was not so much whether Tarak would join him there, but what they would then do.

A confrontation between the Guardians was unprecedented. Just how they could constrain Golkar, even acting in concert, would be something they would have to decide on. Kell had a few ideas of his own and hoped that Tarak had also turned his mind to the problem. Clearly, Golkar believed that one Guardian could overthrow another, the fact that he had acted was proof of that. Kell felt that once it was started, a fight to the death would be inevitable. The fate of the world might depend on the outcome.

"Tell him about this human that Golkar has brought here to help him. That will alarm him enough to ensure that he joins me."

"I hope so," Nim replied. "And then on to Elissa?"

Having gathered what he would need from his desk, Kell turned to face his friend. "Yes, that's right. She must do what she can to resist the sligs by herself for the moment. I'm not sure what he hopes to gain by it, but I think it is clear that Golkar will not hinder them. Neither Tarak nor I will be able to help her for now. Tell her that we will come as soon as we are able."

Opening both arms, Kell clasped his friend to him, feeling Nim respond warmly to his show of affection. After a brief embrace, he stood back with his hands on Nim's shoulders. He knew they would both be lucky to live through what was before them. This could be the last time they would see each other. Looking into the quickling's eyes he spoke softly. "May Mishra guide your way, my friend. Once you've spoken to the Queen, join me in Annwn. If I'm not there, wait for me. It's to there I'll return when I can."

Nim nodded and turned towards the door. He turned back as the wizard spoke again. "Please don't do anything foolish, Nim. If there is trouble in the Vale of Dreams, don't do anything rash. Save your own skin."

"Don't worry," said Nim with a grin. "I wasn't planning on any heroics."

Kell watched his friend till he was out of sight and then headed for his own quarters, anxious to be on his way to Annwn. He had some thinking to do. The news that Golkar had obtained an ally of unknown power or strength had shaken him more than he wished to let on to his companion. He had considered extensively the prospect of a confrontation with Golkar, but this 'champion' he had enlisted from another world created a wild card that he had not allowed for.

He did not know how but he did know what he and Tarak would have to do first if they were to survive the coming battle. They would have to find this human and eliminate him.

CHAPTER 6

With a tug on its rein, Rayne urged his horse on, up over the rocky surface, slowly climbing higher with each step taken. They were leading them now, but the horses were still finding the going hard, constantly slipping on the worn granite surface in the fading evening light. Although they had pushed on through the day, knowing they had to put as much ground between them and their pursuers as they could, their strength was ebbing in tandem with the dwindling light. The mad rush that had begun at the falls had gradually slowed as the afternoon wore on and their progress had now dwindled to a determined slog.

Darkness was falling quickly and Sara could feel her exhaustion sapping the strength from her limbs as she dragged herself along in Rayne's wake. With her eyes cast down, carefully watching every weary step she took on the slippery surface, she nearly walked right into the back of his horse when it suddenly halted in front of her.

"This'll do," said Rayne, as she drew abreast of him. "Let's tether the horses over there." Sara wearily followed his lead. Where he had stopped, the ground levelled out for a short distance among a small clump of trees.

"If you can unsaddle them and brush them down," Rayne added, taking his bow from his gear, "I'll do a quick scout around."

Sara nodded mutely as Rayne headed back in the direction they had come from. Mechanically, she forced herself through the process of unsaddling Nell, then repeated the procedure for the horse Rayne had been riding. Once that was done, she took the stiff brush he kept in his saddlebags and began to groom Nell with long, slow, purposeful strokes, knowing she had to conserve enough energy to do the same for the other horse.

At first, she found herself looking around nervously, peering into the darkness beyond the trees as she worked. She had been tempted to ask Rayne to stay with her, but he'd been off so quickly he hadn't really given her much of a chance to voice an objection. Besides, she had to be braver than that. Rayne was no fool; she only had to think about his response to the attack at the falls to know that. Although Sara had no experience in such matters, she wondered how many grown men in similar circumstances would have acted as coolly as he had. He knew the risks now just as well as she did. He knew that a group of men were out there somewhere, looking for them.

Someone she had hoped never to set eyes on again was leading those men. She had recognised the draghar instantly at the falls and dreaded what might happen should he ever catch up with them. Sara shivered at the thought of becoming their captive again. As she worked, she offered up a silent prayer of thanks to whoever was responsible for putting Rayne in her path. She would already be back in their clutches, if not dead, if it hadn't been for him. For all that, though, Sara knew they shouldn't count on getting away so easily a second time.

Realising her turn of thoughts was only making her depressed, Sara turned her mind back to the task at hand. She had already finished with Nell and was working on the big chestnut coloured colt they had found at the falls. As she brushed his flanks with long sweeping strokes, she started to hum, her spirits rising as she picked up the rhythm of one of her favourite songs.

"I think I'll call you Ned," she said aloud to the horse after a few minutes, having forgotten how the rest of the tune went. "Ned, meet Nell. Nell, meet Ned."

"You're a cool one."

Sara jumped, unable to stifle a small screech at the unexpected voice behind her. Turning quickly, she was relieved to see Rayne, with his bow slung over his shoulder and three or four of the wild tubas he always seemed to be able to find so easily in his hand.

"I thought you'd be worried about me," he said with a grin. "Here you are humming a song and having a nice little chat with the horses. I needn't have worried at all."

"Oh, Rayne," Sara returned, her emotions a mixture of annoyance and relief. "I nearly had a heart attack. Don't do that again."

"I'm sorry," he replied, with a wry grin on his face. "I didn't mean to scare you. You looked pretty relaxed to me."

"Well, that's how much you know. I've been scared out of my wits here waiting for you."

"I truly am sorry," said Rayne, all serious now. "You look like you've done a good job there. Let's hobble them for the night. Give me a hand."

Several minutes later the task was completed and the two horses were left to forage for what foliage could be found among the trees that surrounded their campsite. Rayne then took his saddlebags from among Nell's gear and laid them out on the ground. As he started removing the things he needed for their camp, he turned once more to Sara. "Let's get our gear ready first and then we can talk. Would you bring those saddlebags over from . . . Ned is it? Let's see if there's anything useful in there."

They both busied themselves then. While Rayne laid out his bedroll, Sara began taking out everything she could find from the stranger's gear.

"Cold supper tonight I'm afraid," said Rayne, pulling from his pack some dried meat to add to the wild roots he had found. "We can't light a fire. If they're anywhere close by it would draw them straight to us."

His reference to their pursuers startled Sara, who looked up from what she'd been doing and began nervously scanning the trees that surrounded them. "Do you think they're close?" she asked in a whisper.

"No. It's okay," replied Rayne, leaning across and placing a reassuring hand on her shoulder. "I don't think they could have caught up to us yet. It will take them some time to figure out what went on back there and then get back on our trail. Besides, I did all I could to make it a difficult one to follow. We should be all right for tonight. It's just that we can't take any chances." Sara visibly relaxed as he spoke, but continued to glance around, eyeing the trees suspiciously.

"So, what did you find?" asked Rayne, trying to distract her attention from the darkness that surrounded them.

Although the sun had set some time ago, the moon had risen and was casting enough light through the trees for them to still be able to see what they were doing. They both turned their attention to their new acquisitions.

Sara had already taken the soft leather water pouch and the bedroll which had been tied to the back of the man's saddle and had placed them beside her. The bedroll was particularly welcome, as Rayne had been gallantly letting her use his since the night they had first met.

Turning to the saddlebags, she began to rummage through their contents as well, drawing out the items she found one at a time so that they both could examine them. First out was a little tan-coloured cloth bag with a drawstring top. Opening it, she quickly confirmed that it was, as she had guessed, full of coins, mainly bronze with the occasional glint of silver. Passing it to Rayne, she dug down further, producing in quick succession a tinderbox, a pipe, a pouch of tobacco, and some dried meat wrapped around with cloth. Rayne took the last item. Holding it up to his nose before examining it more closely, he declared it a much-needed addition to their supplies.

Moving to the other bag, Sara found a pair of linen trousers and a shirt, bigger than those she had borrowed from Rayne, but definitely usable. Beneath that she found a small, wooden shovel, a long leather coat rolled up tightly into a roll with a hat of similar material and, right at the bottom, a coil of rope. Rayne said the coat was a weather jacket, similar to one he had. Its tanned exterior would keep out the rain. Taking the rope from her, he examined it closely, measuring it by looping it, as one does with rope, from elbow to palm.

"This is good rope," he pronounced, "and a decent length to boot. I've got some of my own but this extra length may come in handy."

While he was doing that, Sara produced the last of her finds, a grooming brush for the horse and, wrapped in a small leather pouch, a cake of soap and a comb. Sara smelt them both gingerly. She expected them, probably unreasonably, to give off some strange odour, but was pleasantly surprised when she found that they both seemed quite usable. The soap was nothing like the cake Rayne had loaned her a few days previously but would certainly come in handy.

"Not a bad haul," said Rayne as Sara finished and began putting the items back where they had come from. To her surprise, he began to lay out the new bedroll alongside his.

"Mmmm," replied Sara, her hands busy with the saddlebags but her mind on what he was doing. On previous nights they had slept on opposite sides of the fire, with Sara curled up in the bedroll and Rayne stretched out on the bare ground with his saddle for a pillow.

"Is this okay?" asked Rayne in a low voice, interrupting her thoughts. With a start, she realised she had been staring at what he was doing.

"What? Sorry." Sara looked up at Rayne, noticing that he had stopped arranging her bed and was looking directly at her.

"I just thought that, without a fire, and it being dark, and you being a little bit jumpy and all, that you'd feel a bit safer with us next to each other, and not leagues apart. I'll sleep over there somewhere if you'd rather." Rayne pointed vaguely in the direction of the horses.

"No, no, of course not," said Sara. "I . . . I just . . . n-no . . . that's fine, really, no that's fine, really. Oh . . . I mean . . . hell . . . don't mind me. I'm just a bit shaken up by everything. It's a good idea . . . and very thoughtful of you."

She focused her attention on the saddlebags as Rayne went on with what he was doing. Once their two beds were laid out, he placed a saddle at the head of each one, but at opposite ends so they could lie head to toe, beside each other. Sara suspected that he had decided on the latter at the last minute in response to her reaction to what he had done.

Once their beds were laid out, they both sat down on their blankets facing each other. While they chewed on the dry rations Rayne allocated for their dinner, they began to chat. "I know this is a bit distressing, Sara," said Rayne, "but I think we should talk about what we're going to do now. We have to have a plan after what happened today."

"I know," said Sara despondently. "I'm sorry I got you into this, Rayne." She couldn't bring herself to look at him as she spoke. Although she was aware she would have no chance at all without his help, she felt terribly guilty that his life was now as much at risk as hers was.

Rayne reached out and placed his hand over hers as she nervously played with the rope belt at her waist. "Don't worry about it," he said. "You didn't ask for this trouble either, remember. We're in it together now, so let's just concentrate on getting out of it."

Sara nodded, afraid that if she spoke she might cry. She simply couldn't believe the kindness Rayne had shown to her. It stood out in such contradiction to everything else that had happened to her since she'd arrived in this place. Luckily, Rayne seemed to sense her feelings and recognise her need to contain her emotions for the moment. Withdrawing his hand, and sitting back, he went on.

"I won't try and kid you, Sara. We have to understand what we're up against. Things don't look too good. From what I saw, there are at least three of them after us, and they're not likely to give up the chase easily. You already killed one of them, and now I have too. They aren't going to call it off after that, if they ever were going to, anyway. What's more, they've tracked us over a fairly long distance, which means they know what they're doing. We won't find it easy to shake them. Quite frankly, if we hadn't found that second horse I don't think we would have gotten this far."

Sara fought down her emotions and tried to contribute to the discussion. She knew what Rayne was saying was true. "So what can we do?" she asked. "Isn't there anywhere we can go for help?"

"The problem," said Rayne, "is that we're a long way from help. The wilderness is a big place and we're a fair way into it. There are some small settlements here and there, but they aren't places you can count on for help. This is a pretty wild place, Sara. The people we're likely to meet in the settlements may be just as likely to hand us over to the men who are after us as they would be to help us. For all we know, the men who are chasing us have come from one of those settlements."

"But Rayne," cried Sara, her alarm clear in her rising voice, "if that's the case then we don't have a chance. We can't fight three of them and . . ."

"Hang on, hang on," interrupted Rayne. "Don't give in so easily."

Sara drew a deep breath, reminding herself that his advice was the same she had given herself back in her cell. Now was not the time to give up. "Okay," she said. "I'm sorry. What do you think we should do?"

"That's better." He paused before he went on. "Okay, I think we have no choice but to continue to run. Only, we're going to have to change our goal. I've already been steering us in a new direction. If we keep going directly for Algaria, we'd never make it. It's too far to get through the wilderness that way. I think we should take a more southerly route that will get us out of the wilderness much more quickly. It will still take us about six or seven days. Once we're out of the wilderness, we can find a town and a militia post and then we'll be safe."

"That sounds reasonable," said Sara, much more relieved now that she knew Rayne had a plan. "Six or seven days sounds like a lot, though. Can we keep ahead of them that long?"

"Not without a lot of luck. I said I didn't want to fool you about this Sara. I know it upsets you, but we won't make it through this unless we both understand what we're up against. Quite frankly, I don't see how we can keep ahead of them for very much longer. My guess is we'll be lucky if they don't catch up within three or four. But we've got to try. We'll just have to deal with whatever happens when it happens.

"It's not all bad," he went on. "I know the area we're making for a lot better than where we've been. My dad and I did some trapping there a few years back. And hopefully the further we go the further we get away from the parts the people following us know."

"Thank you, Rayne," said Sara, after a few moments. She was grateful, not just for his honesty but for the fact that he was treating her like an adult. "It does scare me to hell, but you're right. If I don't know what might happen, then I won't be ready for it when it does." She knew her words sounded braver than she felt. She also guessed that Rayne was probably more scared than he was actually letting on to her.

Rayne smiled back at her, once more reaching out and touching her arm to comfort her. "Good. Now, some practical things. We're not going to be able to have a fire at night any more and we won't have much time for one during the day. I'll cook us something in the morning if I can find any game. But that'll probably be our last fire for some time."

Sara nodded. She suspected she would quickly come to hate the taste of dried meat and raw roots.

"You can have the bow we took from that man at the falls," he continued. "I want you to make sure that you've got it and your knife with you, or within reach, at all times. Unfortunately, we won't have time for any more practice. From what you showed me, you know what you're doing anyway. Just remember, if you have to use it, do so. Don't hesitate. Don't let what happened at the falls fool you. I got lucky with that shot. Those men are killers and they know what they're doing. If you hesitate, they won't."

"Okay," said Sara. She was glad now that she had pushed him to show her how to use his bow. She'd only had two practice sessions but felt much better for them. Her archery lessons at school might serve some purpose now after all.

They had already proven their usefulness when Rayne had given her his bow one morning after breakfast and told her to have a go, pointing to a tree about twenty paces away. She'd beamed with pride when she had hit it with three out of five arrows. Although he thought the way she held the bow was downright strange, he'd told her he wasn't going to ask her to change anything while she shot like that. "You're a regular Rolfe Harkinson," he had said. When she asked who Rolfe Harkinson was, he told her he was a famous person who'd won an archery contest and saved his son's life. Sara thought he'd probably been trying to build up her confidence, but was quite happy to take the compliment anyway.

"We'll be okay for tonight," continued Rayne, "but from tomorrow we're going to have to take turns sleeping. And we're going to have to pick our campsites very carefully. We'll need spots where we can't be ambushed very easily."

"What if they keep going through the night?" asked Sara. "Won't they catch up very quickly if they do that?"

"They won't be able to do that. They can't track us in the dark. We'll be twisting around a bit so they can't be sure where we're headed. They'll have to wait for daylight to follow us. I've also got some tricks in mind that will slow them down and help us to get some of that extra time that we need."

"Like what?" asked Sara.

"I'd rather not talk about them," said Rayne turning his face from her as he fumbled for something from his pocket. "I don't feel too good about it, but I don't see much choice. Just leave it to me."

Sara looked on in fascination as Rayne averted his eyes to cover his obvious embarrassment. She was intrigued at what he might do that would make him too ashamed to talk about it. Rather than pursue the subject, she sensed it was better left alone.

"Okay," she responded, raising her hand to cover a yawn. She had forgotten how tired she was. "Anything else?"

"No. I think that's enough for one night. Except . . . I think you're the bravest girl that I ever met. I just wish we'd met under different circumstances."

Now it was Sara's turn to be embarrassed. "Thank you," she said, not really knowing how to respond. After the briefest of pauses, she continued, deciding it was best if she changed the subject. "We'd better get some sleep. I gather we're going to have to get going as early as possible tomorrow."

"Yes, I guess so." Rayne's subdued reply indicated that he was equally as embarrassed as she was by what he had said.

They both silently went about preparing for bed. Sara noticed Rayne smile when she put the bow and arrows on the ground beside her and placed Tug's dagger under the blanket she had propped up against her saddle for a pillow. Within a few moments, they were both lying back quietly, tucked into their bedding.

Sara went through Rayne's comment again in her head. It occurred to her he might have been trying to say more than he had. She quickly rejected the idea. She had known for some time she had a bit of a crush on Rayne and could see she was just projecting her wishes onto his actions. Although he had made a few gestures of affection towards her, he was probably just feeling sorry for her. He was clearly an innately kind person after all. She was carrying on like a silly schoolgirl to think it was anything more than it was. She also felt she wasn't being fair to Rayne, who had been so wonderful putting his own life in danger to help her. Rather than responding like a child, she decided that behaving more like an adult would be a better way to show her gratitude in future.

Putting those thoughts aside, Sara lay on her back for a while, staring up at the stars and listening to the sounds of the forest. None of the constellations looked at all familiar to her. The moon, which had been almost overhead earlier, was now low down on the horizon, a thin sliver of silver dripping light into the valley below them. Her thoughts, which had drifted to home and the family she knew would be distraught at her disappearance, were rudely interrupted when an owl hooted suddenly from somewhere close by, back in the direction they had come from. For a few moments, Sara's heart pounded as she wondered what might have disturbed it. Was the owl sounding out a warning?

"Rayne," she whispered. "Are you awake?"

"Yes. Why?" came the whispered reply.

"Do you hear anything?"

"Only you keeping me awake."

That does it, thought Sara. Throwing back her blanket, she stood up and bent to pick up the saddle that she had been resting against.

"What are you doing?" asked Rayne, lifting his head and looking around.

"I'm not sleeping like this. I'm scared." Sara lifted the saddle and placed it at the opposite end of her bedding, beside the one Rayne was lying against. She then proceeded to turn her bedding around so it lay the same way as his. Having completed the rearrangements, she lay down again. This time she was lying right beside him, though on her side and with her back to him. She had taken the opportunity to move her bedding closer to his.

As she settled into place, she felt his hand on her waist. "It's okay Sara," he whispered from behind her. "It's just the noises of the forest."

"Thank you," replied Sara softly, feeling comforted by his proximity.

A few minutes later, the quiet of the night was broken again. This time it was the harsh call of a bird from the trees above where they had camped, answered a few moments later by its mate further up the slope. Noticing that Rayne's hand hadn't moved from her waist, Sara reached up and put her hand into his. As he gently returned her soft grip, she slowly eased her body back towards him, pulling his hand down around her waist as she did so and clasping it to her stomach with both of her hands.

"Is that all right?" she whispered in the darkness.

"Yes," Rayne answered. She felt his arm gently embrace her waist as he spoke.

Sara smiled contentedly to herself as she felt the tension in her body slowly dissipate. Within a few minutes, she was fast asleep with Rayne's arm securely enfolding her waist and his hand firmly clasped within hers.

CHAPTER 7

The settlement looked peaceful enough. A thin trail of smoke from a chimney was the only sign of life Sara and Rayne could see. Two days had passed since the incident at the falls and they had still seen no sign of their pursuers. Now they sat on their horses, just behind the tree line, watching the four cabins that straddled the banks of a small stream.

From what he had told Sara, Rayne knew precious little about the settlement other than its location. He and his father had passed through this area a few years earlier and his father had mentioned its presence then. He had told Rayne that, although it had a small store where trappers could sell a few pelts and re-stock their provisions, he preferred to avoid it. Apparently, he had been there many years earlier, before Rayne had been old enough to join him on his trips into the wilderness. He had said that he had no desire to go back. The family that lived there looked to him like they would be just as likely to knock you over the head and throw you in the river if they thought there was going to be any profit in it as they would be to help you.

Luckily for him, his trip had been a lean one and he didn't have anything on him that would make it worth their while. They'd had a damn good look though, as he told it, particularly when he pulled out a few silvers to pay for some fresh flour and a few vegetables. Then, when he'd come out of the store, he'd caught one of them having a good look over his horse and his gear. He'd made good time getting out of there and had never gone back.

Now here Sara and Rayne were, sizing up whether they should venture in themselves. The four cabins were at the centre of a few acres of cleared ground, the stumps scattered throughout the area and the split logs the cabins were made of testimony to the forest they had displaced. Sara and Rayne could easily have ridden around the settlement, but they were desperately low on provisions. As Rayne had foreshadowed, there'd been no time for them to hunt or cook over the last few days. Their supply of dried meat was almost exhausted and they were running very low on a number of other items. They decided the chance to restock was too good a one to miss. As long as they were careful, and got in and out with as little delay as possible, they should be all right.

"Okay, let's get it over with," said Rayne, urging Ned forward.

Easing their horses out into the open, they slowly walked them down towards the cabins, riding side by side as they discreetly scanned the area, alert for anything unexpected. They had both strung their bows and wore them slung across their shoulders. Rayne had strapped on his sword and had his knife openly sheathed at his waist, as did Sara. He'd assured her it would be best if anyone they encountered could see they were well armed.

As they moved closer to the buildings, the porch of the nearest and largest one came into view revealing two men seated in the sun with their chairs tilted back and their legs resting on the wooden railing that bordered the front of the dwelling. The slip rail corral at the back of the cabin and the large barrels that lined its side indicated this building was the store Rayne's father had told him about. The three smaller dwellings appeared to be living quarters. One stood a small distance behind the large cabin. The other two faced it from the opposite side of the small watercourse that split the settlement in two. A small bridge made up of logs laid side by side and covered in dirt spanned the stream. As the store itself was built on a slope, its front was raised up on short pylons. A few stairs led up to the front porch.

As these were the first dwellings, other than Golkar's home, which Sara had seen in Ilythia, she had no idea whether they were typical of how people lived. To her, they seemed to be ramshackle and desperately in need of repair. Although she'd never seen a shingle roof before, she was certain the shingles weren't supposed to be jammed in at the oddest of angles, as many of these were. It looked as if some had slipped out and only the most perfunctory attempt had been made at repair.

Her attention was soon drawn back to the largest of the cabins. As they approached it, a dog lazily rose from the porch, walked down the steps, and ambled along the road towards them, hanging its head and slowly wagging its tail as it approached. One of the two men rose from his chair, opened the front door, and disappeared inside. The other stayed where he was, scrutinising them closely as they approached the cabin.

"Hello," called Rayne as they drew up to the front of the store. As he dismounted, Sara followed his example, wondering if he was as nervous as she was. They both tied their horses to the hitching rail that ran along the front of the store and walked up the few stairs that led to the porch. The old man, as they could now see he was, had nodded in reply to Rayne's greeting but had remained seated as they had dismounted and walked up to join him. He looked to be in his seventies or eighties. Thin wisps of silvery hair could be seen protruding from beneath his battered hat. The overalls he was wearing stopped short a few inches above his ankles, revealing the cracked and leathery skin of his lower legs. His leather boots looked almost as ancient as he did.

"We'd like to buy some provisions," said Rayne.

"Well, I guess you come to the right place then," said the old man slowly, rising from his chair with some difficulty as he spoke, then shuffling his way to the door. Rayne and Sara waited for him to open it then followed him inside.

If the exterior had presented a dismal appearance to Sara, then the interior did nothing to dispel this image. The cabin was poorly lit and the dirt-smeared windows did little to alleviate the situation. They seemed more of a hindrance than a help. All in all, this was not what Sara had expected. The musty cabin seemed more like a storeroom than a store to her mind. The place was crammed full of barrels and boxes of various sizes with an assortment of other goods stacked beside, behind and over them. Narrow corridors, formed by the high piles of goods, led off among the mess in a number of directions.

"Ya want some pig meat?" asked the old man, who had traversed the small open area adjacent to the door and opened a cupboard that appeared to contain a number of bundles swathed in wet cloths.

As Rayne walked over to join him, Sara glanced around at the junk that was stacked around the room. With a start, she noticed two men seated on chairs in the shadows to one side of the room. "Hello," she said with a slight smile, trying not to show her surprise at seeing them there.

The men, both in their twenties, simply stared back at her, not even nodding in response. From their looks, they were brothers, or at least very close kin. The clothes they wore were dirty and they themselves looked in desperate need of a good wash. One wore a thick beard and the other sported a stubble of hair on his face as if he hadn't shaved for a few days. Their straggly hair showed evidence of having been roughly hacked back to keep it off their ears and collars. As Sara looked at them, the bearded one, quite openly and deliberately, slowly looked her up and down. Sara remembered the look that Golkar had given her, and the thought made her shudder. She quickly turned back towards Rayne, not wanting them to see the flush of embarrassment she felt on her face.

As she moved closer to Rayne, she heard one of the men give a low chuckle and whisper something to his companion, who laughed in return. Sara sat down on one of the boxes on the opposite side of the room, positioning herself so she could see the two men in her peripheral vision while she watched what Rayne and the old man were doing.

" . . . and some salt if you've got any," she heard Rayne call out to the old man, who was scooping something from a barrel into a small sack at the rear of the room.

The old man grunted in reply. Placing the sack to one side he took a smaller cloth bag and began filling it from another container. While he busied himself doing this, Rayne turned and smiled at Sara. Without turning her head, she moved her eyes purposefully in the direction of the two younger men. Nonchalantly, Rayne turned and glanced around the room, obviously taking in the two men as he did so. He then turned back once more to the old man who had shuffled over to him with the two sacks.

Sara watched as the old man placed them on top of a box beside Rayne, alongside a cloth covered mound, which she took to be meat, and another smaller object wrapped in a thin gauze of cloth. She hoped that Rayne had obtained something more inviting than pig meat.

"How much for all that?" asked Rayne, taking a small bag of coins from his pocket.

"Well," said the old man, his eyes fixed on the coin bag, "let's see. There's the oats, the meat . . . and the cheese . . . flour . . . salt . . . bread. That'll be . . . I reckon that'll be four of them silver pieces there and six of them coppers."

Rayne counted out the coins from his bag. When that was not enough, he reached into his pocket and produced a few extra coppers. "There you go," he said to the old man, placing the coins in his hand and pushing the now empty coin bag and his few remaining coppers back into his pocket. Sara was relieved that his estimation of the amount he would need had been accurate. He had hidden most of their money, rolling it up inside his bedroll, only leaving enough to cover what he needed to buy.

"Okay, Sara," he said, picking up the goods from the top of the box and turning towards the door, "let's go."

The old man looked over at the other two men. "You there, Jape, you no good loafer. Go git two bags of oats from the back room and bring it round front." One of the men reluctantly rose and headed for the back of the cabin, mumbling something to himself as he went.

While this was happening, Sara stood up and followed Rayne out through the door, noticing as she went that the remaining man was still staring at her, eyeing her up and down as if she was a piece of meat. As they left, both he and the old man followed them out.

Rayne walked down to the horses and began stowing the fresh provisions into the saddlebags, distributing the extra weight among the two horses. While he did that, Sara stood casually to one side, discreetly keeping an eye on the two men who were now joined by their companion. The latter was carrying two large cloth bags, presumably full of oats.

"Did you say your girl's name was Sara, fella?" asked the old man when Rayne had finished what he was doing.

Sara felt her blood run cold at the man's query. Noticing that Rayne had shown no reaction to the question, she forced herself to walk slowly over to the horses and mount Nell. The man with the oats walked down to them, handing the bundles to Rayne who added them to his gear, tying one to each side of Ned's saddle. Once he had done that, Rayne mounted Ned.

"What's it to you?" answered Rayne once he was mounted. As he spoke Ned frisked around nervously, turning this way and that as Rayne held him in place with a tight grip on his rein. Sara could see that the man who had passed him the oats was looking closely at Ned's flank as he twisted and turned in front of him.

"And would your name be Rayne?" asked the old man in his slow drawl, ignoring Rayne's question.

"What if it is?" asked Rayne, steadying Ned and looking back intently at the old man.

Sara could feel the tension in the air. She wasn't sure whether to be ready to put an arrow to her bow or to turn Nell and take flight. She watched Rayne closely, waiting for one of their prearranged signals. He had given no sign of using either as yet. While she waited and listened to the unexpected exchange, she wondered what could possibly be going on. She didn't see how the old man could know what their names were. She had realised from his first question that Rayne had slipped and mentioned her name, but she had barely spoken at all herself. Even if Tug had somehow been here before them, there was no way for the old man to know Rayne's name. And yet, impossibly, he did.

"Well, I reckon I know someone who's wantin to meet up with ya, young fella," said the old man. "An old fella come lookin for you and yer friend few days back now. Real old fella he was. Even older than me." As he said this the old man gave a short cackle, exposing a few missing teeth. "Said he was yer uncle and askt if I seen ya."

"Oh," said Rayne. "Thanks for letting me know. If he comes back again tell him we're heading up Thompson's Swamp way. He might find us up there if he's not far behind us."

"Will do young fella, will do," said the old man, shuffling back to his chair in the sun.

As Rayne turned Ned, ready to move away, the man who had been examining the horse spoke up. "That's a right fine lookin mount you got there boy," he said. "You had him long?"

"Thanks," said Rayne. "Actually I bought him off of a trapper I met a few days back. My horse went lame and he offered to sell me this one. Well, thanks for your help. We'll be off now."

With that Rayne turned Ned and rode off, with Sara and Nell close behind. Sara noticed as he crossed the creek and headed for the tree line that the direction he took was different to the one they had planned. She guessed he was intending to carry through with his pretence of heading for Thompson's Swamp, at least until he was out of sight.

Once they had cleared the tree line, Rayne risked a quick glance back over his shoulder. "They're not following," he said to Sara as she drew level with him. "Let's get going, I didn't like any of that at all."

They rode on in silence then for some time. The path Rayne took led them single file, affording little opportunity for them to speak further, and it was some time before he finally stopped for a break. By then the settlement was a long way behind them. While the horses rested and cropped the grass nearby, he and Sara sat down on the ground and shared a drink from his water flask.

"What was that all about?" asked Sara. "It didn't make sense. How could your uncle know my name and why didn't you want him to know where we're going?"

"I don't have an uncle," said Rayne. "Least none that I know about. I don't get it, either. The only people who know your name wouldn't know mine and anyone who knew mine wouldn't know yours."

Sara was totally thrown by this new development. She could see no explanation for what the old man had said. "What can it possibly mean?" she asked Rayne.

"Maybe it's Golkar," he replied. "Maybe he has some way with his magic of knowing that you're with me."

Sara shook her head. The description the old man had given didn't fit Golkar at all. "Golkar's not old," she said. "He looked fairly young to me."

"According to my dad, he's centuries old. All the wizards are. I don't see who else it could be."

Sara still wasn't convinced. "I don't think so," she said. "If Golkar could chase after us himself, why would he bother sending Tug and his men?"

"I don't know," Rayne replied in a tired voice, hanging his head and looking at the ground. "It's great isn't it? Just when we think things are really bad, we find out we've got someone else looking for us as well. Then, to add to our troubles, that young guy back there starts looking at Ned as if he knows he isn't my horse. I wouldn't mind betting he recognised the brand. I should have thought about that. Next thing they'll be after us as well."

Rayne leaned back and sighed, running his fingers through his hair, from his forehead to the nape of his neck. Sara could tell the strain was getting to him.

"Hey, c'mon," she said leaning towards him and placing an arm around his shoulder. "Now who's giving up. They haven't got us yet. Remember, it ain't over till the fat lady sings."

"What?" said Rayne looking up with a grin. "It ain't over till what?"

"Never mind," said Sara. "It's a long story. It just means it isn't over till it's over."

"But what's a fat lady singing got to do with it?"

"I'm not really sure, actually."

Rayne's concerns gradually dissipated as the day wore on and they slowly settled back into the routine they had established over the past few days. Despite the absence of any sign of pursuit, they still did their best to make their trail a difficult one to follow. Occasionally they would stop and Rayne would go back over their path for some distance, doing his best to remove any sign of their passage. Wherever they could they followed watercourses, entering at one point and emerging some distance away either up or downstream. If there were wide expanses of rock, they would ride over those.

By nightfall, they were exhausted. Their supper was better than they had had for some days. The fresh bread and cheese was a gratifying substitute for their usual fare of dried stringy meat and stale roots dug up along the trail some days past. Nell and Ned even got their share with some oats in a nosebag for each of them. Rayne said he would have to ration it out for them, supplementing their diet whenever they couldn't get good pasturage.

They called it an early night after that, wanting to push on again at first light the next day. As Rayne had suggested, they had taken to sleeping in turns. Sara drew first watch and it wasn't long before Rayne was fast asleep. She sat down beside him with her back propped up against a tree. The crescent moon was out in force again, lighting up the campsite with its soft, silvery light. Occasionally a cloud would scud across its path, darkening the sky for a short time until it moved on.

Leaning back against the rough bark of the tree, Sara found herself cycling through the three subjects that always seemed to dominate her thoughts, home and how much she missed all of her friends and her family, Tug and Golkar and all of the dread she felt about them, and Rayne. She tended to dwell more on the latter if she could. The other two tended to depress her and had an unfortunate knack of forcing themselves back into her consciousness when she least wanted them to. Her thoughts of Rayne, though childish daydreams, were a welcome escape from the fears and concerns she knew would return the next day.

As she had no watch to guide her, the moon was her timepiece. They had agreed that when it set for the night she would wake Rayne and it would be her turn to sleep and his to keep watch. Not that she really knew what she was watching for. Despite the moonlight, she was sure someone could creep up very close to their camp without her realising they were there.

Rayne had said that, although that might be true, at least they wouldn't wake up with knives at their throats. He had gone on to point out, rather unnecessarily she thought, that in fact, it would only be her that woke up with a blade at her throat. He wouldn't wake at all. No doubt the blade for him would be buried in his back. Although that had shocked her, he had made his point. At least someone awake could alert the other and give them some chance.

The night was well advanced when finally the position of the moon close to the horizon told Sara it would soon be time to wake Rayne. She decided to creep off into the bushes and relieve her bladder before she awoke him, allowing him a few precious extra moments of sleep before it was his turn to keep watch. It wasn't the first time she had done so while he slept. She always made sure that she didn't go far, just enough to ensure her privacy should he wake unexpectedly. Stealthily she rose, picked up her bow and quiver dutifully as Rayne had told her to do, and crept off through the bushes, moving slowly and carefully to ensure she didn't disturb him.

When she had gone not much more than a score of paces from the campsite, she put down the bow. Slipping out of her trousers, she squatted down in a space between two trees. In a few moments, she was done. Silently standing and dressing again, she started to head back to the camp only to freeze in mid-step as she heard a sound off through the trees to her left. It sounded like voices. She had to be wrong, she told herself. She had learnt that the forest could produce the strangest of noises in the dark of the night and she had given up trying to work out the source of most of them.

Then she heard it again. Her pulse rate quickened as she desperately tried to think of the right thing to do. If it was someone preparing to ambush them and she went back to the camp to awaken Rayne, whoever it was would surely see her and move to attack them before she could rouse him. She made a fateful decision. She decided to try to get closer to where the sound was coming from and see if she could identify its source. Taking the bow from over her shoulder, she notched an arrow. Then, slowly, and ever so carefully, she began to creep through the forest, in the direction she thought the sound had come from.

Her progress was agonisingly slow. It seemed that every step would betray her presence. No matter how hard she tried, it was impossible to avoid the profusion of twigs and decaying matter that covered the forest floor, especially out here among the thick of the trees in the dead of the night. Even the slightest sound seemed amplified to Sara as she struggled to divide her senses between the twin tasks of threading a silent path through the darkened forest and remaining alert to whatever it was that was out there.

Her attention was soon drawn back to the more important of her tasks, however. She had only covered a dozen or so paces when she heard the sound again. This time she could identify it. It was a voice, as she had suspected . . . a man's voice. Peering from behind a tree, she could make out the shadow of a man; or was it two? They were very close, maybe a dozen or so paces from her, but partly obscured by some bushes. Then she heard the voice again, much clearer now that she knew where it was coming from.

"Can you see them?" someone whispered.

Another voice whispered in reply. "Yep, they're over by that tree. He's the one on the left. I think that's her lying just to his right." The voice sounded familiar. She couldn't be sure but she thought it might be the man from the settlement. The one who had asked Rayne about Ned.

The other man spoke again. "Have you got a shot?"

"Yep."

"Well take it."

Sara realised she had to do something. She felt paralysed with fear but remembered Rayne's advice: 'Don't hesitate. If you do, they won't'. As she fought with her fear, she saw the shape of a man rise from the bushes, standing up from where they'd been crouching. She watched in horror as he raised his bow to his shoulder, obviously taking aim at Rayne as he lay asleep in the camp. Without thinking, Sara quickly raised her own bow, took aim at the man and let loose the arrow she'd held. As the missile sped from her hand, she shouted out into the night, "Rayne! Look out!"

As her voice rang out, she saw the man with the bow fall suddenly to one side, just as he fired his own arrow. A strange gurgling sound came from where he had fallen, almost instantly followed by a scream of pain from the direction of their camp. Instinctively, Sara looked towards Rayne, but to no avail. She was too far away and it was too dark for her to see anything from her position. The sound of snapping twigs and bushes being brushed aside brought her eyes quickly back to where she'd last seen their attackers.

Sara reeled back in horror as she saw that one of the men was charging directly at her through the forest. He was only a few paces away from her now with a knife brandished in one hand. Dropping her bow and fumbling for the knife at her belt, she felt her legs turn to jelly as she realised she'd left it beside her bedding. As she stumbled backwards, fumbling for the knife she'd forgotten, her assailant crashed into her, knocking her to the ground with the force of his charge. Desperately, she grappled with him, scratching at his face with one hand as the other grabbed on to the wrist that bore his knife.

Sara felt despair consuming her as she realised it would all be over in seconds. He was too strong for her. She couldn't hold him off. Then, suddenly, she felt a sharp crack to the side of her head and she lost all of the strength in her muscles. Her assailant had bashed her with his free elbow, just below the temple, wrenching his other arm from her grip as he did so. As she struggled to stay conscious, her head ringing from the blow he'd given her, she felt the weight of his body slump down upon her, immobilising her. Through the fog that was filling her head, she sensed that he had stopped moving. Then, without warning, she felt his body lift up off of hers, inexplicably swing over on to its back and slump down beside her. As she struggled to gain focus, Rayne's face appeared out of the darkness, looking down at her with a concerned look. Then, as fast as it had appeared, it disappeared again.

Sara desperately tried to get back up onto her feet but could only raise herself far enough to rest on her elbows. The dim shapes she could see around her were blurred and seemed to be moving in various directions. She sensed that if she stood up she would only fall over again. The whole forest seemed to be swinging backwards and forwards before her eyes.

From a short distance away she heard a strangled cry and then, thankfully, a few moments later, Rayne's face appeared out of the darkness again. As he bent down over her, Sara managed to reach up and put her arms around him, letting him drag her up into a seated position.

"Oh, Rayne," she cried, hugging him closely to her, the tears beginning to run down her cheeks as the shock of what had happened hit her. "I thought you were dead." She held on tightly to Rayne as she sobbed. Her stomach was churning with a mixture of emotions.

"It's okay now, it's okay," he replied. His voice was soft and soothing as he gently stroked the back of her head.

"You have to let go of me now," he said to her after a few moments. "Be very careful, I've hurt my left arm."

Looking around at Rayne as she allowed him to gently ease her away from his body, Sara gasped in horror. Protruding from either side of Rayne's upper arm was an arrow. His sleeve was matted in blood.

CHAPTER 8

The gloom that had dogged Nim's trail from the time he had left Cloudtopper lifted as soon as he topped the last ridge and spied the valley below him. The Vale of Dreams was, as always, a glorious sight. Far below him, the cool waters of the Farrofir River glistened and sparkled in the sun. The rich farmland that hugged its banks reminded Nim of a patchwork quilt spread out in readiness for a May Eve picnic. The varying colours of the tilled soils, fallow fields and ripening crops evoked memories of happier days, of his childhood and the fond friends of his youth.

Dotted across the scene were the thatched roofs of the cottages and hamlets of the inhabitants of the Vale. Far in the distance, on the eastern side of the valley, the white stone roof of the wizard's dome glinted brightly in the morning sun. Closer to where he now stood, nestling among the folds of the slope that ran down to the bank of the river, Nim could spy the familiar red clay tiles and ochre walls of the outbuildings of the College of the Medicants.

Even from this distance, Nim fancied he could hear the happy chatter of the young initiates toiling in the herb beds or taking their lessons from the Mistress of Herbs or one of her Instructs. Tarak's enduring monument to his passion for sharing the bounty of his knowledge with his fellow Ilythians never failed to fill Nim with awe. The selfless dedication of this, the third of Tanis' disciples, was truly inspiring. With a momentary feeling of melancholy, Nim wondered how the great mage could have erred so badly in his selection of Golkar. His other two disciples were such models of devotion to the land they served.

Having taken his fill of the view before him, Nim shook off his reverie and strode down into the valley, resting now from the loping run that had carried him more than one hundred leagues in the last two days. Although the sun beat down warmly on his face as he walked, it was the soft sun of Spring, the full heat of Summer was still at least two moons away. And because it was Spring, the fields he strode through were dotted with labourers, planting anew and tending to the newly formed buds on the perennials. Nim found that his path wound its way through a proliferation of colours and scents and he drank it all in, savouring the visual feast and the intoxicating odours.

In one field, a great host of storkbills, a few of them already in bloom, covered the ground from one stone fence to the next. In another grew coneflowers and comfrey, colt's foot and columbine, all laid out neatly in long parallel rows. In the next, a stand of turnsoles had turned their faces to the morning sun, as if in silent worship of the fiery orb. A little further on, he found beds of burdock and valerian, of southernwood and sweet smelling bridewort. And those were the ones he could name.

Despite his strange appearance, and the fact that quicklings were rarely seen in Tenamos, even here in the Vale of Dreams, Nim received nothing but nods and the occasional hearty greeting from the workers who tended the plants, toiling away cheerfully in the scent-filled fields.

As he neared the stone arch that marked the entrance to the College of the Medicants, he couldn't help but cast an admiring glance at the long classrooms with their shutters thrown open to catch the cool morning breeze. It was two years now since the College had celebrated its fiftieth anniversary. Already its impact on Tenamos was far-reaching.

Few now were the Medicants who hadn't learnt their craft here in the Vale, or been taught by one that had done so. And what fine Medicants they were. The craft of healing had begun to make great leaps forward, just as Tarak had hoped it would. The congregation of so many like-minded students and teachers in one place was wetting a thirst for knowledge beyond what even he could teach them. Whole new fields of study were beginning to be opened up now on a regular basis.

Leaving the College behind, Nim covered the remaining few leagues by cart, hitching a ride with a rustic young labourer, Petr by name, who was taking a cartload of goods up the valley in the direction of the Dome of the Wizard. From Petr, Nim learnt, with relief, that Tarak was indeed at home. He'd feared that the wizard might be away. The urgency of his message wouldn't have permitted a delay, and he'd yet to go on to Elissa.

Petr seemed a friendly young fellow and was no more intrigued by the strangeness of the quickling than he might have been had it chanced to snow. "Lots of travellers from the east these days," he noted conversationally to Nim as the cart slowly trundled forward. "You're the first I've seen from the south for a while, though."

"Oh," replied Nim casually, not wanting to sound like he was eager for news, even though he was. "Why is that? What's going on in the east?"

"Trouble in Algaria, so they say. Trouble in Algaria."

"Really? What kind of trouble?"

"Them sligs been brewing up trouble for the farm folk with their raids and whatnot. Least that's what they say." Petr didn't sound very concerned. He might as well have been discussing last year's harvest.

Oh," replied Nim. "Is it anything we should worry about here?"

"Nah," sneered Petr, wrinkling his face as he did so. "I wouldn't put too much stock by it meself. Some people like to make a lotta fuss o'er naught. I'm sure it's nothin the Queen's Rangers won't put right soon enough."

"I hope you're right. I hear the sligs can make quite a nuisance of themselves when they've a mind to."

'Well," said Petr in his slow country drawl. "If they keep on with this nonsense, they'll soon have a Guardian to reckon with, and that'll be that. 'Sides, Tarak won't let 'em bother us."

"Mmmm. Guess you're right there."

As Nim well knew, the people of the Vale took most everything in their stride, trusting in their benefactor, Tarak, to take care of them. The quickling couldn't help but wonder what would come of that trust in the days to come. Would it stand them in good stead in the times of adversity that were bound to follow, or would it be their undoing? Shaking off the negative thought which seemed, like a solitary black cloud in an otherwise clear blue sky, so out of place in the Vale, Nim took in the Dome of the Wizard as it loomed up ahead of him.

The dome was a startling construction, by any standard. Its white marble surface glinted in the sun atop a small hillock to one side and ahead of the road they were travelling by. The hillock itself had once been the site of an old hill fort, with a flattened top surmounted on all sides by a crumbling wall of stone. It was said that many centuries ago, even before the time of Tanis, this was how the people defended themselves. Even now the ruins of long deserted settlements straddled the top of many a hill, silent monuments to the old Ilythians, with nothing to tell of their passing except the crumbling, weed-ridden stones that ringed their peaks, like discarded, unwanted crowns.

Tarak had constructed his residence on the top of the hillock and roofed it over with a white marble dome which followed the line of the hill so that a casual observer might think it just part of the skyline. There was no mistaking the glistening marble, however. No tree, nor weed, nor plant, not even grass, would grow on its surface. It was said that Tarak used it to trap the rays of the sun, ingeniously storing its power for use within. Certainly, Nim had been within the dome and the living quarters did draw on some strange magical power for a number of purposes. He wondered at the drain on Tarak should he be channelling his own power for all of those items.

Thanking Petr for the ride and jumping down as the cart trundled along the road that wound past the hillock, Nim began the final part of his journey, the short stroll up the well-beaten steps to the Guardian's abode. As usual, Tarak stood at the door awaiting him. Nim hadn't yet fathomed how the Guardian managed that trick. When he had mentioned it once to Kell, the wizard had merely replied, "The ways of wizards are varied and wondrous; best not to try to untangle them", leaving Nim none the wiser, as he was sure had been intended.

"Greetings, friend of my friend," haled the wizard as Nim neared the top of the steps.

"And well met to you too, Tarak," replied the quickling in a slightly exasperated tone. "The least you could do if you knew I was coming was have a nice cool drink ready for me."

"The chilled mulberry water's waiting for you in the hall," laughed the wizard, opening the door and ushering Nim into the dome. "And the dandelion tea is steeping as we speak. Come in friend, come in."

Tarak eased back in his chair, relishing its comfort as he sipped away at the warmed glass of mead. It had been a long and demanding day. He hoped the decision he'd finally made would turn out to be the right one.

Nim had left about mid-afternoon and by now would be well on his way to Keerêt. It wasn't Queen Elissa or the Algarians the Guardian was thinking of, however. Elissa would do what she had to do. That wouldn't be where this matter would be decided. His thoughts turned now to himself. He knew only too well that it was what the Guardians did that would decide the fate of Ilythia. As so often before, the fates of many would turn on the decisions of him and his colleagues.

The problem, as he saw it, was that the Guardians had allowed themselves to drift too far apart from one another. They had each gone off in their own direction of late, each pursued his own interests, at the expense, it was now apparent, of their common purpose. If what Kell claimed was true, then the Council itself had become nothing more than a façade. And yet how could it have come to this? How could they, the very ones entrusted with ensuring the continuing peaceful co-existence of the many and varied peoples of this world, have allowed themselves to become enemies?

Or had it really come to this? Was Kell, in fact, being played for a fool by the sligs? Of all the races, they had ever been the most inherently aggressive, the least likely to put aside their differences. It seemed to go against their very nature to live in harmony with their neighbours for long, to share rather than to take what was needed. Perhaps they sought now to divide the Guardians, to distract them while they got up to some new devilry. That at least had to be considered before he and Kell rushed off to condemn their colleague, no matter what their differences.

At the very least, Golkar must be confronted with these allegations. Just how reliable was this informant of Kell's? This talk of opening up a way to another world and acquiring some kind of ally; it just didn't ring true. It smacked of something the sligs would think of, not something Golkar would do.

The pleasant voice of his companion interrupted his contemplation. "Come to bed, my sweet," she insisted. "If you must be away on the morrow, then at least get a good night's rest."

"Soon, Kira, soon." As he spoke, he looked up at his partner with an affectionate smile, taking her hand in his as she reached out to comfort him. Her obvious concern for his welfare never failed to touch his heart.

"Hmmm. Make sure it is soon." Leaning over him as she spoke, Jekira kissed him softly on the forehead, gently gripping his hand in hers as she did so, then turned and walked away. Tarak watched the sway of her hips as she slowly crossed the room to the door. As she tarried at the sideboard beside the door, taking a beeswax candle from the small box they kept there and lighting it to take up to their room, he took in her loveliness.

As always, he found it intoxicating. Her long red hair splayed forward over her shoulders as she stooped at the bench, its lustre catching the flickering light as the candle sputtered alight. The swell of her full breasts pushed against the fabric of her dress as she bent. Although it was still too early to tell, Tarak couldn't resist a glance at the swell of her belly. There was, of course, no sign of the baby he now knew was growing within her. It had been no more than a week since she'd told him the news.

Tarak found it impossible to resist the pang of regret that lanced through him. Had he been wrong to take a mate, especially now, of all times? He knew this wasn't the first time that a Guardian had taken a lover. Both Kell and Golkar had done so before and even he'd had his flings in the past. But Jekira . . . she had become so much more to him than that. And a child! If either Golkar or Kell had gone that far, then they'd certainly never acknowledged it.

He'd told himself a thousand times that this was true love and he was entitled to its virtues as much as any man was. But was he fooling himself? Was it really anything more than vanity? Perhaps it was just the thought of someone desiring him despite his age that had ensnared him. Perhaps this was yet another example of the selfishness the Guardians had degenerated into? Was Jekira just one of his 'pet' projects? With a sigh, Tarak pushed the recriminations aside. Now was not the time for this. Questioning the decisions he'd made in the past was self-indulgence that would do nothing to help the current situation.

The news that Nim had brought had only served to confirm his view that the Guardians were losing their way. But it wasn't too late to put a stop to that; it couldn't be too late, too much hinged on their continuing accord. What did Kell think he was doing, spying on one of his colleagues? Why hadn't he simply confronted Golkar with his suspicions instead of prying into his business like that? The direct approach was always much more satisfactory, and a more appropriate way for a Guardian to conduct himself than skulking around behind another's back. It was that very lack of dialogue between the three that had led them to this, of that he was certain.

As if to compound the error, Kell had allowed himself to sink to dealing with the sligs. Surely that should have sounded warning bells to him, if nothing else had. How could he hope to get anything but lies from the sligs? The whole affair smacked of being mishandled. If Golkar had really got himself involved in something grubby and unbecoming, and Kell for one shouldn't simply take the word of a slig for that, then he should be confronted with it.

Tarak knew what he had to do. Certainly, he would do as he promised. He would join Kell in Annwn, just as he had told Nim that he would. But Kell had allowed the sligs to spook him, rushing off to Annwn, sending messages to the Algarians and Mishra knows who else, all on the word of the sligs. Tarak had no intention of jumping to conclusions himself.

First, he would go to Tu-atha and talk directly to Golkar. Let him answer the charges to his face and then they would know what they were dealing with. Time enough to plan what to do after that. If Golkar really was up to something, then Tarak would know by the way he responded. When you had known someone for half a millennia, you could quickly tell if they weren't being straight with you.

He would take Nate and Arcle with him, and as a precaution, he would send Jekira off to her family for a while. As unlikely as it seemed, if there was to be conflict between the Guardians, then he wanted her well clear of any of the bother. Her people in Keerêt would be only too happy to see her and she would enjoy the fuss they would make over her impending addition to the family.

He would be sorry to miss that himself. With no family of his own, he had come to regard Jekira's parents and siblings with a good deal of fondness. And although he wouldn't admit it to many, he was quite proud of the prospect of becoming a father. He was almost as excited about it as Jekira was and he certainly wanted to share every aspect of the event that he could with her. Telling her family the news would be the first such event and now, unfortunately, he would have to miss it.

Even though it would slow him down, Nim had quite generously offered to take her with him when he left, but Tarak had felt that was being far too hasty. Apart from the fact that it would have worried Jekira to be asked to rush off so suddenly like that, he still wasn't convinced things were anywhere near that dire.

For a while, he considered what to do about the College. It would seem alarmist and pre-emptive to disrupt their lessons until he knew if there really was a problem. And if he did make such a dramatic move, panic would quickly spread throughout the Vale and the surrounding area like ripples in a pond. If there was to be trouble in the end, he hoped he would still be able to throw a protective arm across the Vale. Perhaps it could become a place of refuge for people in need. What more fitting role could there be for it, after all?

Raising his glass and draining the last of the mead, Tarak rose from his chair. It was time for bed. His decision had been made; he at least of the three of them would do the sensible thing and try to talk some sense into his colleagues before matters got out of hand.

A little while later, as he slipped under the bedsheets, sidling up to the warmth of Jekira's body, he wasn't surprised to find she was still awake.

"Is everything done, my love?" she asked, turning over to face him as he joined her.

"Yes. I will leave early. I'll miss you."

"Mmmm. As I will you, my sweet. You will be careful, won't you? Nim seemed to have got himself quite worked up about it all and that isn't like him."

"I'll be fine," he answered with a smile, brushing some hair from her face as he did so. "I do love you so much, you know, Kira. It's you who must be careful. Get Mareek to help you with the packing. If there is anything in what Kell says, we'll sort it out before long. We're overdue for some straight talking anyway and Golkar's always been willing to listen. You just make sure you don't get too used to being spoilt by your family. I'm the one who needs the spoiling."

With a laugh, Jekira reached out and hugged Tarak to her. "I'm the one who deserves to be spoilt," she said with mock petulance as he embraced her. "I am, after all, carrying a future Guardian in my belly . . . and don't you forget it. I should be waited on hand and foot."

"I won't forget it. Don't worry," whispered Tarak, pulling back so that he could gaze into her eyes. "I'll never forget that, Kira."

~~~

The Forest of Annwn was at its best in the springtime. Blossoms were falling like snow from the thousands of budding elms, giving the forest a look of enchantment unmatched throughout Tenamos. Whole drifts of the stuff, cast off by the newly formed buds, filled up the soft folds of the forest floor. With each fresh breeze, thousands more would drift down from the canopy to join their companions below. It was as if winter had returned for a brief moment with a last unseasonal snowstorm. For all of its charm, it did little to lift Kell's spirits.

The cabin had once been a hunting lodge but had fallen into disuse some time ago. Who its former owners were or why they had left had been long forgotten. Fortunately, it hadn't taken much to repair it. The roof had needed mending and the pitch in the walls had decayed in places, but generally, it had still been in fairly good shape. It had berths for six but would sleep a dozen at a pinch if needed. Not that that was likely. Kell was only expecting himself, Tarak and Nim.

The quicklings had undertaken its repair, both as a favour to Nim and as a mark of respect for Kell. Overall, it was quite a comfortable spot and the larder was well provisioned. The generous supply of wine that could now be found in the small cellar had been an added touch that Kell couldn't resist. There was no need to live like a barbarian, regardless of the seriousness of the situation. And there was no telling how long they would be there.

As Kell went about the task of preparing his dinner, he went over once again what he knew of the problems they now faced. The human that Golkar had summoned to this world to assist him would clearly be one of the primary threats. Unfortunately, too little was known about this stranger and there would be precious little opportunity to ascertain more. Kell would have to make some assumptions if he was to have any chance of dealing with this menace.

The one thing he did know was that the being had some form of magical power he could use against Kell and Tarak, and presumably others. Clearly, the two Guardians would be his principal objective. As to what form his power might take, Kell had no idea at this stage but presumed he could expect it to be quite formidable. Golkar wouldn't have gone to the trouble of bringing him here if he didn't believe the stranger could deal with the two of them, or perhaps deliver a crippling blow which would then enable Golkar to finish them off.

At the same time, there must be limits to the human's powers. Golkar had to be able to control him, so he must either have a weakness or Golkar must have some way of restraining him. He would have ensured he had some way to rein his ally in once the deed was done. Perhaps Golkar had offered him a reward in exchange for his help, or they had made some sinister deal. But even if that were so, Golkar would still need some form of insurance, some way of ensuring his accomplice didn't end up turning on him as well.

Whatever that weakness or that control point was, it could be the key to Kell and Tarak's survival. And they had to do much more than just survive. If this human was unable to eliminate them, but still managed to weaken them enough to give Golkar the upper hand, then their doom would still be sealed.

With a growing sense of despair, Kell realised it was an almost impossible conundrum. Somehow they had to manage to defeat a magical being when they had no idea what its powers were, how strong it might be, or what weaknesses it might have, if any. By the Seven Towers of Trinkolai, how was he supposed to solve this riddle?

Not alone, that much was clear. He was going to need Tarak's help to resolve this. He had come at the problem from every angle he could think of and was still no closer to solving it. It needed a fresh perspective. 'What one can never solve, oft clears with two involved', as the old saying went.

With a sigh of frustration, Kell realised he'd allowed his mind to wander from the task at hand and he'd burnt the eggs he'd been frying on the small wood-fired stove. The meat he was grilling was fine, but the eggs were badly singed. Scraping them from the pan and adding them to the small fillet of meat, he hoped Nim would complete his errands and join him here before too long. He'd become quite accustomed to the quickling's cooking and dreaded the prospect of fending for himself for very much longer. Sound thinking required a sound diet and he was unlikely to get much of the latter while he was the cook.

Moving to the table, he placed the plate beside the glass of wine he'd set there earlier. Cutting a small piece from one corner of the meat he tentatively placed it in his mouth and began to chew. It wasn't bad. It wasn't bad at all, he thought, smiling to himself as he ate. At least he wouldn't die from his cooking.

As he sat there, slowly eating his dinner, his thoughts turned to his fellow Guardian, not Golkar this time, but Tarak. They'd never collaborated on anything major before and he wondered how well they would work together. So much would depend on how effectively they could cooperate as it was fast becoming clear nothing short of joint action would save them now.

Given all the unknowns about Golkar's accomplice, it was clear to Kell their only chance for success would lie in both of them tackling him at once. A sustained two-pronged attack was what they would have to devise. If that didn't work, then nothing would. The question to be resolved was what form their attack should take. What spells should they use? Which were most likely to be effective?

All of these questions would need to be resolved once Tarak joined him. They would also need to consider when and where to fight this battle, assuming they had a choice. If Golkar didn't know where they were, and they didn't know where the human was, then it became a matter of who found whom first. They might find their attempt to take the initiative forestalled by pre-emptive action from the other side. It was for that very reason they couldn't afford to tarry.

One thing at least was certain: they would have to use their crystal shards. Dark as the blackest night, the enigmatic crystals nonetheless seemed, by some trick of the way they were faceted, no doubt, at times almost alive in some inexplicable way. On close examination, the blackness within seemed some times to be moving, slowly swirling or twisting, though Kell guessed that the crystal was somehow simply reflecting movement in the surrounding atmosphere.

He had never forgotten Tanis' warning, however, that the shards were to be used in direst need only. His mentor had cautioned that the power within the crystal could be perilous in certain circumstances. It would slowly corrupt the heart and soul of its wielder if over-used. "Use it when you need to. I am giving it to you for that reason. But use it sparingly," he had advised. "And use it wisely. Don't become its slave. Let it serve you, not the reverse."

Kell had adhered to that advice ever since, and he knew that Tarak had too. He had thought that Golkar had as well, but . . . given the recent turn of events . . . well, who knows? Perhaps this was what was behind his colleague's behaviour.

It was something to be discussed with Tarak, but Kell was sure he would agree. They would have to take that risk now and use it against their colleague. But they would do so with as much restraint as circumstances would allow.

Kell turned his thoughts then to Nim. By now he should have met with Tarak and be already on his way to Elissa. And Tarak, in turn, should be on his way to Annwn. Kell wished his colleague luck for he would not only need to move swiftly but also discreetly. It was essential that they unite before either of them encountered any interference from Golkar or his accomplice.

Kell knew that his friends were at risk. All who stood against this maniac would do so at their peril. Unwittingly, his thoughts turned to another dear friend, an ally perhaps for times just like these. He dare not draw him into this mess though, he thought with a shudder. He may be the last of his kind.

What possible purpose can there be to all this? Kell wondered. *What do the gods think they are about?*

He knew from Tanis' teachings that four gods, the Ilaroi, were said to be watching over Ilythia. And he believed that was so, even though he'd never witnessed any direct evidence personally of either their existence or their intervention in the affairs of the world. Tanis had certainly had no doubt and had even claimed to have been chosen by Mishra herself, the most commonly invoked of the four.

Though he couldn't explain why, Kell had always accepted that as fact, without even a hint of doubt. At times he had even felt that Mishra was guiding him, just like she had guided Tanis, speaking to him, advising him when he was beset with doubt, helping him to choose his path in times of difficulty.

But was all this just wishful thinking? Or tricks the mind played to explain one's inner voices? And if these Ilaroi, these gods, did exist, did they really care what happened to mere mortals?

The wizard hung his head in despair. He had no answers to these questions. He simply had to hope that if there were gods they would not forsake Ilythia now in the hour of its direst need.

CHAPTER 9

The rapidity with which the slig camp followers could disassemble a camp and be on the move again was nothing short of extraordinary. All of the jealousies and rivalries of the tent women were put aside as they worked silently but efficiently to strike the tents and pack their belongings in readiness to follow in the footsteps of the Sagath warriors. Along with the children and the old or infirm, they went about the task as if they'd been doing it all of their lives, and they had. The sligs were an inherently nomadic race.

Within a quarter of an hour, the camp had been struck and they were gone. The site they vacated had more in common now with a rubbish tip than the open pasture it had once been. The scattered remnants of their fireplaces, the piles of smouldering litter, the scattered bones and debris, they would all form a lasting reminder of their passage. The sligs weren't the tidiest of people. If they didn't move on in search of better hunting or in pursuit of a foe, then the accumulation of rubbish would eventually provide its own impetus. When the stench and the mess finally became unbearable, even for them, they simply moved on.

Although Mardur knew that the two women who shared the wagon she rode in would be only too happy to usurp her position as tent woman to the Second Warrior, they were the closest 'friends' she had among the slig women. Of the two, Varna was her only real competitor. Her mate, Larnük, was a member of Hrothgar's hunt. Although he was a respected warrior, Mardur knew that Varna would swap Larnük's bed for Hrothgar's as quickly as a warrior could draw his blade. She was also young and willing and more than capable of attracting Hrothgar's eye. Larnük often boasted of her prowess as a bedmate.

With a chill, Mardur knew that if Hrothgar ever tired of her, Varna was just the kind of woman he would turn to. And Varna would have no qualms about displacing her. It was the way of the sligs. What was important was to survive; the cost didn't matter. There were no real friendships among them. Their society was strictly hierarchical. Even the camp dogs had a pecking order.

Her other companion, Drait, presented no threat to Mardur's position. Drait was considerably older than both Varna and Mardur. Her eldest son, Norag, had almost reached manhood. In another season or two, he would undergo his initiation and become a warrior himself. Then he would join the menfolk rather than being left behind to help the women. They would miss his help in setting up and dismantling the tents and loading up the carts. He was a strapping young lad of great strength, like his father. One of them would have to drive the wagon then in his place. Drait's other son, Kradug, was far too young to be of much help yet and her daughter, Hara, didn't have the strength to help with the more physical of the tasks.

Although Drait was frequently grumpy and was a harsh mother to her children, Mardur preferred her company to that of Varna. The younger woman liked to talk more of herself or her mate than of anything else, whereas Drait's place in the tribe was clearly established and she no longer dreamed of how she could rise higher. Mardur had found there was much she could learn from Drait and the older woman didn't seem to mind passing on the benefits of her knowledge or her experience.

Mardur lay in the back of the wagon, dozing fitfully as she sheltered from the heat of the sun. Her babe lay asleep at her breast, snuggled up to the warmth of her body. Idly she listened to the chatter that drifted back from the front of the wagon. Drait held the reins of the two mules that dragged the wagon forward and Varna was sitting beside her, prattling on incessantly about this and that as she usually did. Drait seemed to take little notice, an occasional grunt signifying she was listening even though she was contributing little to the conversation herself. As usual, the conversation was about Varna and her mate.

"Everyone knows that Larnük could lead the hunt himself, of course," she was saying. "Grartok has his eye on him, you can tell. The next time a new hunt leader is chosen he's sure to choose Larnük."

"He is a strong warrior," agreed Drait noncommittally.

"I think he would already be a hunt leader but for Hrothgar," whispered Varna. "Larnük says that Hrothgar is jealous of him." Clearly, Varna believed Mardur was asleep. Keeping her eyes closed, the Second Warrior's tent-mate focused her attention on the two voices. Despite the rumble of the cart and the fact that Varna had lowered her voice, she could still make out what was being said.

"If anything ever happens to the Second Warrior," Varna continued, "then Larnük will be able to show what he is really capable of. I know his day will come."

"Perhaps you're right," replied Drait. Mardur knew what Drait would be thinking. A mixture of boasting and wishful thinking usually fuelled Varna's statements. It was well known that she wanted Larnük to progress so she herself could rise up the pecking order. Drait had no doubt seen it all before.

"I'm certain of it," replied the youngster. "Grartok needs strong leaders and he has a sound eye. Larnük would vie for Second Warrior if Hrothgar were to fall."

Mardur doubted if Larnük was as good as Varna claimed. He was a capable warrior but had little experience at leadership. To be chosen as Second Warrior he would need to be judged the best of all of the hunt leaders. Even if he was as capable as Varna claimed, he would need to prove himself as a hunt leader first. As usual, Varna was allowing her dreams to get ahead of reality.

"Hrothgar isn't worthy of the role," Varna went on when Drait offered no response. Once again, she had lowered her voice. She was on dangerous ground and she probably knew it, thought Mardur, but her prattling mouth apparently couldn't resist pursuing the subject. "Grartok knows that, too," she went on. "His bedding of Mardur shows his contempt for the Second Warrior."

"All that shows," snorted Drait contemptuously, "is that Grartok likes to keep his lance well oiled."

"Well," replied Varna, somewhat indignantly. "If Hrothgar was a true warrior he wouldn't allow someone else to warm his bed for him. And Grartok knows that. That's why he picked her. Because he knows Hrothgar is too weak to stop him."

The older woman laughed openly at Varna's statement. "Don't be foolish, child. If Hrothgar had any idea what was going on, he would call for *Shüglac* without hesitation. I don't think he could best his older brother, but he would acquit himself with honour. Do you think Larnük would do that if it was you that Grartok was bedding?"

"He certainly would," Varna insisted, clearly offended at the suggestion her mate might turn a blind eye to such a thing. "I'm sure of it. Larnük wouldn't want to live with such dishonour."

"Mmmm." It was clear that Drait wasn't convinced Varna's assessment of Larnük was an accurate one.

"Anyway," said Varna, "we'll soon see if you're right about Hrothgar."

"Why is that?" asked Drait, obviously tiring of Varna's nonsense.

"Because," responded Varna smugly, "Larnük is going to tell Hrothgar what Grartok's been doing."

Mardur couldn't stop the gasp that escaped from her mouth at what she'd heard. She felt a chill run up her spine and had to fight down the urge to jump up and grab a hold of Varna and shake her until she told her everything she knew. Restraining herself, she hoped that by continuing to feign sleep she may hear more than if she openly challenged the young fool.

"You dolt," spat Drait angrily. "What does he hope to achieve by that?"

"Hrothgar is . . . is his hunt leader . . . his . . . his loyalty is to him." It was clear from the uncertainty in Varna's voice that she hadn't expected the response she'd got from Drait. "Besides," she went on, "if Grartok kills Hrothgar, then Larnük will profit."

"You put him up to it, didn't you?" accused Drait. Her annoyance was palpable, even to Mardur at the back of the wagon. "You stupid little idiot. All you've done is ensure the Sagath will lose a good warrior at a time we can least afford it. And Larnük will be lucky to keep his own head. If Hrothgar doesn't slay him in a blind rage, Grartok will when he finds out who told his brother about him. Where will that leave you then?"

"H-Hrothgar will be grateful for Larnük's loyalty." It was clear Drait had rattled the girl. If what Drait said was true Varna would find herself without a mate. And if Grartok had the slightest suspicion of her involvement in any of this, she might even lose her own head. "N . . . no one will know. No one will know who told Hrothgar."

"Well, I'll give you this girl. You play a dangerous game. Too dangerous for my liking."

Mardur's mind raced as the two women fell into silence. It was clear that Varna was wondering now whether she had done the right thing after all. Not that Mardur cared about her; her own safety and that of her child was her paramount concern. She knew Hrothgar well. Drait was right. Larnük would be lucky if the Second Warrior didn't slay him on the spot when he told him about her and Grartok. Surely Larnük must know that too. Hrothgar's rage was well known. Maybe what Varna said had been just more of her dreams; maybe she hadn't really put Larnük up to something so perilous.

Unfortunately, Mardur knew she couldn't take that chance. If Varna had told the truth, Hrothgar would go straight to Grartok looking for vengeance. Or, if she were anywhere close by, he might seek her out first. By the blood of her fallen ancestors, she had hoped somehow not to have to deal with all of this. She had no choice now; Varna's stupidity had forced her hand. She would have to do something, and quickly.

Grartok was the only one who could protect her now. But what reason did he have to do that? She wasn't bearing his child, she knew that, and he wouldn't lift a hand in her defence until or if she did so. That was it! It suddenly dawned on her what she needed to do. She must go to Grartok and tell him she was with child, his child. He would be elated. She could then ask him to acknowledge her as his mate, to take her into his tent and under his protection. He would certainly do so. Then, as long as he could deal with Hrothgar, her safety would be assured, as would her babe's.

Desperately, she tried to quell her beating heart. Mardur was frightened, very frightened. She was in great danger now. She had to hope she could get to Grartok before Hrothgar heard what Larnük had to say and returned to their camp in the blind rage that would inevitably follow. It was uncertain when they would link up with the warriors again. Certainly, it would be within the next few days, but exactly when would depend on their own movements and those of the Algarians. In the meantime, Mardur's life would be at risk. All because of a stupid, scheming, fool of a girl.

If Varna only knew how precarious life became the higher up the tree one rose. Despite the lowly position Drait held in the tribe, at least she had little to fear from ambitious rivals. The higher one rose, the more one's time was spent looking over one's shoulder, no less for the women than for the warriors. At least the warriors were the masters of their own fate. Mardur hadn't really chosen the position she'd found herself in. She'd never really sought Hrothgar's favours; it was he that had been attracted to her. Once he'd singled her out for his attention she'd had little choice in the matter. The same went for Grartok, only more so. He had simply stepped into her tent one night and that was that. And where had all this led her? Now she was fighting for her life, and that of her child, as grimly as any warrior did in battle.

Having resolved on her course of action, Mardur wondered what would come next. She needed to get pregnant, quickly. Her ruse would work for a short time, and hopefully, it would carry her through her current dilemma, but she couldn't feign pregnancy for too long. If she couldn't find some way of truly becoming pregnant then she would have no choice but to run away and take her chances on her own. Any hope that she might have been able to pass another child of Hrothgar's off as Grartok's was now gone. Curse Grartok. If he had impregnated her as he'd been trying to do, she wouldn't be in this mess. And who else was there to fulfil the task?

As the wagon rolled interminably forward, slowly taking them deeper and deeper into the lands of their enemies, Mardur turned her head to gaze back at the hills they were leaving. Behind the wagon, a dozen or so paces in its wake, walked Drait's two children, her young daughter Hara and her elder son, Norag, who was carrying young Kradug astride his broad shoulders. Mardur's eyes fixed on Norag, taking in the muscled torso of the young lad she knew would soon join the ranks of the warriors. He was a striking specimen, no doubt about it. Perhaps, thought Mardur, there are more things for Norag to learn than what the warriors will teach him.

~~~

Hrothgar leaned over the side of his horse with one hand firmly gripping the pommel of his saddle and spat. He was tired of his assignment already and it had barely begun.

Of the twenty warriors in his hunt, he had quickly moved to position three to keep a watch over the approaches to Cloudtopper, and a further three to keep an eye on the Vale of Dreams. That would provide him with some insurance should his prey escape the net and try to win through to either of the Guardians. He and the remainder of the hunt had then pressed on for the wilderness.

Late on the previous day, they had reached the edge of the Western Wilderness and this morning he had divided his resources even further. Two groups of four warriors had already left, bound for their allotted portion of the area to be searched. The third group was now ready to depart as well. Once they were about their task, he and the remaining two warriors would form a fourth group. Over the next three days, each of the groups would comb a specific sector of the wilderness. Should their quarry still be at bay when they regrouped at an agreed location on the evening of the third day, then they would be allotted new areas and the search would continue.

"Good hunting and may the will of Zar be with you," growled Hrothgar to the leader of the third group as they prepared to depart. Although he said the words, there was no real depth of feeling behind his statement and the recipient of his commendation knew it.

"May the God of Battles show me the path to courage and victory," replied Larnük, giving Hrothgar the traditional response as he placed his right hand across his chest with his clenched fist just below his left shoulder.

"I'll see you three days from now at the ford," grumbled Hrothgar, unable to shake off his exasperation at what he saw as the menial task that his brother, Grartok, had given him. "Let's hope we're done with this accursed mission by then."

"Don't worry, Second Warrior, if our first sweep doesn't find the human, then our second should."

"It'd better," snapped Hrothgar angrily. "I won't be wasting my time on any more than two."

"What will we do if we still haven't found her then?"

"We'll give it up and rejoin the assault. I have no intention of rotting here while our brothers cover themselves in glory in Algaria."

Although Larnük tried to hide his concerns, it was clear he wasn't comfortable with the idea of open disobedience of Grartok's orders. "I thought you said Grartok saw this mission as critical to his plans," he replied. "The First Warrior won't be happy if we come back empty handed."

"I don't care what he thinks about it," roared Hrothgar. "I'm the hunt leader here in the field and I'll make the decisions. If my brother thinks he can sidetrack me here, while he reaps all the glory for himself, then he underestimates me badly. Just be at the ford in three days' time and leave the thinking to me, Larnük. I'll let you know when I need your advice."

"Yes, Second Warrior."

Although Hrothgar knew he had insulted the warrior, he was unconcerned. Larnük's place was to take orders from his hunt leader, not to question his decisions. Besides, in his current frame of mind he didn't care who he insulted, Larnük least of all.

For the briefest of moments, Hrothgar wondered what was troubling Larnük. He was a capable warrior, no more so nor less so than any of the other members of the hunt, but undoubtedly capable. A number of times over the last few days Hrothgar had felt Larnük had been about to say something, and then, just when he had seemed about to speak, he'd checked himself and kept whatever was troubling him to himself. Maybe, thought Hrothgar, he would rather be back at camp with pretty little Varna. There were times when he envied Larnük his possession of that one. Still, 'rutting is rutting and killing is killing' as his father used to say. There'd be time enough for rutting when the killing was done.

With the conversation so abruptly concluded, Larnük and his companions rode off in silence, leaving Hrothgar and the remaining two sligs alone. With a sigh, Hrothgar turned his own horse and kicked it forward. "C'mon then," he called out grumpily over his shoulder to his two companions. "Let's be on with it. I want to get this over and done with as soon as we can." It was their turn now to focus on the task that Hrothgar found so belittling.

The task would not be an easy one. Scouring the wilderness in a search for one human child would be like finding one particular beast in a herd of brugon. Their only real hope of success would be if the girl followed one of the more direct routes out of the wild in her flight from Golkar. The assumption was that she would make her way to Kell or Tarak. Grartok had told Hrothgar he should be able to intercept her somewhere along that line. Combing the whole of the wilderness would have been an impossible task, even if Hrothgar had ten times the number of warriors at his disposal that he actually had.

This wasn't the work that a slig warrior was trained for. Hrothgar and his men knew only too well that the rest of the Sagath warriors would have already moved down from their winter camps in the mountains onto the plains of Algaria. Even now, they would be making their first assaults on the villages and towns that were scattered along the eastern border of what the Algarians had come to regard as their 'sovereign territory', as their queen was accustomed to calling it. The only consolation was that the first week or two of the slig offensive would bring them little real opposition.

It was only when the Algarians realised the true extent of the onslaught the Sagath had launched that they would begin to marshal their forces and present some real form of resistance. Once they realised this was no longer a case of isolated raids but a full-scale war, they would mobilise every fighting man they could. That was when the real fighting would begin.

And Hrothgar was determined to be part of that. By the time the conflict had reached that point, he was determined to be back where he and his men belonged, in the vanguard of the slig assault force. To achieve that he would need to find the girl quickly. Then, if he still had time, he could take her to Golkar himself and see what price he could extract from the wizard in exchange for his merchandise. If he took too long in finding her, however, he might need to delegate the task to Norvig, assuming the snivelling little coward had rejoined them by them.

Although Hrothgar wouldn't admit it, even to himself, he was already well on the way to persuading himself that would be the more sensible course to take. That way, he told himself, he could return to the tribe to join in the assault on the Algarians as soon as he and his hunt had found their prey. Norvig was much more experienced at bargaining with these wizards than he was, in any event. And if Golkar didn't take kindly to Hrothgar's proposal, then Norvig could be left to extricate himself from the mess as best he could. The Guardians had a tendency to get quite ruffled if rubbed the wrong way. Hrothgar didn't have the time to deal with that sort of nonsense right now. Not when the greatest offensive the Sagath had ever initiated was underway.

Hrothgar was determined. When the slaughter began he intended to be in the van of the slig host. Until such time as Kell acted on the information supplied by Hrothgar and reined in the Sagath, as Golkar clearly would not, he intended to make the most of what was an all too infrequent opportunity: a chance to wreak havoc on an under-prepared adversary.

~~~

The unexpected sound of a horse approaching drew Dain's attention from his work. Looking up from the rich brown soil at his feet, and the rows of young corn shoots that stretched out across the field in front of him, Dain spied his nephew, Erl, coming across the field towards him on his brother's big bay. That something was up was immediately clear. Erl was pushing the horse hard. He was in a hurry, there was no doubt of that.

As Dain waited for Erl to reach him, he leaned on his hoe, taking in the darkening sky at his nephew's back. A big storm was brewing in the east and the dark, rain-laden clouds were coming this way. Like all farmers, he welcomed the sight. Spring rains were generally the harbinger of a good season to follow. His family could do with a decent harvest. The last two had been disappointing with much drier summers than they'd been accustomed to. A good crop this year would certainly be welcomed.

As Erl drew near, Dain lifted his arm in greeting. "Hey, Erl, what's up? What's the rush?" As Dain spoke, Erl drew his horse to a halt, only a few paces away from him. For the first time, he could see the harried look on the youngster's face. The bay he was riding was blowing hard. Whatever had brought them here in such a rush, Dain feared it wouldn't be good news.

"Sligs," panted Erl breathlessly, his eyes wide with fright. "Lots of them. Da sent me to warn you. He said there's a big push on. He's packin to leave."

Dain's heart sank. He and the rest of the farmers out here in the eastern provinces had been hoping last year's slig raids had been nothing more than an aberration. The news that they were out and about again was the last thing he needed to hear. What concerned him most, however, was the suggestion that his brother was packing up and planning to leave. Jorl didn't spook easily. For him to be fixing to move out meant he was expecting much more than the isolated raids they'd seen in the past.

"What sort of push? What's happened?"

Erl seemed to have recovered slightly from his earlier panic. Having got his primary message out seemed to have calmed him a bit. "We got word last night, from Harald, that they was comin. Then this mornin we seen the smoke from Brand's Ford. Right after breakfast, Pep rode in and told us the sligs had burnt it to the ground last night. He said that word was there was nearly a hundred sweepin across from the river and still more comin."

"Brand's Ford attacked and burnt? But there's upwards of a score of folk in Brand's Ford. What happened to them?"

"I dunno, Uncle Dain. But da said we're gittin out, and quick. Said you should do the same. Said don't wait for him, just git Aunt Kared and Thom and git. We're gunna make for Kurandir. There's Rangers there."

Dain tried to calm his racing thoughts. The sligs must be up to something big to attack a village. He couldn't remember the last time that had happened. Usually, they harried the outlying farms and such but they rarely had the numbers, or the daring, for a direct assault like that. Although Dain doubted the suggestion there were hundreds of them on the way, Jorl was right. If something big was coming, he would be much better off getting his family to some safe place until he could find out what was really going on.

Kurandir was the logical choice. Although its walls hadn't been needed for many a year and had fallen into disrepair, there was a squad of Rangers stationed there. That was the place to head for, no doubt about it. If the sligs were attacking and burning villages then they meant business. His heart went out to the folk of Brand's Ford. He had friends there. Or he used to.

"Alright. Thanks, Erl. You get yourself back home quick then. Pass my thanks on to your da and tell him I'll see you all in Kurandir. May Mishra guide your path." As his nephew made to turn his horse around, back in the direction he had come from, Dain called out to him again. "Erl!"

"Yes uncle?"

"Go safely boy, go safely. And keep your wits about you on your way back."

"I will, uncle." With that, the boy spurred his horse forward. Dain watched him for a few moments and then quickly turned and started towards the farmhouse. After a few paces, he started to run, throwing his hoe to the ground as he did so.

When he arrived back at the farm, he went straight around to the back. His son Thom was there, mending the fence around the pigpen. Once Dain had repeated Erl's news, he told Thom to stop what he was doing and to saddle up.

"Get the wagon ready, Thom," he said, as they strode back towards the barn together. "As fast as you can. I'll get it out of the barn, but I want you to hitch up old Harna for me while your ma and I pack. Once you done that, get Bess saddled up and get yourself over to Luc's place and tell him what's goin on. Don't worry 'bout your stuff. We'll pack that. After you told Luc, go on down to Prard and tell him. Then make straight for Kurandir. Don't come back here 'cause we'll be gone. And don't stop for nothin boy."

"What about Jinny?" the boy pleaded. "I gotta let her and her dad know."

Dain allowed himself a smile. He'd suspected for some time that Thom was sweet on young Jinny, but the boy had been unwilling to acknowledge it. "Okay. But that's all. Go to Jinny and Rem first, they're furthest east. Then Luc. Then Prard. And be careful. Your ma will fret until she sees you safe and sound in Kurandir, you know that."

"I will da."

"And Thom!"

"Yes da."

"Take your bow."

"Yes da."

Having sent Thom on his way, Dain broke the news to his wife Kared. Once he'd convinced her that there was nothing they could do about the spring crop now and that it wouldn't even be worth having if the sligs came while they were still there, they set about packing what they could take as quickly as they could. They knew they couldn't take much. Food and fresh clothes came first, followed by blankets and bedding. Dain took down his old sword from the wall, and his bow and a few tools from the barn, things that might come in handy in Kurandir.

Once that was done, Dain let all of the animals out of the paddocks and pens. It would be a nuisance rounding them up again when they came back, but at least the animals would have a chance at finding something to eat that way. There was no sense in leaving them penned up with no one to feed them when they had no idea how long it would be before the trouble had passed and they could come back again. Hopefully, a show of force from the Rangers would put things to rights pretty quickly, but it wouldn't pay to count on that.

In some ways, the talk of a hundred or more sligs wasn't really surprising. Dain knew that people always overestimated trouble when it first hit them. But sligs had never been seen in those numbers. That would suggest a degree of cooperation that was entirely uncharacteristic for them. There had been a couple of big raids back when Dain was a boy, though. That had involved a few dozen sligs and his dad had said that had only been put to rights when one of the Guardians had intervened. The Rangers had been overwhelmed on that occasion and, although the squadron in Kurandir was bigger now than it was then, it still only numbered two dozen.

Within no time, Dain and Kared had loaded up the wagon and were on their way. As they turned down the track that led away from the farmhouse, they both spied the streams of smoke curling up into the darkening sky in the east. Something was definitely burning out there, no doubt about it. It was a long way away from them, but there were at least four separate fires that could be seen from where they were.

"I hope Thom is careful," exclaimed Kared anxiously, with her eyes nervously scanning the eastern horizon.

"Don't worry about him," replied Dain, placing his left hand on his wife's wrist as he urged the horses forward with a flick of the reins from his other hand. "It's the folks out east of us I'm worried about. I hope Jorl has time to get out with Erl and Nika. Thank Mishra he thought to send word to us, but I hope it doesn't delay him getting away."

For a while, they were alone on the road, but soon they began to see signs of others either preparing to leave or already, like them, fleeing westwards. By mid-afternoon the number of refugees on the road was increasing noticeably and their progress had begun to slow. It was at that point that Dain really began to worry, though he said nothing as yet to Kared. From what they heard from others they met, theirs wasn't the only part of the province that was reeling from the sudden appearance of slig raiders. Dain began to wonder about the number of sligs that might be involved.

When they topped a gentle rise around dusk and looked down at the walled town of Kurandir, they were no longer surprised at the scene before them. A steady trickle of refugees was making its way into the town through each of the three gates that could be seen from their vantage point. Many drove wagons like themselves, while some were on horseback and many more were on foot, carrying what few of their precious belongings they could on their backs. Everywhere were worried looks. It didn't take much foresight to realise that the trickle was bound to increase in the days to come. In the fields between them and the town, Algarian Rangers were at work driving pointed stakes into the ground. Although they couldn't be sure of the exact nature of the work from this far away, it was clear that attempts were also being made to repair the walls. Lanterns had been lit to enable the work to continue on into the night. Already thoughts had turned to the defence of the town.

Dain's concern was whether Kurandir could offer them the protection they sought. If the slig raids were as widespread as they now seemed, would even Kurandir be able to withstand them.? Unless the Rangers had sought reinforcements from the west, they could be hard pressed with only two dozen trained men at their disposal. Their best hope would be if the sligs contented themselves with looting the abandoned farms. No one in living memory had seen a slig assault on a walled town. Dain hoped that they wouldn't be the first to do so, though it was clear from the work that was going on someone considered it a real possibility.

Of greater concern to him was Thom. He hoped the boy would follow his instructions to the letter. He could end up in grave danger if he tarried anywhere along the way. Thom was a sensible boy, but even the most sensible of men could make the wrong choices when put under pressure. Dain suspected they would all be put to that test before this threat was over.

As they edged forward towards the eastern gate of Kurandir, Dain and Kared felt the first sprinkles of rain. The smell of it had filled the air for some time and now it was upon them. Dain cursed as he pulled a tarpaulin from behind the seat up over their heads. He had hoped to be within the walls before the foul weather caught them. As the rain began to splatter against the tarpaulin, his prayers went out to his boy. With a deep sense of foreboding, Dain prayed that the gods would guide his footsteps. He sensed that it wouldn't be his last call on the gods in the trying days that lay ahead of them.

CHAPTER 10

Taking a hold of Rayne's free arm as a support, Sara put all of her effort into lifting herself up from the forest floor. Getting up was one thing, however. Moving from that spot once she had achieved that goal was another altogether. With one hand firmly clasped around Rayne's wrist and the other braced against the rough bark of the tree, she concentrated on keeping her legs from collapsing beneath her.

"What happened?" she asked, looking around suspiciously at the forest once she'd steadied herself. "Are there any more of them?" As she spoke she let go of the tree and managed to take a few tentative steps, all the while keeping a firm grip on Rayne's wrist with her other hand. Now that she'd regained some limited physical control, she was beginning to gather her thoughts as well. They couldn't stay where they were for long.

"I don't think so," answered Rayne. "You got one of them in the throat with an arrow and I finished him off. The other one's got my knife in his back. It was those two men from the settlement." Leading Sara around the corpse that lay beside them, he began to steer her slowly back towards the camp. "And anyway," he continued as they picked their way carefully through the trees and the bracken, "if there are any more of them out there, I'm afraid neither of us is in much of a state to do anything about it."

Once back at the camp, Sara slumped down on her bedding. The short walk back to the camp had taken more effort than she had thought it would. Rayne squatted down beside her and started to unbutton his shirt.

"Can you get a knife, Sara," he said, wincing with pain as he gingerly eased his shirtsleeve away from his shoulder. "I need you to cut this sleeve for me."

Sara's head was still throbbing from the knock that she'd taken but she knew she had to help Rayne; his injury was much more serious than hers. Rather than try to stand by herself, she allowed herself to drop to the ground. With some effort, she slowly crawled over and grabbed the knife she'd left beside her bedding.

Looking at the blade as she pulled it free of its sheath, she wondered what use it would have been had she had it with her earlier. The image of Ruz with Tug's blade in his belly flashed through her mind, followed quickly by that of the stranger lunging at her with a knife in his hand and bowling her over onto her back. Her head spun as the images flashed through her mind and for a brief moment she had to fight down her nausea.

Pushing those thoughts from her mind, she tried to clear her head so she could concentrate on what needed to be done. Once she was steady again, she crawled back to Rayne and knelt beside him. As soon as he'd finished unbuttoning his shirt, she took the knife and carefully cut the sleeve away from the rest of the garment. Once the sleeve was discarded, the extent of the wound to his arm became more apparent.

The arrow had pierced the flesh on the underside of his upper arm and had gone right through and out the other side. The blood-smeared head and a short length of shaft showed on one side of his arm, while the bulk of the shaft and the feathers protruded from the other. He was lucky it had missed the bone. As it was, Sara almost fainted when she saw the nasty wounds it had made and the blood that was seeping out, particularly from where the arrowhead emerged from his skin.

Rayne examined the wound carefully, flinching as he touched his hand to the shaft of the arrow. "Grab those extra clothes we found," he gasped between winces. "We're going to need something to bind the wound once we get the arrow out."

Sara scrambled back to the saddlebags, moving more quickly now that she had seen the extent of Rayne's injury. Her stomach churned at the thought of removing the arrow from his arm. Once again, she pushed the unwelcome thoughts from her mind. Focusing on the task at hand, she quickly found the clothes where they had put them, down at the bottom of the stranger's gear. Taking the knife, she cut the trouser legs into long strips of cloth and then returned to Rayne.

Sara could see that his face had already lost some of its colour and he was starting to sweat profusely. He was also clearly in a lot of pain. "Now," he said to her. "I need you to slice the feathers from the end of the shaft with the knife. You'll have to hold it steady with one hand so it doesn't move around in me too much while you're doing it. You've got to slice them right down level with the shaft so we can pull the whole thing through the wound."

"I've got to do something about that bleeding first," said Sara, taking a closer look at the underside of his arm. Taking a strip of cloth she wrapped it around his upper arm and tied both of the ends in a knot. She then took a small length of branch from the ground and inserted it under the cloth. Twisting it around and around, she drew the cloth tighter and tighter, asking Rayne to hold it in place once she felt it was tight enough. "That should help to reduce the flow of blood for the moment," she said when she was done.

"Where did you learn how to do that?"

Sara sat back on her haunches. "I'm not totally useless," she replied, giving him a forlorn look.

Rayne managed a weak smile. "I know that, Sara. If you hadn't shot one of those men we wouldn't both be alive right now. What were you doing out there, anyway?"

"Going to the toilet," she mumbled, turning her head away as she spoke.

Rayne laughed at her response, grimacing with pain once again as he did so. "Thank Mishra you did."

Ignoring his jibe, Sara turned her attention to the arrow. As carefully as she could, she began trimming the feathers from one end. She soon found it was impossible to do so without jiggling the shaft, every movement of which drew fresh expressions of pain from Rayne. Sara herself was on the verge of bursting into tears and she could feel the moisture beginning to pool in her eyes, threatening to hamper her efforts to complete the task at hand. Somehow, she managed to finish the job. Then it was over to Rayne to carry out the more painful task of removing the shaft.

Trimming the feathers had been bad enough, but this was much worse. Sara looked on helplessly as he began to slowly draw the shaft through his arm. As much as she wanted to help him, she knew that she couldn't. It was all she could do just to support him as he slowly drew the arrow through his arm and out the other side.

Once that grim task was done, she was ready to take over again, washing the ghastly wounds on either side of his arm clean with water from their flask. Releasing the makeshift tourniquet seemed to have little effect on the flow of blood, which continued to ooze from the holes left by the arrow. Sara guessed that this meant no significant veins had been severed. She proceeded to apply pads of cloth to the raw wounds and then bound his arm tightly with the long strips of cloth she'd prepared.

Once she was finished, Rayne eased himself back down on to the ground. Sara moved around so he could lay with his head in her lap while she leant back against the trunk of a tree. Her head felt clearer now, though it still ached a little if she tried to move too quickly. She knew her troubles, however, were nothing compared to how Rayne must be feeling. Looking down at him as he smiled wanly back at her, the hold she'd put on her emotions finally gave way. She wiped her face as the tears began to flow freely. The image that kept coming back to her was the one of that man charging at her through the trees with his knife in his hand.

She felt Rayne reach up and take a hold of her hand. "It's over now Sara," he whispered.

"If only it was," she sobbed.

The sounds of the forest awakened Sara with a start. To her surprise, she realised they'd both fallen asleep and slept through the night. Rayne still lay asleep in her lap and, as she stirred, he awoke as well, grimacing as he turned his head to look around. Sara had no idea how long they had slept. The sun had risen, but by how far was difficult to tell. In contrast to the day before, thick clouds covered the sky.

With a little help from each other, they managed to rise from the spot where they'd spent the night. Neither of them was in very good shape. Sara ached all over, as did Rayne, and as soon as she moved she realised she still had a dull headache from the knock she'd taken the night before. Rayne complained that his arm was throbbing.

Despite their ailments, they knew they had to get moving. After a quick breakfast, they divided up the tasks that had to be done between them. Sara got the lion's share. While she packed their gear and saddled the horses, Rayne went to examine the bodies of their assailants.

Within a very short while, Sara had completed all of her work and had both the horses saddled and ready to go. A few moments later, Rayne reappeared. To her surprise, he was leading two more horses. He'd found them tethered to a tree some distance away. They both knew without a word being spoken what had happened to their owners. As they were still saddled as well, they mounted them and led their own horses, giving Ned and Nell a rest after the constant work they'd been put to over the last several days. Rayne hoped that this might gain them some much-needed time. By his reckoning, Tug and his companions couldn't be far behind by now.

That day was a long and depressing one. They spoke little, each engrossed in their own thoughts. As the day progressed, the pain in Rayne's arm seemed to worsen. When they stopped by a stream in the middle of the day, Sara bathed and re-bandaged his wound. It was still bleeding a little, but it wasn't that which worried her. From the look of the skin around where the arrowhead had emerged, she feared the wound had become infected, despite her attempts at cleaning it. The pain, which had at first been localised, seemed to be spreading out from the wound and Rayne now found that the whole of his upper arm, from his shoulder to his elbow, was tender to touch. He was also beginning to show some signs of running a fever. Even with her limited experience, Sara could see he needed rest and better medical attention than she could give him.

Unfortunately, it was impossible for them to stop and allow him the rest he needed. It was enough that they had to spell the horses from time to time, but that was all they could afford. Even those spells were becoming less frequent now that they had two extra horses. After they re-dressed Rayne's wound, they changed over once more, mounting Ned and Nell again and leading the new horses as they pushed on.

Sara felt the despair she had slipped into back in her cell returning. Try as she could to maintain hope, deep down she felt sure it was only a matter of time now before Tug and his friends would catch up with them. She chided herself for having allowed Rayne to be shot by their attackers when she was supposed to be keeping watch. If she had been doing her job properly she would have heard them approaching, and she knew she should never have gone off by herself like that without first waking Rayne.

She toyed with the idea of giving herself up to Tug and his men. She knew Rayne would never allow it, but thought about waiting until he was asleep and creeping away, back along their trail, until Tug found her. If recapture was inevitable anyway, then at least she could save Rayne. There was no point in him throwing his life away senselessly on a lost cause.

With a deep sense of shame, Sara knew she wouldn't be able to do it, that to give herself up to Tug meant her certain death, and probably much worse before that. She also knew that her cowardice was probably dooming Rayne to a similar fate. As she struggled with her conscience, she reminded herself of her resolution, to not give in, to fight, to the bitter end if she had to. Rayne would have to make his own choices. He knew what they were up against just as well as she did.

She tried to think more positively, turning her mind to what they should now do. From what Rayne had told her, she figured they must be only two or three days away from getting out of the wilderness. With the additional horses they now had access to, perhaps there was a chance they might yet be able to keep ahead of their pursuers for long enough. If Rayne could keep going, that is.

Her own headache had finally cleared. The side of her head was still sore to the touch; otherwise, she was fine, just a little bit tired. Rayne was in pretty bad shape, though. What's more, if his arm was infected he would only get worse. Somehow, she would have to help him to keep going for the moment, and then get him some medical attention as soon as they cleared the wilderness. Presumably, the nearest decent sized town would have someone who could attend to his wound.

Sara also resolved that she would have to start taking over some of the responsibilities Rayne had been bearing until now. Although there was no avoiding their dependency on his knowledge of the wilderness, she could do more of the thinking for them from now on and start to make more of the decisions. He had been looking after her up to this point. Now it was time for her to look after him.

At their next break, she questioned him about where they were heading and what path he had planned for them over the next few days. When they resumed, having swapped horses again, she took the lead, allowing him to follow along in her wake while she kept an eye on the trail. She'd already noticed that the twisting and turning which had typified their path on earlier days had been given up since Rayne had sustained his wound. He'd been finding it difficult enough just to stay mounted, without the added burden of trying to conceal their trail. With her in the lead, Rayne seemed content just to sit back and rest. He was tiring quickly now and Sara realised her decision to take the initiative had been a timely one. His fever was obviously worsening.

To add to their troubles, rain set in about mid-afternoon. It was only drizzle, but they quickly donned their wet weather gear anyway. Rayne had his own and Sara put on the hat and coat she'd found in Ned's saddlebags. As the evening approached, it began to bucket down and they both felt their spirits sinking as they trudged along through the mud and the slush. Despite their coats, the rain still managed to get in under their clothing and by the time they stopped for the night they were both soaked to the skin. They made camp under the lee of a cliff, a slight overhang providing some relief from the downpour.

Fortunately, the rain cleared for a while then, giving them a chance to change out of their wet clothes and make decent arrangements for a dry night. They used one of their groundsheets to make a rough tent, small though it was. Once they'd tended to the horses, they both squirmed into it, glad to be finally under some shelter. After a quiet meal, they lay down for the night, both of them huddling under their blankets. Sara lay on her side, with Rayne right behind her, clinging closely to her in an attempt to keep warm.

They chatted for a while. Although they were both very tired, neither was ready for sleep. They'd already agreed they'd dispense with a lookout. The risk they ran had to be balanced against their need for rest.

Sara took some heart when Rayne told her the storm should help them by washing away their tracks. She was aware they hadn't made much more ground that day than they had on previous ones, despite the fresh horses. Slowly their talk turned away from their immediate concerns. For a while Rayne talked of his father, telling Sara of his life as a mercenary before he had settled down with Rayne's mother on the Marches.

"Rayne, tell me a story," Sara asked when he seemed to have finished. "I'd love to hear about something that doesn't involve wars or fighting for a change."

Rayne thought for a while. He told Sara that although he'd heard many stories from his father over the years he wasn't used to telling them himself. "All right," he eventually said. "I'll tell you about Jesec and Ranoran."

Sara rolled over to face him, propping herself up on one elbow. Her eyes twinkled with a mixture of interest and expectation. Rayne did the same, propping himself up on his good arm as he lay facing her. Because of the limited space available in the makeshift tent, there was only a small gap between them. Outside they could both hear the wind as it gusted through the surrounding trees.

"Ranoran," began Rayne, as a shower of water, shaken loose from the branches above them, rattled across the roof of their tent, "was a wealthy man with many servants and vast properties. One day he was out walking near the boundary of one of his estates, where his land merged with the wild woods, when he spied an old oak tree, almost ready to fall over. As he had a number of his servants with him, he ordered them to gather stakes to prop the tree up, saying it was too elegant and beautiful a thing to be allowed to fall to the ground.

"The nearby woods were said to be as ancient as the hills themselves and had always been known as a mysterious and magical place. Unbeknown to Ranoran, a nymph, who had come down from the woods many years ago, now inhabited the oak, and she had been on the point of perishing along with the ageing tree.

"His servants soon finished their task and returned to the house, leaving him alone, gazing up at the old tree. As he stood there, admiring its grace and beauty, he was astonished to see the nymph emerge from the trunk of the tree, stepping out on to the ground right before his very eyes. The nymph took the form of a maiden and she was the most beautiful girl Ranoran had ever seen."

Sara was fascinated by the tale. She hadn't been sure what to expect, but the story Rayne was telling reminded her of the fables her mother used to read to her in bed when she was much younger.

Rayne continued. "Ranoran fell to his knees. Knowing the creature before him was a magical being, he was afraid he had offended it in some way and that it had come forth seeking retribution. Instead of chastising him, as he expected, however, the nymph bade him to rise and when he did so she stepped forward and embraced him, kissing him lightly on each cheek and then hugging him to her. Standing back again, the nymph thanked Ranoran for saving her life and told him she would grant him a reward for his kindness."

"Is this a true story?" interrupted Sara when Rayne took a brief pause.

"Are there really tree nymphs in Ilythia? Have you seen one?"

"I'm not sure if it is," replied Rayne. "I've certainly never seen one, but I've heard they have been seen in some places." Sara nodded thoughtfully at his response.

"Ranoran," he went on, "was besotted by the nymph's beauty and boldly asked for her love as his prize. To his delight, she readily agreed and immediately lay down with him beneath the bows of the tree. There she willingly yielded herself to his desire. When they had finished making love, Ranoran asked the nymph if he could see her again, telling her he'd never met anyone like her before. She agreed, but on the condition that Ranoran remain a faithful and constant lover.

"From that day on they became lovers. The nymph told Ranoran she would send a honeybee to him as her messenger. Whenever it arrived, he would know to come to the grove where she would be waiting for him. The bee came often to Ranoran's villa, and whenever it did he would rise from whatever it was he was doing and go out to the edge of the woods for a tryst with the nymph, lying down with her beneath the creaking limbs of the old oak tree.

"This went on for some time. At first, Ranoran was delighted and his heart swelled with love for the nymph. As time passed, however, his passion cooled. One day, when the bee came to summon him, he was playing at dice with a friend. He was so engrossed in his game that he took no notice of the bee, idly swatting at it as it buzzed around his head. Eventually, the bee gave up trying to get his attention and returned to the nymph.

"The nymph waited for Ranoran in the grove. When the bee returned to her and she found out what had happened, she flew into a rage, casting a spell on Ranoran as she did so. The spell rendered Ranoran blind, in that very instant, and the nymph decreed that he would remain so until he learnt the value of love and constancy."

"So it's not just the Guardians who can cast spells?" asked Sara, interrupting him again. "There might be all sorts of beings in Ilythia who can do that."

"I don't know," said Rayne with a slight frown. "You could be right. But remember, I said I didn't know whether this was a true story. I haven't seen a nymph myself."

"I suppose you'd like to," teased Sara. "Especially if they're all as friendly as this one was."

Rayne blushed in response to her jibe. Ignoring her comment, he quickly went on with his story. "Ranoran and his friend were confounded at what had happened to him. When Ranoran finally guessed what had happened, however, he bade his servants to lead him to the grove. Upon arriving at the oak, he begged the nymph to come forth and forgive him, but to no avail. He stayed there for much of the day, pleading with the nymph to listen to him and to forgive him for his thoughtlessness. Eventually, when she showed no sign of responding, he returned to his villa, full of despair. Though he returned to the oak many times in the coming days, the result was always the same.

"As time passed, Ranoran, through his blindness, began to lose all of his wealth. His business associates cheated him and he could no longer properly oversee the work on his properties. In a very short time, he lost everything. He soon ended up as a pauper, forced to wander the land with a cane, begging for food and shelter.

"One day, his wanderings brought him to the home of a young widow. Her name was Jesec and she took pity on him, offering him shelter for the night. When he told her his story, she felt so sorry for his condition that she allowed him to stay on in her house. While he gave her what help he could with the chores, she cooked for him and looked after him, sharing her meagre earnings with him in her pity for his plight.

"Over time, Jesec began to fall in love with Ranoran, who had changed as a result of his fate. Instead of the proud and haughty landowner he'd once been, he had become a more humble and compassionate man. He began to find that he cared for Jesec as well. Finally, they began to fall into a deep love for each other and, as their love grew, Ranoran found that his blindness slowly began to diminish.

"At first he began to be aware of light where once there'd only been darkness. Eventually, the light coalesced into shapes and, on the day Jesec asked him if he would marry her, his full vision returned. The happy couple rejoiced at this and married that very day in celebration. Their love for each other continued to grow and they stayed together for the rest of their days. They had two children together, a boy and a girl; but that is another story."

Sara smiled at the stylised ending to the story. For someone who usually concealed his feelings, to her surprise, Rayne had told a very tender story about love and the capriciousness of the gods.

"I'm going to miss you Sara," blurted Rayne suddenly, interrupting her thoughts. Looking up she found that he was looking straight into her eyes.

"What do you mean?" she replied, uncertain as to what had brought this on.

"It's not fair," exclaimed Rayne. "No matter what happens to us, I lose you. If the people chasing us catch up with us, I lose you. And if we escape, you'll eventually find some way to get back home and then I'll lose you that way. Either way, I'm going to miss you very much when you're gone."

"Oh Rayne, you're so sweet." Sara felt her eyes blur as she reached out and caressed his cheek with her hand. To her surprise, she saw a tear fall from the corner of Rayne's eyes and run down his cheek. Turning his head slightly, he opened his lips and gently kissed the fingers touching his cheek.

Sara gasped at his touch. "Oh Rayne," she cried. Leaning over closer to him, she tentatively opened her lips, closing her eyes as she saw him do the same. As their lips touched, she felt the spark of desire flame into passion. Without a further thought, she hugged Rayne to her, allowing the feeling that was sweeping through her to guide her. They lay together like that for a few moments, kissing passionately as their bodies entwined, twisting and pressing against each other in the close confines of the tent. Then, with a gasp, Sara broke off the kiss and lay back. Her chest heaved as she looked up at the roof of the tent.

They both lay there panting until Rayne broke the silence. "If I said I was sorry, I'd be lying," he finally said between breaths.

Sara rolled over towards him and kissed his lips once more, pulling back as his kisses became more ardent again. "I'm not sorry, either," said Sara, looking down at him with sparkling eyes, her face only inches from his. "It's just that I need to take things a bit slower. Okay?"

"Okay," said Rayne, taking a deep breath.

"Let's just talk," said Sara, lying back. "I need to calm down."

"At least I forgot about my arm for a while," replied Rayne with a smile.

CHAPTER 11

Tug was worried. He didn't dare go back to Golkar without the girl and yet it had been ten days now and they still hadn't caught up with them. He knew they were close, but they'd been close before and still not managed to close the trap. Whoever it was that the girl had latched on to, he wasn't making their job an easy one.

Twice now they'd been lucky not to lose a horse to those damned traps he'd been setting. The first time, Tug himself had taken a fall when his horse had been brought down by a vine stretched across their path on a steep decline, about fetlock high. It was a miracle the horse hadn't broken something and Tug himself had been lucky to escape serious injury from the tumble he'd taken as the horse had come down.

That had slowed them. Then, two days later, luck once again was all that had prevented them from losing one of their horses. They'd been spelling their mounts and Rewin, their tracker, had been leading his on foot. By pure chance, he'd sighted a beaver trap, partially hidden by a smattering of twigs and leaves, right in the middle of their path. That had slowed them even further. And now, just when they were starting to make some progress again, the rain had set in.

The three of them had camped for the night and were now sheltering from the rain in their tent. As Tug unwound from yet another long day in the saddle, he considered his mismatched helpers. He'd known both of them for a few years now and they'd worked together a number of times.

Rewin was a master of forest craft. Tug had found that there wasn't a living thing he couldn't track. To look at him, though, with his wiry frame, his pinched cheeks and receding hairline, he didn't seem like he'd be much of a help if it came to a fight. Tug knew better. Rewin could handle himself when he needed to as well as anyone Tug had ridden with.

Ter, on the other hand, was a big oaf by comparison, all brute strength with little finesse. He had his own uses, though. More than once his single-minded determination had gotten Ruz and Tug out of tight situations. And he fought like a demon. He didn't know how to lose or when to give up.

"I don't like it," said Tug, more to voice his frustration than seeking a response from either of his companions. "This rain is gunna make it damned difficult to track them now."

"That depends on how soon it lets up," responded Rewin, as he slowly chewed on a piece of dry meat. "Soft ground can make it easier, as long as the rain doesn't wash the tracks away before we find them."

"They can't be far ahead now, anyways," snarled Ter, as he sharpened his knife on a stone. "We gotta be right on their hammer. Tomorrow, next day at the latest, we're gunna catch the villain that did Kyrt in. He's got a lot to answer for, the cur. When I git my hands on him I'm gunna give him one, not just for Kyrt but for old Jard as well."

"You're right there, Ter," said Tug. "He's got it comin to him. But let's not underestimate him. I thought that might have been a lucky shot he got Kyrt with, but bringing down both of Jard's boys, that was no mean feat. I wonder how long before old Jard figures they ain't comin home."

"He's injured now," said Rewin, focused as ever on the chase. "That arrow we found left a big hole somewhere and he might still be losing some blood over that. I reckon his days is about to come to an end real soon now."

Tug wasn't so sure, or maybe it was just that he had a lot more riding on this chase than Rewin and Ter did. For them, it was just money, although he knew it had become very personal for Ter when his brother had been killed at the falls. When the girl and the man with her had jumped over the edge, the big man had gone mad with rage. He'd been off to his horse and after them before Tug and Rewin could do anything to stop him. Tug wondered if they'd still have fallen for the trick if it hadn't been for that. He and Rewin had raced off after him and they'd lost half the afternoon before they'd thought to check the top of the falls again and found they'd been back that way. Kyrt's horse had been what had really done it for them, though. They'd have caught up with them easily again if they'd still only had the one mount between them.

"I hope you're right," he said to Rewin. "They've given us a long chase already."

"Yeh, but they're running out of tricks. We'd have got them already but for those traps. That slowed us down a lot keeping an eye out for them. They'd be getting pretty tired now, and with him being injured and all, he must be getting weak. Those horses they got from the boys will have helped them, and the fresh provisions they got, but you can tell they're slowing. Remember, while we're sleeping sound here, they're out there worrying about us chasing them. The chaser always sleeps easier than the chased. They can't afford no fire either, so they're cold and they're eating cold rations. They're slowing real quick now." Rewin paused, nodding thoughtfully before he went on. "We got em."

Tug nodded. "He's yours," he said, turning to Ter, "once we get him. As much as I'd like to see the runt get what's comin to him, you got the right."

"You bet I have." The look on Ter's face was a murderous one. "And he ain't gunna git it quick like Kyrt did. He's gunna be beggin me to kill him before I'm done with him."

"How do you reckon he got the drop on Jard's boys?" asked Tug again, looking back at Rewin. He knew Rewin had ways of telling things like that from the tracks. While Ter was as good as anyone when it came to a scrap, or a bit of larceny for that matter, it was Rewin who did most of the thinking. Not that Tug would admit it; he was the boss and he liked it that way. It made for a nice change seeing as it was him that was usually the one taking orders from Ruz. Tug had learnt enough from Ruz to know his own limitations though. He was quite happy to let Rewin be the brains as long as he called the shots in the end.

"I don't think he did, you know," answered Rewin, looking up at the draghar thoughtfully. "It looked to me like that girl might have put an arrow in of one of them and then her fella finished him off with a knife. The other one . . . I don't know. The tracks didn't make much sense to me, I have to say. I know he got hit though."

"You could be right," said Tug. "She showed a lot of fight getting away from me and Ruz. I hadn't figured her as being anything but a harmless little thing until then, but she showed she sure ain't harmless. Just ask Ruz. If he ain't dead by now."

"Yeh, well I think this one's going to be a lot more of a handful than that last one we picked up for Golkar. Whatever did happen to her?"

"She's dead."

Rewin nodded as if he'd expected that answer. "Pity," he said. "She was a pretty thing."

Tug nodded silently in response. There wasn't much Rewin and Ter wouldn't do for money. Kidnapping, murder, stealing, it didn't seem to matter to them as long as Golkar's gold was somewhere at the end of it. In some ways, Tug looked down on them for that. He regarded Ruz and himself as professionals. They did it because they enjoyed it, not because Golkar paid them for it. Not to say that there weren't some perks that went with the job.

The thought of Golkar turned his mind back to the task at hand. "How far now to the edge of the wilderness?" he asked Rewin. "I want to catch up with them before they get out into open country."

"Maybe three days at the pace we been going," said Rewin slowly, clearly thinking about the ground they would need to cross between here and there. "A lot depends on this rain. That might slow us down, or, like I said, it might make it easier to track them. With us so close now, I think we'll get them before they clear the wilderness." After a slight pause, Rewin spoke again. "Yep, I don't think they'll get that far."

Tug lay back down on his bedding, listening to the soft drum of the rain that had begun to fall once again on their tent. Once more he hoped that Rewin was right. There was no way he was going back to Tu-atha without the girl. No way.

~~~

All through the next day, Sara and Rayne plodded on through the intermittent rain. As he rocked back and forth on Ned, with his eyes fixed on the rump of the horse in front of him, Rayne found that the depression, which had previously gripped Sara, now had a firm hold on him.

He cursed himself for the foolishness that had driven him to venture into the settlement. His father, with all of his experience, had warned him of the place and still he had done it. And then, to compound the error, he'd given little thought to their choice for a campsite that night. If it hadn't been for Sara's brave response to their attackers, he'd be dead already. As it was he still didn't give much for his chances of making it out of the wilderness alive.

Their only hope now lay with this rain. Rayne doubted if it would be enough to save them, however. They had a long way to go and it was taking all of his energy just to stay mounted. Instead of leading them forward at a time when they should be pushing on with all speed, he'd become nothing more to Sara than a dead weight. He was just slowing her down. If only his cursed arm would begin to show some sign of improvement.

Rayne realised that, far from improving, his arm was getting worse. It was clearly infected, and the fever that was muddling his thoughts was also worsening. If things continued the way they were going, Sara might have to tie him into the saddle. The dull ache in his arm had progressed till the pain had become a permanent distraction. It throbbed constantly from shoulder to wrist and it had taken all of his will not to scream out in agony when Sara had last re-dressed and bathed it. Even if by some miracle they did get out of the wilderness, he'd be lucky to retain the use of his arm.

And what of Sara? Rayne knew that he'd let her down, and badly. The poor girl was depending on him to save her from a horrible fate and yet it was all he could do to just to keep from falling off his horse as he followed along behind her. When he had said that he wanted adventure, he hadn't planned on it turning out like this. He was supposed to rescue her and here she was looking after him. What would his father think of him now? What must Sara think of him? He'd had his first chance to do something, to make his own mark as a man, and he'd failed.

Rayne wondered if it had become his fate to lose everything he loved. Was he cursed in some way, as Ranoran had been by the nymph? He'd lost his mother, and then his father, and now, just when he had dared to feel something for Sara, it seemed he was going to lose her as well.

He remembered how his father had once said to him that life was anything but fair and he should never expect anything more from it other than what he got. He'd never truly understood why his father had felt that way, wondering whether it might be bitterness over the loss of Rayne's mother that was behind it. Now he could see that his father was right. If there had been anything fair about life then he wouldn't have been given the opportunity to meet someone as lovely as Sara only to have her snatched away from him just when he realised he cared for her.

Rayne considered his feelings for Sara. He knew he'd only known her for less than two weeks, but he was fairly certain of what he felt for her nonetheless. He'd known other girls back on the Marches, pretty ones too, but none of them had intrigued him as much as Sara did. She was far more intelligent, and worldly, than the girls he was used to. At times that daunted him, but it also added to her mystique.

Looking up as they rode on, he took in her lovely form. Her long ponytail hung down to the small of her back, ending just above her slender waist. He smiled as he remembered how it had felt when he'd placed his hand there, remembering how much he enjoyed snuggling up behind her at night with his hand round her waist. She had her back to him now, but he had no difficulty picturing her face. He'd spent enough of his time admiring it. He loved her smile, especially the way that it seemed to light up her whole face. That was the thing that he liked more than anything else. When she was happy it struck a chord somewhere deep within him that made him feel happy as well, content that something was pleasing her. Rayne thought her simply the most beautiful girl he'd ever seen.

He thought back to their first few days together. As he'd started to feel something for her, he'd tried to dismiss it but had found that he couldn't. Then he'd told himself that someone as beautiful as she was wouldn't be interested in someone like him. What was he after all? Just a trapper. He was just someone she had turned to for help. It could have been anyone. It just happened to be him.

And then, last night, when they'd kissed, everything had changed. He had never felt such a strong desire for someone before in his life. She certainly wasn't the first girl he'd kissed, but none of the others had affected him as she had. He was just grateful she'd been stronger than he had been. The last thing he wanted to do was to hurt her.

To add to Rayne's depression, he now knew that she felt something for him as well. Her response last night had made that clear. The irony of the situation galled him. Instead of the elation he should have been feeling, frustration was eating away at him like a canker. He couldn't bear the thought of losing her.

Rayne's thoughts were interrupted as he felt something shaking him. With a start, he looked up. It was Sara. She had turned Nell around and ridden back to him and was shaking his arm.

"Rayne," she said with a look of concern on her face. "Are you okay?"

"Y-yes," he replied, a little uncertainly, wondering why she was asking. "Why, what's wrong?"

"I've been trying to get you to answer but you wouldn't respond. I think you're getting tired. We'd better stop for a bit."

Looking around, Rayne could see they were close to the top of the ridge they'd been ascending. The drizzle had stopped for the moment. "Let's get over into the next gorge and stop there," he replied. "Less chance of being seen by someone following then." He was glad he was still aware enough to be of some use to them.

"Good idea," said Sara. "I didn't think of that. Follow me."

Turning Nell around, Sara led the way again. Rayne followed, urging Ned on so that he kept close behind. He looked about him as they climbed, determined not to let his thoughts drift away again. A few minutes later they reached the crest of the ridge, stopping as they did so to look down at the valley below them.

The scene before them was similar to many they'd viewed before, the broad mass of trees which spread out in front of them was broken here and there by a few rocky outcrops. A shallow river bed snaked its way across the floor of the valley below them. Rayne cast his eyes to the horizon, searching forlornly for an end to the wilderness. The low clouds which hung over the forest ensured that his vision was limited. Perhaps on a better day he might have been able to see further.

"Oh my god," whispered Sara as his eyes scanned the horizon. "Quick, get back."

Before Rayne had a chance to react, Sara turned Nell and, taking hold of Ned's rein, quickly led them back off the crest of the ridge, returning to the valley they'd just climbed out of. The two spare horses, which had been tied in a line to the back of Rayne's saddle, turned with them. Once they were all safely behind the ridgeline again, she stopped and dismounted.

"Wait here," she whispered urgently to Rayne, who still hadn't worked out what was going on. As he watched, she dismounted and warily crept back up to the top of the ridge, peering over into the valley on the other side from behind the safety of the ridgeline. Intrigued and confused, Rayne somehow managed to clamber down from Ned and scramble up beside her.

"What is it?" he whispered, painfully aware of the ache in his arm as he knelt down on the ground beside her.

"Down there," said Sara pointing, "in the bed of that stream. There are some men down there on horses."

Rayne looked down at the spot Sara was pointing to, trying desperately to focus his vision. He didn't see how Tug and his men could have gotten in front of them. Following the line of her arm, he could see there were small shapes moving about on the bed of the shallow watercourse. They were mounted . . . but they weren't men! Rayne felt a chill come over him as he realised what they were looking at. He'd never seen one himself before but they fitted his father's description perfectly. "They're sligs," he whispered, his voice betraying the horror he felt.

Sara squinted, trying to get a better look at the shapes she had seen. "My god," she said after a few moments. "They look horrible. I thought you said that they lived far away? What are they doing here?"

"I don't know," he whispered, wondering why he did so when the sligs were far too far away to hear them. "Let's get out of here."

"Which way should we go?" asked Sara as they quickly made their way back to their horses. Rayne could see she was as shaken as he was by this unexpected development.

He struggled to clear his head. "I don't know," he responded, stopping and looking around as he tried to gather his thoughts. "We can't go back. We'll just go straight into the arms of Tug and his men if we do that."

"Well," said Sara. "We have to either go further up this valley then, or lower down."

"Let's continue down the line of the valley we're in and try to cross over further down," he decided. "They looked like they were headed up the valley." He hoped he was right. They would have no hope at all if they ran into a band of slig warriors.

"Okay," said Sara, quickly mounting. She was obviously anxious to get moving.

With an effort, Rayne remounted Ned. Letting Sara take the lead once again, he concentrated on following along in her wake. The appearance of the sligs wasn't something he had considered. He couldn't begin to fathom what they were doing here in the wilderness; they were certainly a long way from their normal haunts. What really alarmed him, however, was what they'd been doing. He couldn't be sure, but he'd gotten the distinct impression that they were searching for tracks, like they were following or searching for someone. He wondered what it meant, hoping that whatever it was it had nothing to do with them.

As quickly as they could, they made their way along the line of the ridge, keeping sufficiently below the crest to ensure they couldn't be seen. While Sara kept peering nervously over her shoulder, Rayne tried to keep an eye out for Tug and his men. Although they weren't going back on their former trail, they were effectively travelling at right angles to it. His father used to have an expression which Rayne thought fitted their current circumstances perfectly. 'Between the hammer and the anvil,' he called it. Rayne now knew how desperate a place that could be.

After a while, they halted again and crawled up to the crest of the ridge once more. They were further down the valley now and the ridgeline itself wasn't as high as the spot from where they had seen the sligs. They lay there watching for some time but could see no further sign of the creatures. Cautiously, they re-mounted and crossed over, making their way down into the next valley, both of them anxious to be down and up the other side as quickly as could. Neither said a word as they made their way down through the trees; they were afraid they could run into more sligs at any moment. Rayne forced the pain in his arm to the back of his thoughts. The prospect of an encounter with slig warriors was now foremost in his mind.

It took them some time, but they finally reached the edge of the shallow stream, halting as they did so and peering nervously up and down the watercourse. Nothing could be heard but the babble of water as it gushed over the stony creek bed. After a brief pause, they urged the horses out from the cover of the trees. Rayne held his breath as they moved out into the open, only releasing it with a gasp of relief when they finally gained the cover of the trees on the other side. Sara, who had waited for him on the bank, reached out with her hand as he drew level on Ned.

Taking her hand in his, he gently squeezed it, trying to give her a reassuring smile as he did so. He could see that Sara was just as scared as he was. Neither had said a word from the moment they'd crossed over into the valley. The tension was becoming unbearable. The brief linking of hands lifted Rayne's spirits and he could see Sara drew inspiration from it as well.

With a nod to each other, they moved on, only to halt again abruptly a moment later. Somewhere, close by, a horse had snorted. They had both heard it and pulled up at the same time. Turning to Sara, Rayne placed his index finger to his lips, indicating that they should be as quiet as possible. His heart thumped furiously as he looked around, frantically trying to see where the sound had come from. He desperately hoped that their own horses wouldn't make any unexpected noise.

Both of their heads snapped to the left as they heard voices and the splashing of horses wading through water. The sounds had come from downstream. Quickly they urged their horses away from the bank, anxious to gain the cover of the trees before whoever, or whatever, it was got closer. To Rayne's horror, as they moved forward two mounted slig warriors appeared from between a clump of bushes, directly before them. They were only ten or so paces away. As Sara screamed, Rayne quickly turned Ned and kicked him into a gallop, knowing Sara would follow his lead.

Even as they bounded forward, Rayne knew that they wouldn't make it. The two spare horses tied behind him would ensure that what little chance he had of outrunning the sligs was doomed to fail. As Sara drew level on Nell, Rayne suddenly spun Ned about, calling out to Sara as he did so. "Fly Sara, fly and don't look back."

Drawing his sword, Rayne determined to make a stand in an attempt to give Sara what chance he could. Slashing futilely at one of the sligs as its horse veered around him, he knew it was hopeless. The slig had ignored him, intent on racing after Sara. Before Rayne could make any attempt to turn and follow the warrior, he screamed out in pain as the second slig crashed into him, springing from its horse and knocking him to the ground in one movement.

Rayne felt a searing burst of pain shoot up his arm as he fell. It seemed to him as if everything had slowed down. As his shoulder crunched sickeningly into the floor of the forest, driven down by the weight of the slig on top of him, Rayne experienced an unexpected sense of calm. As darkness swept over him, he realised he was blacking out. His last thought as he lost consciousness was one of relief. It was finally over.

CHAPTER 12

Swirling tongues of flame surged up from the crackling logs, thrusting up into the darkness, like the hands of some infernal demon, desperately straining upwards, ever upwards, in a futile attempt to grasp a hold of the very firmament itself. Their seeming endless struggle threatened to mesmerise Sara as she sought to lose herself in the chaotic rhythm of their dance. Try as she might, though, she could not achieve her aim. The dread circumstances she now found herself in stubbornly resisted all her attempts to deny them.

Not for the first time during her brief stay in Ilythia she found herself bound and at the mercy of others. She had thought that nothing could be worse than returning to the clutches of Tug. That was before she'd had a close encounter with a slig warrior.

Nothing in Rayne's description of the sligs had prepared Sara for what they actually looked like. The slig warrior that eyed her sulkily through the shimmering heat that rose from the flames that separated them looked like something out of her worst nightmare. Like Rayne, his long hair was pulled back into a short ponytail at the nape of his neck. That was where the similarity ended, however.

He was tall, at least a head higher than Rayne, and his broad chest was covered in a shirt made from small metal rings, linked together over a padded, dun-coloured vest. Sara guessed it was a form of chain mail. His breeches were made from toughened leather, as were his long boots, which were laced up to the top of his shins. Where his skin was visible, which was only his arms and his neck and face, it appeared to be scaly and was greyish in colour. It was his face that really frightened her, however.

It looked closer to that of a boar than a man. The end of his short nose was flat and his two nostrils pointed forwards from either side of its surface. His brows stood out like ridges below a forehead that rippled with corrugations of skin right up to the line of his greasy, black hair. His deep-set eyes seemed to glimmer in the firelight. She'd seen them earlier, in the daylight, and knew that the irises were yellow, like those of a beast of the forest. When he spoke or opened his mouth to eat, he revealed sharp, interlocking teeth that reminded Sara of a wild dog.

All in all, the sight was a thoroughly frightening one. Her skin prickled and the hairs on the back of her neck rose whenever she looked at him or his companions. The memory of the coarse touch of their skin on hers rekindled a dread, empty feeling in the pit of her stomach. She'd wanted to shriek in terror when they'd dragged her from her horse. Now at least she could look at them, though her pulse rate still quickened whenever she chanced to make eye contact.

Sara found it hard to distinguish the four sligs from each other as they sat around the fire, chewing away at the meat they'd been roasting. slight differences in their clothing or their weapons were all she could see that identified one from the other. They paid her little attention as they sat there eating and talking, an occasional glance the only indication that they were even aware of her presence.

She knew that struggling against the bonds that held her wrists behind her back was useless. Her attempts to free herself had already brought her one teeth-jarring smack to the side of her head and she didn't relish another. In any event, her more subtle attempts to test the efficacy of her bonds had already proved that further exertion was futile. Even should she have been able to overcome that hurdle, her ankles were bound as well. Sara tried not to swallow, despite her hunger. The vile taste of the cloth gag that had been forced into her mouth was bad enough as it was. A moan from nearby drew her attention away from her own problems.

Rayne's body lay slumped on the ground beside her. He was similarly bound, but with the added imposition of his ankles being drawn up behind him and tied to the bonds at his wrists. Like her, he was gagged as well. The large bloodstain on the arm of his shirt indicated that his wound had re-opened during their brief tussle with the sligs. It was clear he was losing blood again at a rapid rate.

Sara hadn't known till they'd stopped to make camp whether he'd been killed at the creek or brought with them. The sligs that had captured her had thrown her bound body sideways across the back of Nell and tied her in place like a sack of chaff. The painful trip to their current campsite that had followed had afforded her a view of little else than the side of the horse and the ground as it passed below her. It was only when that torturous trip had finally ended and the sligs had stopped to make camp that she'd seen they'd brought Rayne with them as well.

He had been unconscious when taken from the horse he'd been tied to, or at least that's what she'd assumed at first. When, after a long time, he still hadn't moved, Sara had begun to fear he was dead. Although the occasional muffled groan he was now emitting had dispelled that dread thought, Sara wondered how long it would be before they both wished that the sligs had killed them right where they'd caught them.

As she looked down at Rayne, she saw his eyelids finally begin to flutter open. At first, he screwed up his face in obvious pain, and then he groaned once more through his gag. After a brief moment's respite, another wave of pain seemed to course through him, right on the heels of the first. When it had passed, he peered up at Sara through glazed eyes that showed no sign of recognition. With another heart-rending groan, he began to struggle against his bonds. One of the slig warriors looked up from his meal and called out with a snarl. "Shut up you. And quit your wriggling."

Rayne seemed not to hear them, continuing to moan as he twisted and turned in a vain attempt to free himself. The warrior who'd spoken threw his meat to the ground in obvious anger. Rising from his place by the fire, he strode over to stand over Rayne. "I said shut up," he growled as Rayne writhed on the ground at his feet. When he showed no sign of desisting, the warrior lashed out at him with his hard leather boot.

Sara watched helplessly, choking back the scream in her throat as she saw that he'd caught Rayne's injured arm as he viciously kicked into him two or three times in quick succession. With a piercing shriek, Rayne convulsed in pain, then fell into silence again as his body went limp. Sara hoped he'd merely lost consciousness. She prayed that the slig hadn't killed him.

"That's better," growled the slig, spitting at Rayne's prostrate body before he returned to his place by the fire. As he sat down, the other warriors muttered something to him, then they all laughed cruelly, looking at Rayne as they did so. Sara watched as the slig took up the meat he'd thrown in the dirt and commenced to chew on it again. She felt sure she was going to be sick.

She cried for a while then as she thought of poor Rayne. His brief moment of consciousness must have been a painful one, especially with his injured arm pulled back behind him. She guessed he must have thought he'd awoken in hell. The knowledge that it was a hell she was responsible for didn't help her at all. If only she had stayed where she was, with Ruz and Tug and Golkar. She would have been no worse off than she was now, and Rayne wouldn't have been dragged into her nightmare.

She should have crept away from their camp when she'd thought of it. So much for fighting to the bitter end. The end was certainly bitter, but there had been precious little fighting. Oh, Rayne had tried. Sara felt a lump in her throat as she remembered what he had done. She wondered if there had ever been a braver move than the one that he had made as he'd turned back to face the sligs. Unfortunately, his attempt to give her a chance to escape had been a futile one. The sligs had just snapped her up like a child. She realised now what a fool she had been to think she could possibly escape from the fate this world had reserved for her.

She sat there sobbing and drowning herself in her sorrows like that for some time. The sligs took no further notice of her, or of Rayne for that matter. They continued to talk among themselves, laughing and cursing as they went about their meal.

She wondered about the sligs. What possible motivation could they have for deciding to take her and Rayne captive rather than kill them on the spot?

Rayne had told her little about the fell creatures other than that they were involved in raids on the Algarians' eastern frontier. He had also been vague about where they came from; somewhere out beyond the eastern mountains, he had indicated dismissively when she had asked. Although she had thought at the time that he'd been reluctant to let on how little he actually knew of the world beyond his own experience, it occurred to Sara now that perhaps he had actually been unwilling to share with her the real horror behind the sligs. For all she knew, they were cannibals and had taken her and Rayne captive as a source of fresh meat. Sara felt a moment of terror as she tried to shake off that notion. She couldn't afford to believe that was the case. She'd go mad if she allowed herself to seriously entertain that thought.

Regardless of what they planned for her and Rayne, her situation was clearly a hopeless one. Even if she could have been able to free herself, Rayne was so seriously injured that they would never be able to escape. With that thought, Sara began to despair again . She didn't want to die; she was so young and had so much she still wanted out of life. What had she done to deserve this nightmare?

Her previous existence seemed so far away that she was beginning to wonder now which was the real world and which was a dream. This place she was in seemed so real it made her wonder if the parents and friends she missed so much were, in fact, the dream. Did they ever really exist, and if they did, would she ever be likely to see them again? She had long since given up hope of awakening from this nightmare existence. For now, it was as real as anything got. With that forlorn thought, she fell to sobbing again.

Sara had almost cried herself to sleep, her eyes felt heavy and she was trying to work out how to lie down, bound as she was, when a movement on the very edge of the fire-lit area caught her attention. Looking out into the darkness, the forest around the campsite seemed as impenetrable as ever. It must have been some small animal moving about in the undergrowth on the periphery of the firelight. The sligs were chatting softly between themselves now and they didn't seem to have noticed anything unusual.

After a while, the need for sleep began to drag her eyelids down once more. A flicker of movement off to one side drew her drowsy head up again and slowly around to the right. As she turned her head, she was astonished to see an old man step out of the darkness beyond the campsite and into the light. It was as if he had suddenly appeared out of thin air. The slig warriors had seen him too and they quickly scrambled to their feet, drawing their weapons as he approached them.

The man was old, so old that he stooped as he walked, relying on a short, gnarled walking stick to support him. He was dressed in a long gown that was belted at the waist. The garment was a simple one, faded brown in colour and plain, with long sleeves that ended just above the wrists. Below its frayed and dirty fringe, Sara could see that he wore leather boots. The skin on his hands was wrinkled and cracked, and his face was lined and mottled. His head sported a shock of white hair above a thin but kindly face. He seemed quite unperturbed by the sight of the four armed slig warriors that stood before him.

"I've come for the girl," he said slowly in an even voice. As he spoke, he raised his stick, waving it vaguely towards the fire.

All of a sudden, a piercing light flashed out from the flames. Sara's body reeled back in an instant defensive reaction. With a shock, she realised that the flash had blinded her. Swirling shapes swam across the void that had displaced her vision. She was aware of yells and curses from the direction of the sligs. Struggling to rise from where she had fallen, she flinched as something touched her, an involuntary gasp escaping her lips as she did so. A moment later she felt a hand, more gently this time, passing over her eyelids. At the same time, she heard someone say something, a few mumbled words, unexpected and indecipherable, from just above her.

As the hand drew away, she opened her eyes, finding, incredibly, that her vision had been restored. The old man was crouching over her and looking down through crinkly eyes with a kindly smile. "You'll be all right," he whispered. "Let's get you out of this." As he spoke, he took a knife from his belt and cut the bonds at her ankles. He did the same for her gag and then eased her forward and reached over to cut the bonds that secured her wrists behind her back. As she rubbed the soreness from her wrists, she saw him glance back at the sligs. Following his gaze, she was amazed at the wild scene being played out on the opposite side of the fire.

One of the sligs was blindly stumbling about, recklessly swinging his broad axe before him in a vain attempt to connect with their attacker. A second was on his knees, crawling on the ground, groping with his hands in desperation, trying to establish where he was. As she watched, a third stumbled into the fire, screaming as his clothes caught alight. As he lurched away from the fire, the first warrior caught him a glancing blow across one arm with his axe, drawing another scream that seemed to reverberate right down the length of Sara's backbone. The fourth was nowhere to be seen.

"Quickly now," said the old man, turning his back on the mad scene before them. As he helped Sara to her feet, he whispered in her ear. "Help me with Rayne."

"Who are you?" whispered Sara in return, stooping to loosen Rayne's bonds and trying to keep an eye on the sligs at the same time.

"Time enough for explanations later." As the old man spoke, he sliced through the last of Rayne's bonds and together they managed to lift him to his feet. It took all of Sara's strength to support him under one shoulder and she could see that the old man was wheezing as he struggled to do the same on his side. Somehow, they managed to drag him away from the fire and the sligs and into the shadows of the forest.

Sara had no idea where they were going, but she knew that they wouldn't get far. Rayne was too heavy for her. The old man was struggling too, seemingly barely able to stay afoot under the dead weight of Rayne's body. After they'd gone a short distance, he spoke again, panting for breath as he did so. "I can't go any further with him," he gasped. "We have to stop here."

Once they'd stopped and lowered Rayne to the ground, the old man bent over from the waist, sucking in air in long, wheezy gulps. Leaning heavily on his wooden stick, he coughed a few times and then slowly began to straighten, grimacing from the effort as he did so. Sara looked on in amazement, wondering at the contrast with how easily he'd dealt with the sligs.

"Wait here," he whispered once he had regained his breath. Without waiting for a reply, he turned and walked away, quickly disappearing into the darkness.

Sara didn't know what to do. She had no idea who their strange benefactor was or what his intentions were. As she kneeled nervously beside Rayne in the darkness, however, she realised she had no choice but to trust him. She would have no chance of escaping alone, on foot and at night in the forest, with no idea of where she was. And she couldn't leave Rayne, at least not in the condition he was in. If the stranger turned out to be someone that Golkar had sent to retrieve her, she would just have to try to convince him to first of all help her to get Rayne to some place where he could be cared for; or, at the very least, to take her and to leave Rayne alone.

The old man had been gone for some time and she had begun to wonder if something had happened to him when she heard the sounds of someone approaching. Letting Rayne slump to the ground, she quickly threw herself down beside him, trying to lie as flat as she could. To her relief, it was the old man again. This time he had three horses with him. Recognising Nell's dappled grey, she could see that two of them were hers and Rayne's. He must have gone back to the camp to get them.

With the old man's help, she managed to get Rayne up again and, after a good deal of effort, they finally got him onto Nell. Sara climbed up behind him, struggling to hold him in place as she did so. The old man mounted the third horse, a sorrel with a striking blonde mane. With a wave of his hand, he motioned for Sara to follow him. Then, turning his mount, he headed off through the trees, away from the slig camp.

Although the rain seemed to have stopped, the sky still hadn't cleared and the interposing clouds muted what little light the moon and the stars would normally have provided. Sara could barely make out the old man's shape as he rode off into the dark of the night. For a moment, she hesitated, knowing that this might be her last chance to escape. The occasional cry of anguish from the direction of the slig camp indicated that pursuit was unlikely from that quarter for some time. She and Rayne could turn and ride off now and hope that the old man wouldn't be able to find them again in the dark.

As she urged Nell forward, following him, she knew that would be pointless. He had already managed to find them once in the dark. If what he had done back at the slig camp was any indication, he would have little difficulty finding them again. Besides, she already had enough enemies here in Ilythia. She had to hope that maybe she'd finally found another friend.

Sara struggled to keep up as the old man rode on through the forest ahead of them. She had never ridden at night and was finding it difficult to know what needed the most of her attention. Between hanging on to Rayne, keeping an eye on the path and looking out for overhanging branches that seemed to appear suddenly and with little warning directly in front of her, threatening to knock them both out of the saddle, she had little time to consider where they were going or what they should now do.

Occasionally, she risked a glance backwards. Although she could neither see nor hear any sign of pursuit, she didn't feel very reassured. She felt sure it wouldn't be long before someone or something was after her again. She'd spent the whole of her time in Ilythia either running away or planning to run away from someone and there seemed little reason to hope this would change now.

After what seemed like hours, the old man's horse slowed to a walk. They had traversed a considerable distance from the slig camp and had begun to climb again. Finally, he stopped and dismounted in front of her. Uncertain as to why they had halted, Sara stayed where she was. As she looked on nervously, the old man slowly walked back to where she waited. *Is this it?* thought Sara, moving her hand stealthily to where the hilt of her knife would normally protrude from her belt. Had he brought them this far in order to kill them here, alone, in the dark? She felt her body tense as she realised how helpless she was, unarmed and barely able to hold Rayne upright in the saddle before her.

"I'll hold him while you dismount," the old man said to her as he reached her side. As he spoke, he reached up and grabbed a hold of Rayne with both of his arms.

Sara did as he suggested, not knowing what else she could do. She dearly wished that Rayne was conscious; she was sure that he would know how to handle this situation. To her relief, the old man made no attempt to harm either of them. Together they managed to get Rayne down from Nell and to prop him up between them. Then, with one of his arms wrapped around each of their necks, they began to move up the slope together, half dragging and half carrying their injured companion between them.

As before, Sara could see that the old man was tiring quickly from the effort. She still had no idea where they were going and she felt the cold grip of fear returning to her limbs. Although it was dark, she could see enough to establish that there was nothing in front of them except more trees and rocks. Where was he taking them?

As Sara struggled with her fear, too afraid of what his answer might be to ask the obvious question, their progress came to a halt when a rock wall loomed up in front of them. To her utter amazement, they halted directly in front of it, close enough to reach out and touch it. Looking up, Sara wondered how they would ever manage to scale it, for that was now their only option. Even if by some miracle she could get Rayne up its face, the old man seemed utterly incapable of such a climb.

As she began to consider why he had saved them from the sligs, led them miles and miles away through the dark of night, then dismounted and led them through bracken and bush to a stone cliff face in the middle of who knows where, the old man reached out in front of them with his walking stick. Using it to push aside the bushes that lay against the cliff face, he revealed what appeared to be a dark opening in the rock.

Sara felt the skin on her arms prickle with apprehension as they stepped forward into the black void. The forest had been dark enough but now she couldn't even make out her own hand as she held it up in front of her face; she was totally reliant on touch as they edged forward cautiously into the blackness. When they suddenly halted after only a few steps, Sara felt her whole body begin to tremble. If she'd been scared before, she was petrified now. They were in pitch darkness. What were they doing here? What madness had driven her to follow this stranger?

As Sara reached out with her senses, smelling the earthy dampness of the air that surrounded them, a sudden sound startled her. It was the old man. He was muttering something. Once again the words were indecipherable, running together and at such a low volume she just couldn't quite make out what he was saying, though she felt that if she listened closely enough she might be able to understand him. Before she could do so, she gasped in awe as his muttering stopped and his stick started to glow, lighting up the interior of the cave they'd stepped into with a soft light.

Sara stood there gaping, both at the feat he'd performed with his walking stick and at the wide cavern that opened up before her. In the dim light, she could see that it went back some distance into the cliff face. It was clear it offered room for their horses as well as for them. This was no chance finding. Some distance in from where they stood she could make out the remains of a fireplace and a scattering of possessions. From the rear of the cavern came the sound of the steady drip of water splashing on to rock. Looking behind her, she could see that they'd turned slightly as they'd entered and that a large boulder, which lay between where she now stood and the outside, obscured the entryway itself.

"Let's get him over there," grunted the old man, gasping for breath and waving with his stick towards the burnt remains of the fireplace as he spoke.

With some effort, they managed to carry Rayne the remaining distance and then gently lowered him to the floor of the cavern. With that task completed, the old man turned to Sara again. "I'll look after him. You get the horses inside." Without waiting to see her reaction to his order, he turned and shuffled toward a pile of blankets and old clothes that lay a few paces away from the fireplace.

Sara hesitated for a moment and then moved to obey his instructions. What else could she do? Whatever he intended, for the moment, her fate, as well as Rayne's, was in his hands.

When she returned a short while later, leading Nell, she saw that the old man had got a fire going. It was already blazing away fiercely, despite the shortness of her absence, and he'd covered Rayne with a blanket. He had propped his head up with a bundle of cloth and was leaning over him examining his arm. When he heard her return, he stopped what he was doing and silently directed her towards the rear of the cave with a wave of his arm. With the additional light cast by the fire, she found it went back further than she had realised. Right at the rear, she found a spot for the horses. There was already one there, a big brown horse that neighed in welcome to Nell.

Returning for the other two horses, she was startled to see the old man leaning forward over Rayne once more, muttering and swaying slightly as he did so. She watched, fascinated, as he reached out and ran his hand along Rayne's arm. As his hand passed along the limb, the skin he touched started to glow with a soft, unnatural light. Within moments, Rayne's whole arm was glowing from wrist to shoulder. Moving to Rayne's forehead, he did the same there, with similar effect.

Approaching the two men in awe, Sara found herself unable to draw her eyes away from the incredible scene she was witnessing. As she got closer, she could see that the glowing skin was pulsing, as if in rhythm to the flow of Rayne's blood. His skin had become translucent. She could see the veins and the muscles and tendons of his arm now as clearly as if his skin had been made of glass. She had never seen anything like it in her life.

"What are you doing?" she whispered, turning from Rayne to the old man and back again, her eyes wide with amazement.

"I'm doing what I can for his injuries," replied the old man wearily, as if there was nothing exceptional in what he had done. As he spoke, he looked up at Sara for a moment and smiled gently. It was clear that he was close to exhaustion himself.

As he turned back to Rayne again, Sara forced herself to return to her own task. The last thing they needed now was for their hideaway to be revealed by the presence outside of the two remaining horses. When she returned a few minutes later, she saw that the old man had stopped what he had been doing to Rayne and was fussing about with more blankets.

On her third and final trip, she was surprised to find their new companion wrapped in a blanket and stretched out, apparently fast asleep, by the fire. Rayne lay asleep on its opposite side. A third blanket, which had clearly been left for her, lay beside him. Anxious to join them, she hurriedly tended to the horses.

When she had completed her work and returned to the main part of the cavern, she found that they were both still sleeping soundly. As the skin on Rayne's arm and forehead continued to glow she couldn't resist sitting beside him for a while and marvelling at the pulsing of the veins in his arm. His face looked more peaceful than she had seen it for some time, with no sign of the pain that had been etched across it back at the slig camp.

Sara wondered what she should do, not knowing whether she should be outside keeping watch or whether the old man himself might need help. He looked peaceful enough as he lay snoring softly beside the fire. Who was he and where had he come from?

Whatever his intentions, he had looked after Rayne, or at least it would seem so, and that eased her mind greatly. She thought she could bear whatever else might come if she could just see Rayne safe and well again.

As she sat there, mulling over the events of the last few hours, the suspicion that had already formed in her mind began to grow stronger. He had to be one of the remaining two Guardians, either Kell or Tarak. If what he had done at the slig camp had not involved magic, then there was no doubting the power he had used to deal with Rayne's injuries. Sara had felt that same dryness she'd sensed in the air as he worked on Rayne once before, during her encounter with Golkar.

What did he want with her and how had he known how to find them? How had he known Rayne's name, and could she trust him? Although Rayne had said the Guardians worked for the good of all of Ilythia, she knew that Golkar had already betrayed that trust. Perhaps this one was similarly tainted.

She decided, once again, that entertaining such fears was pointless. With Rayne as badly injured as he was, she needed to trust the old man. He had, after all, given no indication of any desire to hurt them. Far from it. He had rescued them from the sligs and brought them to what seemed to be a secure hideaway. He had even tried to do something about Rayne's injuries. Maybe he was going to help them get out of the mess they were in.

It occurred to Sara he might even be able to help her to get out of Ilythia. She felt her skin prickle with goosebumps at the prospect of being able to go home. She didn't know what she would do if the old man offered her that choice. To leave Rayne at this point, after all he had done for her, would clearly be a betrayal. She resolved that if such an opportunity did arise she wouldn't leave him until she was absolutely sure he was both safe and well. The notion that she might not want to leave him at all was pushed away to one of the further recesses of her mind. She wasn't ready to deal with that thought yet.

After a while, she realised she needed sleep as badly as her two companions did. The events of the day had exhausted her more than she had realised. Before long, she was stretched out alongside Rayne. It didn't take long for sleep to claim her.

CHAPTER 13

Sara awoke with a start. She'd been dreaming of home. Rayne had been there with her and somehow they were married. Everyone that she cared for had been there as well, and they had all been so incredibly happy. As pleasant a thought as that was, she forced her mind to return to the present.

As she lifted her head up from the floor of the cavern, supporting herself on her elbows while she looked around, she wondered how long she had slept. A small patch of filtered light, peeping through from the outside onto the floor near the entryway, suggested the sun had already risen. Rayne still slept soundly beside her. His arm and forehead still glowed eerily, though she thought his skin had become more opaque than she remembered it being during the night. She hoped that was a good sign, that it meant it was healing.

The fire still burned beside them, though the flames were much lower than they had been when she'd fallen asleep. It looked as if someone had added some more wood to it at some stage while she'd slept. Further inspection of the cave was interrupted by a voice from behind her. It was the old man.

"Good morning," she heard him say in a croaky voice. "I hope you're feeling better after a good night's sleep."

Turning back towards the entryway, Sara watched as he shuffled slowly across the floor of the cave towards her, leaning heavily on his walking stick for support as he did so. He had obviously just returned from outside and still looked very tired. "Yes thank you," she replied, stretching her arms wide as she sat up on her bedding.

It took him some time, but the old man slowly returned to his own bedding and sat down opposite her, resting his stick across his knees as he did so. Sara noted the effort he seemed to expend in carrying out such a simple task. Once he was seated, he reached out and warmed his hands in front of the flickering flames. Taking a blanket and wrapping it around his shoulders, he turned to face Sara, looking across at her with a gentle smile on his face.

"Who are you?" she finally asked, too intrigued to leave the question unspoken any longer. As she spoke, she noticed a small loaf of bread, a knife and some cheese that lay on a flat rock beside her. An earthen mug filled with liquid sat beside the food. "Is this for me?" she asked, eyeing the food hungrily.

"My name is Josef," the old man replied in a weary voice. "Of course," he went on, gesturing towards the food, "I guessed you'd be hungry when you woke." His smile accentuated the creases that lined his face. Sara hadn't fully realised before how old he really looked. He seemed ancient, like someone who belonged in a wheelchair in a nursing home, propped up with a pillow to support his head and a blanket wrapped around his legs. His presence here in the middle of the wilderness, in the situation they were in, seemed terribly out of place.

Unable to restrain her hunger, Sara reached out and broke off a piece of the bread. Taking the knife, she pared a few slices from the cheese. As she slipped the food into her mouth and began to eat, she contemplated what the old man had said. She had been certain he would identify himself as one of the two Guardians. Perhaps he didn't want her to know who he really was. She decided to approach the issue head-on.

"I thought you might be Tarak . . . or Kell," she said casually, keeping a surreptitious watch on the old man's face to see how he might react to those names. "I didn't know there was anyone else in Ilythia with the power to do what you did last night."

The old man sighed deeply, looking down at the ground as he did so. After a few moments of silence, he responded to what she had said. "There wasn't. Not until recently, anyway. Things seem to have changed a bit in Ilythia of late, though."

"What do you mean?"

The old man drew in his breath again, looking down into his lap and shaking his head slightly as he did so. Sara watched as he lifted one hand and rubbed it across the cracked and wrinkled skin on his forehead. His face had a pained look, as if he was dreading answering her question. Eventually, he lifted his head. Looking directly at Sara, who had stopped eating and was watching him intently, he started to speak again. "I guess this is where it starts," he said as his eyes locked on to hers. "I had hoped this could have come later. After you had come to know me a bit better. There's no time for that now." When he paused, Sara waited expectantly, not wanting to interrupt him now that he had begun. Besides, he still wasn't making any sense.

"My story is a long one," he said before a sudden coughing fit prevented him from going on. After a minute or two, he recovered. Regaining his composure, he wiped some spittle from his lips and went on. "I came to this place by the same means you did. I came through the portal."

"What? How? Why?" Sara was stunned. She hadn't expected this at all. She shook her head as she blurted out her questions. She'd been convinced he was one of the other two Guardians. If he had come through the 'portal', as he called it, then he must have come from another world, like her. He might be stuck here, just like she was. Was he on the run from Golkar too?

With his eyes riveted to hers, Josef continued. "I opened the portal and came to this place looking for you. I need your help."

Sara couldn't believe what she was hearing. It had to be some kind of sick joke. "You need *my* help?" she replied incredulously, almost laughing as she spoke. "That's rich. I can't even help myself. I was sort of hoping you might be able to help me."

A pained look passed across Josef's face as she spoke. "I know it seems strange," he responded, almost apologetically. "I hadn't wanted to tell you all of this straight away. But I have no choice now. The Spell of Portal drained me immeasurably." He paused for a moment as he bent forward, racked by coughs yet again. Sara could see now that he really didn't look well. His whole appearance was of someone who had been greatly weakened by excessive effort. She hadn't noticed before, but his eyes were bloodshot and his hands were trembling slightly. When he spoke again he seemed to be almost pleading with her. "I'm dying, Sara. What I've done has only served to shorten the brief time I have left."

Drawing her hands up to the sides of her head, as if to block out what he was saying, Sara shook her head. This couldn't really be happening to her. She had begun to think that all of her troubles might be behind her. Obviously, she had been too hasty. The old man was on his deathbed. Instead of one person to look after, she now had two. Even as they sat there talking, the sligs were probably combing the area searching for them. Taking a deep breath, she told herself to get a grip. It wasn't Josef's fault, whoever he was. And he *had* rescued them from the sligs. The least she could do was show him some courtesy.

"I'm sorry," she said, looking back at Josef and trying to force a smile to her face as she spoke. "I can't begin to thank you for saving us from the sligs. But I don't see how I can help you. I'm just a young girl, and a lost one at that. Other than 'somewhere in the Western Wilderness', wherever that is, I have no idea where we are. I'm really sorry you're not well and I'll do whatever I can to be of help. But you've got the wrong person."

Josef's face lit up with a broad grin, the corners of his eyes crinkling endearingly as he did so. "I should have guessed you'd be a kind person," he said. He sat there looking at her silently for a few moments with a fond look in his eyes that totally confused Sara. She had just told him he'd got the wrong person and now he was looking at her as if she was a saint. It was very disquieting. Perhaps he really was crazy. After an uncomfortable pause, he went on.

"I haven't got the wrong person," he said, shaking his head. "And you're wrong. You're not just a girl. You're much more important than that. Hear me out. Please. What I have to say is going to be difficult to believe. I knew it would be, but just give me a chance to explain. I can see from your face that you think I'm mad. Maybe I am. Maybe this whole idea was crazy right from the beginning. But you're my only hope. At least hear me out."

Sara nodded reassuringly, despite her misgivings. "Alright," she said. It wouldn't hurt to hear what he had to say. It couldn't be any more confusing than what he'd said so far.

Placing his hands in his lap and gripping his walking stick, as if seeking reassurance, Josef took a deep breath. He appeared to be preparing himself for an ordeal. Although he seemed a bit more relaxed than he had been before, his hands continued to tremble slightly and his voice, when he spoke, had a gruff tone to it. She sensed he still hadn't managed to clear his chest properly. He spoke slowly and carefully, as if he was finding it difficult to stay focused on what he needed to say.

"I don't know how much you know about the portal, Sara," he said. "Very little, I presume. I know a lot about it. I've studied the spell that controls it for a long time. For nearly ten years, I would guess. I found that it doesn't just open up a way between worlds, as it did between yours and this one. It also has some amazing qualities, not least of which is its effect on anyone who travels through such a portal. It enables them to understand and converse with anyone they meet whenever they enter a new world.

"You probably don't realise it, but you are not speaking in whatever language you used at home in your own world. Both you and I are speaking using the Common Tongue which almost everyone in this part of Ilythia uses. Because of the spell, you are able to do so without even trying. It just happens. If I spoke to you now using one of the more obscure languages used in a few of the nations in Ilythia, you would understand and be able to converse just as easily in those too. Of course, some of the idioms we both use don't make much sense to each other; they are culturally based. But that isn't the only amazing thing about the portal. It can also be used to move across time.

"I come from Ilythia," he went on. "But the Ilythia that I live . . . no . . . lived in . . . lies many years into the future. Over eighty years into the future, in fact." He stopped for a moment, waiting for what he had said to sink in.

Sara didn't know what to make of his claim. Although she was prepared to believe almost anything after what had happened to her to date, the concept of time travel took her incredulity to an altogether new level. She wished Rayne were awake to help her.

"If that's true," she responded cautiously, after a few moments silence, "then why did you come back here and how did you know about me? How do you know my name? And Rayne's?"

"I'm getting to that," he replied, sighing again as he did so. "I'm getting to that. Hear me out. You see, I know your limited exposure to Ilythia has been anything but pleasant. It isn't such a bad place, though. It really is the most beautiful of worlds, full of wonderful things and wondrous places." He paused for a brief moment before he went on. "It isn't going to stay that way, however. You," he said, emphasising the word, "and your presence here will be the harbinger of great change."

Sara's eyes opened wide at his reference to her. Before she could respond to what he had said, he continued.

"Golkar's behind it. In my time he rules Ilythia with an iron fist, he and those accursed sligs. It all happened very quickly. Within a few short years of your arrival here in Ilythia, all of the existing kingdoms were swept away in a short and bloody war. Once that was done, Golkar and the sligs set about destroying everything they could. It was as if anything that was decent, or had beauty, or that wouldn't bow down in homage to Golkar or the sligs, had to be wiped from the face of the land. The slaughter went on for years without end. The wanton destruction that accompanied it seemed to have no other purpose than the appeasement of some sick part of Golkar's mind.

"Within a few decades, there wasn't one major town that hadn't been ravaged and burnt to the ground. The people were thrown into slavery, great swathes of the forests were set alight and left to burn until only charred stumps remained, the waters were polluted and great rents were opened in the earth. The sligs seemed to delight in the destruction, not caring that much of the land was rendered uninhabitable as a result of their efforts. The people were cowed into submission, quickly losing both the means and the will to resist. Using the great power he'd acquired, Golkar made an example of one of the major towns very early on. He simply opened up the ground and allowed the whole place to slide into the chasm he'd created. It was horrendous. There wasn't one single survivor. Keerêt no longer exists in my time. When news of that spread, what limited resistance there had been quickly crumbled.

"By the time I departed to come here, there was nothing left. Apart from the sligs, who still roam the land with impunity, I would guess there might be less than a thousand souls out of all of the sentient races that are still alive. All of the ones that had been taken into slavery had died years before. The only ones that survived were those that had taken to the hills and the forests, eking out a wretched existence in the wild. Even the sligs were beginning to diminish in number. The land would no longer support even them.

"Resistance was pointless. Certainly, some tried in the earlier years. My father was one of them. He was a brave man . . . a brave man. But they all fell. Even him. I lost him before I reached manhood." As he spoke of his father, Josef stopped, looking down as he idly twisted the wooden stick that he held in his lap. After a few moments, he lifted his head, wiping a tear from his eye as he looked, first at Rayne where he lay sleeping beside her, then up at Sara.

Sara was appalled. What Josef had said confirmed her original conviction, that she was caught up in a nightmare of hellish proportions. It also destroyed the faint hope she had been nursing, that somehow things might still turn out all right, despite everything that had happened to her. The story Josef had told had crushed that hope in one foul stroke. Sara felt totally gutted.

The mental picture she had formed from his description of what was to come was of something akin to the aftermath of a nuclear holocaust. From what she knew of Golkar, and had seen of the sligs, his story, though shocking, was quite believable. The sligs alone seemed capable of anything, let alone Golkar. Besides, she could see no reason why Josef would want to invent such a tale. No wonder he had fled from his own timeline. Her heart went out to him. She could see that he was filled with remorse, both from his recollection of what had happened to his land, and at the memory of the loss of his father.

After allowing him a few moments of silence, Sara finally came up with the question that had been burning away at her since he had begun his tale. Despite her fear of his answer, she had to know. "But what have I got to do with this?" she asked.

Snapping out of the contemplation he had sunk into once he had finished his tale, Josef lifted his head again, sighing deeply as he did so. His eyes glistened with moisture. As he started to speak again, his voice took on a gentler tone. "It was no coincidence that all of this happened shortly after you arrived in Ilythia, Sara," he said. "Golkar pursued you from the moment you escaped. It took him nearly two years before he finally caught up with you. The destruction of Keerêt occurred a few days after that." Sara couldn't believe what he was saying. It couldn't be right. His next few words seemed to reverberate in her skull. "He used the energy residing in you to cause the great cataclysm that resulted in that destruction."

"Nooooooo!" Sara screamed, jumping to her feet. "You're lying," she shouted at Josef. Turning away, she stumbled blindly across the cavern. "You're lying," she cried again as she burst into tears. "You're lying," she repeated for a third time, her voice slowly dwindling. Slumping to her knees, she buried her head in her hands, sobbing uncontrollably as she did so. *He's crazy*, she told herself. *None of it's true. I won't allow Golkar to catch me. I will get away. I will.*

As her mind frantically struggled to come to grips with the picture Josef had painted, Sara felt a soft touch on her shoulders. Spinning around, she quickly stood up and backed away from the old man, retreating across the floor of the cavern. "Get away from me," she hissed. "It isn't true. You're making it up. You just want to hurt me."

Josef stayed where he was, allowing Sara the space she sought. "I'm truly sorry, Sara. But it *is* true. No. It *was* true. I've come back here in an attempt to change all of that."

With her chest heaving, Sara looked at Josef silently for a few moments, then slumped to her knees again. She knelt there sobbing for a while, trying to bring her emotions under control. Raising her head once more, she slowly looked up at the old man, who had stayed where he was, gazing across at her with a look of concern on his face. Maybe he was telling the truth, she thought. Hadn't she admitted to herself so many times before that she was doomed, that there was no real chance of escape? But all of those deaths, not that. "I . . . I'm not responsible," she gasped between sobs. "If he did do that . . . it's not my fault. It's not."

"I know, I know," soothed Josef, cautiously approaching her. When he reached her side, he bent down and put a hand under her arm, helping her to her feet. "I know that," he said quietly. "None of us are responsible for Golkar's insanity. We are all just victims of it. But I'm one victim who won't give up." As he spoke he led Sara back to the fire, helping her to take her seat once more. This time he sat beside her, holding her hand in his. She could feel his wrinkled, leathery skin against the smooth skin of her own hands. Somehow it comforted her. It reminded her of her grandfather.

Her thoughts were a jumble. Each day in this world seemed to bring some new horror. It wasn't enough that Golkar and the sligs were after her. Now she was being told that the wizard intended to use her against the people of Ilythia. Worse than that, Josef claimed that her fate was sealed, that Golkar would eventually capture her and use her to commit appalling atrocities against not only the Algarians but the rest of this world's inhabitants. Surely it wasn't really possible. Surely someone would stop him before he could do all of that.

"What about the other Guardians?" beseeched Sara, breaking the silence. "Surely they can stop him?"

"He killed both of them before he caught up with you."

"How do you know all of this?" asked Sara, scrutinising him closely. "If there are so few free people left, how do you know all of this? And how did you get to use the portal?"

Josef sighed deeply. "There is more to my story," he replied. "Are you up to hearing the rest?"

Sara sighed and lowered her eyes to the floor once more. "I don't see how it can get any worse," she mumbled softly. "Go on."

"The reason I know so much about what happened is that I found out directly from Golkar." As he said the name of the wizard, Sara pulled her hand away in alarm.

"No. It's not what you think," he went on. "He didn't speak to me. I read it in his diary. You see, some ten years or so before I left my time, Golkar disappeared. He hasn't been seen since."

Sara couldn't conceal her consternation. Josef's story just seemed to get more unbelievable as it went on. If Golkar had left Ilythia and hadn't been seen for ten years, then why had Josef come back in time looking for help? Each time Sara absorbed one part of his story, it just seemed to become more and more complex.

Josef took a gulp of water from the cup beside him before he continued. "At first no one knew he was gone. But slowly, word filtered out. When I found out, I carefully made my way to his stronghold. He made no secret of where he lived. He had Kell's residence, Cloudtopper, pulled down and a magnificent castle built in its place; all of it done by slaves, brought here for that single purpose from all over Ilythia. None of the sligs had dared to enter it since he had gone, even though they suspected it was deserted. I think their awe of Golkar far outweighed any curiosity they might have felt.

By that stage, his power had risen quite substantially. Even the sligs lived in dread of him. I slipped in unseen one dark night and found out that it was true, that he'd gone, that Ilythia was free of its tyrant. I searched and searched that dread place for days, not knowing what I was really looking for. Somehow, inexplicably, I felt driven to go on, and eventually, I uncovered his diary.

"It wasn't really his. It had belonged to Tanis before him, but he had taken it for his own. It was from there that I found out what had happened, how he had caught you in the end, how he'd used you to destroy Keerêt, how he'd then brought others of your kind to Ilythia and how they'd shared your fate, augmenting his power ever further, how eventually, when the land was crushed and the last drop of its usefulness had been squeezed from it, how he'd then used the portal to leave Ilythia and seek out other worlds, just like Tanis had done before him." Josef stopped and took a deep breath, closing his eyes and sagging forward, as if a great weight had been lifted from him.

Sara was too stunned to say anything. She had found the final part of his story as chilling as the beginning. Incredible as it was, however, she believed him. For some reason, she had no doubt that what she had heard had been the truth. But what could she do about it? Why did he have to tell her all of this? All he had succeeded in doing was to destroy her will to fight. It all seemed so pointless now, the flight from Golkar and Tug, the desperate attempts to retain hope; she might just as well give up right here and now.

They both sat there quietly, each lost in their own thoughts. "So why are you telling me all of this?" she asked him after a while, not knowing what else to say. "If Golkar has gone, why have you come back here?"

Josef stared back at her. "I told you," he said in an even voice. "I've come back to seek your help. Where I came from, though Golkar has left, it's too late for Ilythia. The sligs now hold the land in their own evil grip, and it's just as bloody a grasp as the one Golkar had. Certainly, there are still those who resist. I was one of them. But they are far too few in numbers. They have no chance at all. It is all they can do to survive now. The sligs number in the tens of thousands. They control the whole of Ilythia. The land reeks of their carnage from one end to the other. The resistance, if you could call it that, number in the scores, perhaps a few hundred at the very most. It's only a matter of time before it is snuffed out, forever. Even if, by some miracle, the sligs could be overthrown, the land itself is broken. It's been poisoned beyond redemption. Ilythia is nothing now but a muck heap."

Sara nodded despondently, weighed down by the hopelessness of the situation they all faced. "You keep saying that you've come back to seek my help," she finally said, her voice almost a whisper. "What could I possibly do about all of this? From what you've told me, Golkar will destroy the Guardians with or without me. You said that he was well advanced in what he was trying to do, even before he caught up with me."

"Yes," said Josef, "that's right. There's only one way to stop all of that from happening. That's to defeat Golkar. Even if you somehow manage to elude him, he'll still wreak havoc on Ilythia. And he'll probably just go and take someone else from your world in your place and do to them what he intended to do to you."

Sara felt herself beginning to cry again as he spoke. "I don't want to hear any more of this," she cried out in anguish. "You're just tormenting me. Why? What's the point? First of all you say that I'm responsible, and then you say that if I get away he'll only do the same to someone else." She was working herself up into a frantic state, almost screaming the words at Josef by the time she finished. "Why don't you just leave me alone? I can't take any more of this."

"Because I have to," Josef shouted back at her angrily, coughing again as he did so. "I have to make you see. I can't stop all of this from happening. *You*. You're the key. You can stop him."

Sara looked back at him blankly. Both his own emotional reaction as well as what he had said had stunned her.

"I'm sorry, Sara. I'm sorry," gasped Josef as she stared at him with her mouth open. "Don't you see," he went on, pleading with her now. "I've lived through that horror. It took everything from me, my parents, my friends, everything. I've been fighting it all of my life; all of it, from the day I was born till now, trying to do something about it. And there was nothing I could do. Nothing at all. Until I found his diary. And then I saw a chance, a faint one, but a chance. A chance to stop all of that misery, to stop all of those thousands and thousands of deaths from happening. I had to try. I had to. Don't you see?" As he finished he slumped forward, bending right over so that his head rested on his knees.

It was Sara's turn to feel sorry for him. She could see now how horrific it all must have been for him. In many ways, if what he said was true, then she'd be one of the lucky ones. Much better to die early than to have to live through a lifetime of that. She could understand the desperation that Josef must be feeling.

"How?" she asked, her soft voice breaking the silence of the cavern. "How can I possibly do anything about all of that?"

Slowly Josef raised his head. Lifting the blanket he'd thrown aside when he'd gone after her earlier, he wrapped it around his shoulders once more. "I feel so cold," he said, shuddering as he did so.

Sara had forgotten how unwell he looked. He was shivering now, despite the blanket, and yet the cavern seemed quite warm to her. "Are you okay?" she asked, concerned that the emotional exchange they had just had might have taxed him too much in his weakened state.

"No," he replied in a quavering voice. "I don't think I'm well at all, actually. But I need to finish this. Then I'll get some more rest, I think."

Sara took her own blanket and wrapped it around him. Taking the cup of water that sat beside him, she helped him to take a few sips. Once that was done, she added another piece of wood to the fire.

"Thank you," he said, still shivering slightly. "Let me finish what I have to say and then I'll rest."

Sara nodded in response and waited for him to go on.

"I believe that you, Sara," he said looking directly at her once again, "have enough power within you to defeat Golkar and to stop him from turning this world into a wasteland. Although where you come from you were just an ordinary citizen, here in Ilythia you have the capacity for incredible power. That power resides in you. It's sitting there, waiting to be tapped. That's why Golkar wants to get his hands on you, so he can tap into it for his own purposes. I believe you can be shown how to access that power yourself to defeat him instead."

"How can you be sure I have this power?" asked Sara. Although what he said seemed ridiculous to her, if Golkar believed it as well, then that would certainly explain why he wanted to bring her here in the first place, and why Tug had come after her when she'd escaped. "I don't feel any different now to how I did before I came here."

"There is no question that you have it. Golkar's diary makes it quite clear that he tapped it to destroy Keerêt. The only question is whether you can learn to use it yourself."

"But even if it were true and I could learn how to use it, Golkar's been a wizard for centuries. How could I learn in . . . what . . . days . . . months? How could I possibly learn enough to defeat a mighty wizard like him?"

Josef winced at Sara's response. "I don't know whether you could," he admitted. "It's a long shot, I agree. I just don't see any other way. Surely we have to at least try. The power within you is immense. I think you could learn enough to do it." He didn't sound very convincing. All of a sudden Sara sensed some uncertainty in what he was saying. He was guessing, she realised, clutching at straws.

"You think? Just supposing what you say is true, and you're saying you don't know that it is, that this is just a theory of yours, but supposing it was true. Who's going to teach me?"

"I will," said Josef. "That's why I've come back here. I can teach you."

"But that's one part of your story I don't understand, that doesn't make sense. How is it that you have such power yourself? If you're not one of the Guardians, then how were you able to use the portal to come back here, diary or not? And why can't you fight Golkar yourself?"

"I can't explain how I have such power. I just have. I didn't even know I had it at first. And even when I realised I could do things others couldn't, it wasn't till I found Golkar's diary and had studied it that I began to realise I had access to some of the same power that he and the Guardians had. As for why I don't go up against Golkar myself, I don't have anything like the power that resides in you. I wouldn't have a chance. Besides, even if I could have, I'm too weak now. I exerted much more energy than I thought I would in opening up the portal and coming here. Rescuing you and Rayne just capped that off. I think I'm dying, Sara. I don't feel like I've got too long left. If I thought it would make any difference, I *would* go up against Golkar myself, gladly. But I know my time would be better spent helping you . . . helping you to defeat him."

Sara thought about what he had said for a while before she responded. She just couldn't put aside that one discordant note, that one part of his story that didn't ring true. He was hiding something from her. She wasn't sure why, but she knew she was right. "How did you come to realise you had this power yourself?" she asked him. "I'd like to hear more about that."

They talked on for at least an hour after that, with Sara pressing him over aspects of his story, constantly seeking to clarify those bits that weren't clear to her. She even told him of her own experience, of how she had been brought to Ilythia, of her meeting with Golkar, of Rayne and the sligs. Every now and then she would bring the conversation back to how Josef came to acquire his powers. Each time she did so, he would say a few words, usually revealing little that hadn't already been said, and then would subtly turn the conversation to other parts of his story, deflecting her efforts to find the answers she sought.

She did learn that as a child he had done some strange things he had thought little of at the time but which he had later come to realise were portents of the power that resided within him. At first, it was small things, like the time that he and his father had hidden from the sligs in the forest, under cover of an old tree that had been knocked down in a storm. The sligs had walked right past them; one of them had even looked right at them, and yet they had seen nothing. It had been as if they were invisible.

Gradually, over a period of many years, Josef had come to understand he had an ability others did not. It was something to do with illusion, he realised, the capacity to prevent others from seeing things he didn't want them to. When he wanted to conceal his presence, or that of those with him, he could do so. People, particularly the sligs, would see what he wanted them to see. It had become a very useful talent, even if he couldn't explain it. Without it, he and the small band he lived with after the death of his father wouldn't have been able to elude capture for as long as they did. It had even enabled them to put up a limited form of resistance, striking at the sligs occasionally and then quickly melting away, hiding again until the next opportunity arose.

As the years wore on he had perfected the ability. He had used it here to help Sara and Rayne to escape. The flash in the fire, covering their tracks to ensure they couldn't be followed, even concealing the entryway to the cave. All of these things were done with the power he'd discovered within himself.

Healing had been his other forté. Once again it was a skill he had stumbled on. His father had broken his ankle and been knocked unconscious while they were out together in the forest. Josef had been only seven or eight years old and had sat beside him all through a dark and lonely night, idly stroking his father's leg as he sobbed and pleaded with him to get better. He hadn't understood the mysterious glow that had formed around the wound but somehow it had comforted him. Incredibly, his father had woken in the morning with his leg still sore but well on its way to mending.

Josef hadn't realised at first that it had been him that was responsible for the miraculous recovery. When he finally did realise that this was another of his 'special' abilities, he had worked hard to develop it further, to perfect it. In both cases, it would seem, necessity had been the mother of invention. Great need had either revealed or awakened specific abilities.

Until he had gained access to Golkar's diary, his powers had been limited to those two uses. It was only through study of the diary that he'd come to realise there was a source of power within him that was behind his abilities and that with training and understanding it could be channelled in specific directions. Unfortunately, it had been too late for him to make much use of this knowledge. He had concentrated instead on the Spell of Portal, seeing there a chance far beyond what he could achieve in any other way.

Although he claimed to have no idea where his power had come from, something told Sara he knew more than he was telling. He showed it in so many ways when the issue was raised, in the tone of his voice, in his sudden loss of confidence, even in his body language. She suspected he did know, but for some reason he was either unwilling or unable to speak of it. Perhaps he was ashamed. Maybe, theorised Sara, he was an illegitimate child of one of the Guardians. Whatever the truth was, she couldn't prise it from him.

For some reason, he didn't seem to want to talk about his parents any more than was necessary either. The loss of both of them at a fairly early age had clearly been a source of great sorrow to him, the fact that he was still bitter about it at this late stage in his life was a clear indication of that. He said little at all about his mother. She'd apparently died shortly after his birth and his only knowledge of her seemed to have come from his father. He spoke more of the latter, or at least of the man he knew as his father. Sara harboured a suspicion he may have been fostered out at an early age. If his father had actually been one of the Guardians, then that would explain his extraordinary abilities, and yet the man he described as his father was clearly no Guardian.

When Josef had heard Sara's own story, he drew her attention to something that she herself had done. He believed that she, like him, might have tapped into her own power without knowing what she was doing. In her case, he believed that she'd used it to repulse Golkar when she hadn't wanted to be touched by him during their initial encounter. The dramatic result only confirmed his view of the potency of the energy he believed she held within her.

That had certainly set Sara to thinking. Josef got no further, however, with his suggestion that she might be able to tap into that power to destroy Golkar. Such talk was, in her view, madness. Even if she could come to learn some of the 'tricks' Josef had mastered, useful though they were, she knew she could never be a match for Golkar.

Every so often, Josef would maneuver the conversation back to his proposal, and each time he did so she would rebuff him. She just couldn't see that the idea stood up to any rational consideration. By Josef's own admittance, Golkar had defeated the other two Guardians before he had caught up with Sara. If they couldn't resist him, then it seemed senseless to her to assume that she might be able to.

Even the Spell of Portal seemed to be denied her. Although Josef thought that she might be able to learn it, he acknowledged that it had taken him years of study and experimentation before he had finally mastered it himself. It was clear to Sara that he saw this as a selfish option. Even if she could open the portal and she might be able to save herself, her departure would mean that Ilythia itself would be doomed. There would be no one left who could hope to resist Golkar. It was also an option that would provide no guarantee of safety for her, in any event. She couldn't be sure if she did return to her world that Golkar wouldn't simply do what he had already done: use the portal to bring her back yet again to Ilythia.

Eventually they both tired, each seeming to realise they had reached a stalemate. Just as Josef couldn't get Sara to seriously consider his suggestion that she try to learn how to fight Golkar, Sara was having the same difficulty in trying to discern the source of his power. Although it was unspoken, they both seemed to realise they needed to rest.

Josef, in particular, had begun to cough again intermittently. It had become a rather nasty, hacking cough and it concerned Sara greatly. Unfortunately, he couldn't use his healing power on himself, or at least if he could he didn't know how to. In the end, Sara helped him to lie down again and made him comfortable enough that he could get some more rest. It wasn't long before he slipped into a deep sleep.

~~~

Rayne was confused and disoriented. The last thing he could remember was turning his horse to face the two slig warriors who had stumbled upon him and Sara as they'd been attempting to traverse a shallow creek bed. He'd awoken to find himself lying on the floor of a cavern. The warm fire beside him had obviously been burning for some time and was desperately in need of more fuel. Thankfully, Sara was sleeping peacefully nearby, as was an old man that he'd never seen before in his life.

Rayne felt rested, though weak. If the gnawing feeling in his stomach was any indication, it had been some time since he had eaten. He was most gratified to find that someone had taken the trouble to leave him some bread and cheese. It had been placed close by to where he lay. A mug of water sat beside the bread. After helping himself to some of the food, he got up, tentatively stretching his cramped muscles, and proceeded to explore the cave.

Several minutes later, having completed his examination, he returned to the fire, adding some extra pieces of wood from a small pile of faggots that he had found. It was then that he realised his arm had healed. The terrible pain had gone and he could move it quite freely, as if it had never been injured at all. Examining the limb, he could find no trace at all of the wound, not even a slight mark to show it had healed. Surely he couldn't have slept for that long. Although he knew it was impossible for his arm to have healed that completely, he could think of no rational explanation for how it appeared now.

He was relieved though to see that they still had Nell and Ned. The two other horses he had found at the back of the cavern weren't the same as the ones they'd taken from the two men who had tried to ambush them. He guessed they must belong to the old man, whoever he was. He presumed he was a friend. Perhaps he had rescued them. In any event, it didn't seem that Sara was under any coercion to stay with him.

Venturing outside briefly, he found that it was late in the afternoon. The weather had improved and clear, blue sky was a welcome sight after the dreary rain. The bright sunshine quickly forced him back into the cave. Although its warmth was refreshing, his eyes were in no state to cope with the glare.

Retreating inside, he prepared a small meal for himself from the food he found with their gear. Once that had been consumed, he sat by the fire for a while, watching his two companions. Sara appeared well and was sleeping quite soundly. His movement about the cavern hadn't disturbed her slumber. Although he was dying to talk to her, he decided not to make any attempt to rouse her. He had no idea how badly she might need the rest she was now getting. For all he knew, they had arrived here only a short while ago, but that seemed unlikely from what he had seen. It appeared that they might have been here for a few days at least. There were signs that the area where the horses were kept had been cleared out at least once since they'd arrived.

Gazing down at Sara's lovely face, with her smooth, clear skin and her long, black hair pulled back and braided into the ponytail she favoured, Rayne felt a calmness growing within him, one which he had not felt for some time now. The gentle flicker of the firelight, the compelling silence of the cave, the warm earthiness of his surroundings, the very sense of security their place of concealment gave him, all of these combined, providing him with a clarity of thought that had eluded him up until now. For the first time, he realised that what he felt for the girl before him was much more than just affection.

Amazingly, though he had known her for only such a short time, he knew that he loved her, dearly. It didn't matter any more how little time they might have together. He had long since resigned himself to the hopelessness of their situation. As long as they could spend what time they had together, then he would be happy.

His pleasant reverie was interrupted as the old man began to moan softly from where he lay on the other side of the fire. Getting up to check on him, Rayne found that he was shivering, despite the fact that he had two blankets over him and that he was lying close to the fire, which was blazing away quite strongly now. Every now and then he would moan and shudder, twitching under his blankets as he did so. From the way his eyelids were fluttering, he seemed to be drifting in and out of consciousness. He was clearly very unwell, which wasn't surprising given his appearance. He had to be ninety if he was a day, thought Rayne. Where in the hell he had come from and how he had ended up with Sara was a total mystery. Rayne realised his earlier assumption that he might have had some hand in saving them from the sligs couldn't possibly be right. Unless . . .

Unless he was one of the Guardians. Perhaps he was Tarak, or Kell. He had to be the person the old man at the settlement had said had been looking for him, his 'uncle' the settler had called him. That would explain a lot. Although, it wouldn't explain his condition. He looked far from being a man of power. This wasn't what Rayne had expected a Guardian to look like.

Putting those thoughts aside for the moment, he found another blanket for the old man and then set about doing something about his obvious infirmity. Setting some water to boil over the small fire, he delved into his pack for what remained of the herbs he'd been carrying. Once the water was boiling, he steeped a mixture of willow bark, sweet-flag, alfalfa and dandelion, a concoction his father had assured him was as good a tonic as any that a Medicant would sell you.

When it had cooled enough to be drinkable, he helped the old man up into a sitting position and managed to get him to drink some of the mixture. Even though he could barely speak, he managed to express his gratitude in a thin and croaky voice before he lay down once more. Within minutes he was fast asleep again. Rayne wasn't sure whether the tonic would be of much help, but at least the old man's sleep seemed more peaceful for the moment.

It was some time later when Sara awoke. When she rolled over and saw Rayne sitting there gazing at her, her face lit up with the broadest grin that he had ever seen. With a squeal of delight, she jumped up and embraced him, almost bowling him over as she threw her arms around him, hugging him to her and burying her face in the crook of his neck. When he could finally get her to let go he saw that she was crying.

"Oh Rayne," she said as he wiped the tears from her eyes. "I've missed you so, so much. And I was so worried about you."

Leaning forward, Rayne kissed her tenderly on the lips, cupping her chin as he did so. "It's all right now," he assured her soothingly as they both sat back again, looking into each other's eyes as they clasped their hands with outstretched arms. "Tell me what happened. I don't remember anything at all after we saw the sligs. My guess is that you've been through a lot since then and I'm dying to know what happened. And who's your friend here? He's not very well, you know."

It took Sara some time to relate the events of the last two days. Rayne's heart went out to her when he realised the anguish she must have endured at the hands of the sligs, particularly as he could see she had quite reasonably assumed that, at that point, there was no further hope of escape. His astonishment at the intercession of Josef was only exceeded by her revelation of who he claimed to be and where he claimed to have come from.

Rayne found the old man's story hard to believe and wasn't as convinced as Sara had been that the major part of what he had said had a ring of truth to it. He certainly thought her observations regarding Josef's evasiveness were good grounds for suspicion. He was grateful nonetheless for what Josef had done for them and agreed with Sara that, as he had both saved them and healed Rayne of his wounds, he deserved their gratitude until such time as circumstances indicated otherwise. As to his counsel regarding Golkar, Rayne agreed with Sara that his proposal was ludicrous. It was his view that, assuming Josef's story was true, his own grief and despair must have marred his judgement. For Sara to go up against Golkar would be like deliberately stepping into a bear trap. It would be suicide.

"But what can we do?" asked Sara with a hint of desperation in her voice. "If Golkar is bound to catch me, or to turn Ilythia into a wasteland, then there's nowhere to hide and nowhere to go."

"My dad," replied Rayne, "always said 'the future ain't written yet'. Look, even if what Josef says is true, *he* obviously believes it can be changed. Isn't that what you said he wanted to do? So, let's change it. Let's not follow the path Josef said we took."

"I guess that could be right."

Although Sara sounded doubtful, Rayne could see that she wanted to believe in what he was saying. He knew he was clutching at straws but they had to try something. "What if we try to get to one of the Guardians before they have it out with Golkar?" he suggested. "Josef might be able to tell us how to do that. They should know what to do."

"Yes. I like that," returned Sara. "I was so confused after listening to Josef. I didn't know what I should do."

They talked on for some time, considering what to do next and going over what Sara had learnt from Josef. They both knew that it was all very well to say, 'let's go find one of the Guardians'. Even if they could find out where they were, they still had the small problem of getting there. Presumably, the sligs were still looking for them, and Tug and his men were undoubtedly still out there somewhere as well.

Rayne felt very uneasy about staying where they were for much longer; he didn't feel reassured by Josef's claim that he had concealed their tracks, but he also didn't relish the prospect of being back on the run again, constantly looking over their shoulders like they had been doing for so long now. And neither of them knew what to do about Josef.

What would the old man do when he realised Sara couldn't be persuaded to help him with his plan? He could, in fact, become a real millstone around their neck. His claim that he was dying was certainly believable. From his symptoms, Sara wondered if he hadn't contracted pneumonia or pleurisy. She wasn't a doctor but she had seen her grandmother almost die from the former, and that was with access to modern medicines and hospitals. Her symptoms had been remarkably similar to those Josef was now experiencing. Even should he recover, it was doubtful whether he'd be up to further travel.

After some talk, they decided that the only option open to them for the moment was to try and nurse him through his current malaise. They certainly couldn't abandon him, particularly after what he had done for them. As frustrating as it was, for they were both anxious to get moving again now they had decided on a course of action, it seemed they would be stuck where they were for a while yet.

As they talked, they kept a close eye on Josef. It was hard to tell whether his condition was improving or worsening. He continued to slip in and out of consciousness as the day gave way to night. At times he would appear quite lucid and be on the verge of getting up and walking around. At others he would almost seem to slip into a coma, shivering and shaking on the verge of delirium. In one of his more rational moments, they managed to find out some useful information from him, the location of Cloudtopper, Kell's home.

It was during one of these brief periods that they outlined their plan to Josef. To their great surprise, he immediately acquiesced. He seemed resigned to the fact that Sara wasn't prepared for an encounter with Golkar and acknowledged that, even if she were, he was in no state now to teach her what she needed to know.

He agreed that an attempt to link up with the Guardians was their best chance, but warned them that Golkar would be trying to do exactly the same. They ran the risk of putting themselves in greater danger than if they simply tried to hide out in some far corner of Ilythia. Rather than head for Cloudtopper, he suggested they make their way to the Forest of Annwn. Golkar's diary indicated Kell had fled there when he became aware of the train of events Golkar had set in motion. It had taken Golkar some time, but eventually, he had found him there and defeated him after a great struggle. If they went there now with some haste they may pre-empt Golkar and be able to warn Kell of the danger he faced.

"It's all gone wrong," Josef lamented despondently. "My grand plan has proved to be nothing but the foolish dreams of an old man. I can't see what will happen now." Looking up at Rayne through bleary eyes he went on. "My arrival here has already started to change things. You never got shot by an arrow in my time. I think my visit to the settlement did something to change what happened. I can't see where it will all lead any more."

That gave them some hope. Clearly, the future could be changed. Rayne was puzzled, however, by what Josef had said. He thought it strange that the old man could know anything of what had happened to him. Surely Golkar wouldn't have put anything about Rayne in his diary, even if he had known about it, which would also seem unlikely.

In his more demented moments, Josef spoke as if his parents were with him, pleading for them to forgive him for his failure to stop the destruction of Ilythia. Although it was heart-rending to see the way he was tormenting himself, the guilt he obviously felt at least partially explained his reluctance to speak of his parents. He seemed to believe that he had failed them, that he had not lived up to their expectations.

Eventually, they needed to rest again themselves. When Josef fell asleep once more, they decided to join him. Sara quickly slipped into a deep sleep and Rayne felt himself drifting off shortly after her.

He was the last to fall asleep and the first to awaken, although the latter was not a natural process. His sleep was rudely interrupted by someone shaking him. When he opened his eyes and saw Josef kneeling over him, he tried to sit up only to find he couldn't move his body from its prone position. Some strange force held him in place. It was as if he was bound with rope, though he could neither see nor feel any actual physical restraint.

As he frantically struggled against his unseen bonds, Josef's soft voice grabbed his attention. "Don't struggle, Rayne," he whispered. "I've put a constraint over you so you can't rise from where you are." Rayne felt a chill run through him as he wondered if it had all been part of an elaborate trap. Had Josef simply lulled them into a false sense of security, feigning infirmity merely to put them off guard? He had them at his mercy now. What would he do to them now that he had rendered them helpless? Whose side was he on after all?

When Rayne tried to speak, he found his ability to talk had also been denied him. It was as if his tongue was glued to the roof of his mouth. He felt panic rising within him. "Don't worry," whispered Josef, apparently sensing his apprehension. "I intend you no harm. It's just that I mean to leave and I don't want you trying to stop me, or to talk me out of what I intend to do."

Rayne realised that he had no choice but to lie there and listen to what the old man had to say. Once it was clear that he had abandoned his attempts to struggle against the compulsion, Josef spoke again. "This is my last gasp, Rayne. I've managed to push my physical ailment to one side for the moment, though I know I won't be able to keep it at bay for long. It is taking a great effort and I don't have the strength to keep this up for more than a little while. I hope it will at least be long enough for me to create enough of a diversion for you and Sara to escape.

"I can see now that my plans for Sara were ill-conceived. I'm glad that at least I've alerted her to what she is capable of, but I should've known she would need much more time than is available to come to grips with that, and to accept it. My hope now is that you can safely make your way to Kell, or to Tarak, and that one or both of them may be able to assist her; or failing that, that she might be prepared for one of them to use her power against Golkar on her behalf.

"At the very least, you two must escape from here. It is my intervention which has brought on your current danger. In my timeline, it was many months before Golkar even got a hint of what had happened to Sara. I owe it to you both to at least help you to escape from the wilderness. After that, well, it's in the hands of Mishra after that, I can do no more, that's clear to me now." Josef paused for a moment and reached out to take a hold of Rayne's wrist, gripping it firmly while he looked down at him.

"I'm going now. I'll draw the sligs well away from here. Make the most of the opportunity. Don't let what I'm doing be in vain. Please. But before I go, there is one last thing I must get off my chest. I couldn't tell Sara, but I feel I must explain myself to you. You'll see then why I've been so circumspect. I hope you'll understand. You see, Sara was right. I do know more than I've revealed."

A short while later, when Josef had finished his story, he rose and left. Although Rayne knew the restraint that Josef had imposed on him would wear off very quickly, he didn't bother with plans for pursuit. He understood now why Josef had done what he had. He also knew that Josef was right. It wasn't something he could share with Sara. She had enough to deal with already. Once he was able, he would wake her. It was essential that they pack up their own gear and get going. The sooner they were away the better. The trail to Annwn would be a dangerous one.

CHAPTER 14

"Here they come." The cry went up from a number of points as the screaming wave of slig warriors bore down on the eastern wall of Kurandir. Dain swallowed nervously. He could feel a raw emptiness in the pit of his stomach as he looked out at the blood-curdling sight that confronted the defenders. There were so many more of them than he had thought there would be.

Looking around at the men on either side of him, Dain knew that they would be just as afraid as he was. They were farmers, merchants, labourers, not trained fighters like the horde bearing down on them. With a shaking hand, he managed to draw an arrow from the quiver strapped to his back. Notching it, he tried to quell the shivers that were coursing through his body. His movements were sluggish. Desperately, he fought to overcome the disabling fear that threatened to cramp and bind his muscles just when he needed them most.

"Hold your fire," came the cry from the ranger assigned to their section of the wall. "Don't waste your arrows. Remember the drill."

What good will the drill do us now? thought Dain. *This is for real. Those are real sligs out there with real axes and real swords and they mean to kill us.* All along the wall, he could sense that other men were shuffling nervously, just like he was, awaiting the sligs with a dread you could smell. It was the smell of fear and it covered the parapet like a shroud.

Below the wall, only some eighty paces away and narrowing the gap at a rapid rate, rushed the line of slig warriors, the bane of the Algarians, sweeping towards them with their enemy's doom in their hands. The deadly weapons swinging above their heads were already stained with Algarian blood and the defenders of Kurandir knew it.

They could see their faces now. They looked like beasts, wild beasts with a lust for blood in their gleaming eyes. The din of their screams and curses preceded them, washing over the waiting Algarians, like waves pounding on a rocky shoreline, incessantly, irresistibly, with a potency that suggested they would not be denied.

Here and there, dotted among the horde, were warriors with ladders. Their intent was clear. They meant to come right up over the walls and it looked like nothing could stop them from achieving that aim, least of all the ragtag band of farmers and townsfolk that awaited them here on the walls of Kurandir.

Dain drew a bead on one of the warriors. It no longer mattered if he held his aim steady. There were so many of them and they were so tightly bunched, he could hardly miss. They were less than forty paces away now.

"Fire!" Dain could barely hear the command over the roar from the sligs as they approached the wall. He loosed his arrow. With no time to check whether he'd hit his target, he fumbled for another shaft. Quickly he fired again. This time he definitely caught a slig in the chest. It didn't stop him though, he kept on coming with the arrow sticking out of his scaly skin.

The sligs were almost right up to the wall now. Those bearing ladders were preparing to raise them. Dain fired again. Now they were right below them. A ladder slammed against the wall beside him. The man beside him pushed it back. As he leaned over the wall to shove the ladder away, a crossbow bolt pierced his neck. He fell forward, over the wall and into the mass of attackers below. Dain had no time to see what had happened to his companion as he drew and fired again.

The roar from the sligs was deafening now. He could feel the timber walls shaking. The parapet below him shuddered and creaked. He kept shooting, somehow managing to fire down on the mass of warriors below without exposing himself for too long to the crossbows borne by the second line of sligs. A momentary glance showed ladders up all along the wall. Although some were being pushed back, sligs were streaming up others. A slig head came over the wall only a few men down the line from him. A ranger with a short spear quickly dispatched the beast, driving him back. The ranger almost went with him, having to let go his spear as the slig clenched onto it as he fell back.

There was no longer time to think. Fire. Draw another arrow. Fire again. Turn alarmingly as a slig warrior loomed up over the wall right in front of him. He hadn't even seen the ladder. The man beside him lunged at the slig with his broadsword while Dain stood frozen in horror. The slig easily battered his opponent aside. Dain felt his bladder release as the slig turned and looked straight at him. Without thinking, he raised his arms from where they had hung loosely in front of him. He loosed the arrow he held, right at the slig's face. Point blank range. Slig blood spattered his face and chest as the arrow drove into the terrifying visage before him, piercing flesh and smashing bone as it punched through his opponent's head. The slig fell back with a scream, disappearing from sight as quickly as he'd appeared.

Dain drew another arrow and lent over the parapet, catching another slig as he was halfway up the ladder. That one fell back with Dain's arrow driven deep into his neck, knocking a third slig on the ladder behind him to the ground as he fell. Dropping his bow, Dain reached down and grabbed a hold of the ladder, thrusting it out from the wall. As it fell, a crossbow bolt thudded into the wall beside him, a hair's breadth from his arm. Quickly he pulled himself back up behind the wall again.

His heart was pounding. As he reached down to pick up his bow, he realised he was no longer shaking. His bow lay in a pool of blood, whether slig or Algarian he had no time to check. He picked it up and started firing again. A series of shouts and screams drew his attention to his left. A slig warrior had made his way up over the wall and was on the parapet, laying about him murderously with his axe. A second or two later and he was reeling, peppered with arrows. He screamed as he fell forward into the street behind the wall.

The lads who had shot him were there for just that purpose, a second line of defence. Two of them rushed over and plunged their knives into the body as it crashed to the ground. Dain doubted whether that was needed. The slig was surely dead already. He understood the need to make sure, though. They were brave lads. With a pang, he thought of Thom. Where was the youngster? He should have got here by now?

Dain didn't allow himself to follow the thought. Turning back to the wall, he drew another arrow and fired again. The sligs still hadn't breached the line. Here and there warriors were making it to the top, but not in sufficient numbers to overwhelm the defenders. They were being brought down quickly. They hadn't counted on this many defenders. They must have thought there would only be the two dozen Rangers. They hadn't allowed for organised resistance from the rest of the citizens, their ranks swelled by the rural refugees.

As Dain drew and fired again, it seemed to him they weren't making any impression on the number of attackers below them. They might be holding the sligs for the moment, but how long could that last? Thank Mishra they'd sent the women west, he thought. At least Kared would be safe, for now. He'd been given the opportunity to go too. They all had. Only a few of the men had left, though.

The ranger captain had given them a stirring speech. He'd said that if they could hold the sligs here for a while it would give the rest of the province a chance. The sligs had driven all before them over the last several days and the Algarian farmers had run like cattle being herded towards a slaughterhouse. The only chance for the refugees lay in someone making a stand. That would ease the pressure on the surrounding area, the captain had said. It would give the farmers some chance to get away without hindrance from the sligs and it would enable the defenders further west to form a proper line of defence. There was no one else to do it but them, he'd claimed.

There were over one hundred armed men in Kurandir to add to the two dozen Rangers. The captain had said the sligs wouldn't be expecting that. They also had the advantage of the walls. He'd gone on then to point out the debit side of the ledger, how the sligs were a fearsome foe, how they didn't like to lose, how once they'd taken up a fight they rarely retreated, how all they could hope to do was to delay them, not to beat them, not if they were determined to keep on coming, not unless they satiated their desire for killing and plunder before they reached Kurandir.

The men of Kurandir had taken it all in. Incredibly, of the one hundred and seven able-bodied men available to fight, only two had refused the call. Not one person condemned those two. They left silently and without harassment. Those that stayed knew they'd made a grim choice. In a way, they knew it had taken just as much courage to resist the call as it did to respond to it. If anything, the two were envied. Few of those that remained expected to see their loved ones again.

And now, here they were, fighting for their very lives. How many now regretted their decision? How many now wished they'd been the ones to flee? How many wondered how much longer they could last?

The fighting seemed to go on endlessly. Twice Dain had been called on to draw his own sword and fend back sligs from the top of the walls. He was tiring. Then, just as he was wondering how much longer he could keep going, he heard a shout go up, all along the walls. As he drew and fired again, someone grabbed a hold of his shoulder. "Stop firing," his neighbour was shouting. "They're pulling back. Don't waste your arrows."

A cheer went up from along the walls. Dain felt the goose bumps rise all over his body as he began to cheer himself. They'd done it. They'd turned them back. He couldn't believe it. They'd turned back an army of sligs.

After a few moments, when the shouts began to die down, he felt an insidious weariness start to creep up over his limbs, commencing at his feet and continuing right up till it consumed his whole body. It was if it had been hidden there, covered by a blanket, and someone had pulled back the blanket to reveal his fatigue. As his companion slumped down on the wooden floorboards beside him, he did the same, leaning back against the wall for support.

"Get your breath," he heard a ranger call out from nearby. It wasn't the one that had been assigned to their portion of the wall. Dain didn't know what had happened to him and was too tired to try and find out. "Waterboys," the ranger called out. "I want water up here for these men. Now!"

"We did it," exclaimed Dain, raising a slight smile as he turned to his companion. He couldn't recall his name but did remember he was a cooper, from right here in Kurandir.

"Yep," gasped the cooper, clearly out of breath. "I didn't think we were going to make it."

After a while, the waterboy appeared, carrying a bucket and offering ladles of water to the tired defenders slumped along the parapet. Once Dain had taken a long drink, he raised himself up enough to look about him. As he peered along the wall, all the elation he'd felt at their success ebbed out of him. It was a pitiful sight.

Perhaps a quarter of the men who had been with him at the start of the battle were no longer there. Below them, in the street that ran along the inside of the wall, a line of stretcher-bearers was carting bodies away, back into the town. It was clear that some of the bodies were dead men, not just the injured. On the parapet itself, a number of wounded were being tended. Limbs were being bandaged, wounds cleaned, and the more seriously hurt were being helped towards the stairs. It looked like at least half of the defenders had either been wounded or killed in the assault. Here and there the bodies of slig warriors lay. He knew there'd be many more of them that hadn't made it this far. Their bodies must litter the ground at the foot of the walls. Although they had done well, Dain realised the Algarian success had been bought at an appalling cost.

A shout from nearby caused everyone to look up from what they were doing. "They're coming again. Get ready."

Dain's heart sank. It hadn't occurred to him they might come again so quickly. In fact, he'd hoped they might have had their fill. Wearily he dragged himself to his feet. This would be it. They couldn't hold them off a second time.

~~~

Thom dared not move. He lay as still as he could while the sound of marching, booted feet slowly receded into the distance. It had been a close call. He'd been about to cross the road as he made his way across country, back to Jinny and her dad's place, when he'd heard the tramp of feet from over the rise ahead of him. He'd barely had enough time to throw himself over the wooden rails of the fence and into the long grass behind it before the sligs had appeared. From his hiding place he had seen there must have been fifty or more of them, marching three abreast, right down the middle of the road, as if they owned the place.

To all intents and purposes, it seemed to Thom they now did. The folks from all around were clearing out and leaving everything to them. What could they possibly do to stop them anyway? *It would take a lot more than a bunch of hayseeds with pitchforks to do that*, thought Thom. That wasn't his concern right now, though. He had to get back and help Jinny to get away, he had promised her he'd be back for her. As scared as he was, he had got himself into a right pickle. There was no turning back now.

When he'd arrived at Jinny's place earlier in the day he hadn't been able to convince her to leave. Her dad wasn't home. He'd left the previous day to visit his brother over at Brand's Ford and hadn't returned, and Jinny wasn't prepared to leave without him. All Thom could do was get her to pack up some things and wait for him while he fulfilled the promise he'd made to his own father and got a warning to Luc and Prard.

He'd done that, but now there were sligs all over the place and he was having the devil of a time getting back to her. He'd had to abandon his horse some time back; it was impossible to find quick cover from unexpected bands of sligs with a horse to hide as well. Although that had slowed him down considerably, he knew he would never have made it back any other way. Now he was almost there, his thoughts were turning more to Jinny's safety than to his own.

He hoped she had taken his advice about not waiting at the house. He had told her to wait in the orchard where she could keep an eye on the house in case her dad returned. She should be safe there if it was trouble that turned up instead. Thom was glad he had given her that advice. From what he had seen since then, it was clear the sligs were clearing all of the farms and not just concentrating on the villages and settlements.

Although Thom had almost made his way back to her now, it was getting on towards dark and the storm that had been brewing all day was so close he could smell it. Poor Jinny, he thought. If her dad hadn't turned up, and Thom didn't hold out much hope he would, not after what Erl had said about the slig raid on Brand's Ford, then she'd be distraught by now. That's if she hadn't been caught herself.

As he pulled himself to his feet and started to move forward again, Thom felt the first spatters of rain on his head and back. Before he had gone a score of paces, the rain was driving into him, whipped on by the strong easterly wind the storm had brought with it. *At least this will slow down the sligs*, thought Thom, trying to find something positive to lift his hopes. He knew it would also reduce the chances of his running into a raiding party as he made his way across the fields to the orchard. Only a fool, or someone desperate to get someplace in a hurry, would be out and about in this kind of weather.

By the time the orchard came into sight, he was soaked to the skin. The rain had eased slightly after its initial onslaught, or rather, the wind that had been whipping it up into his face had eased, but that hadn't saved him from a total drenching. From where he stood, he could just make out both the orchard and Jinny's house through the curtain of rain that shrouded the open fields in front of him. There was no sign of life at the house. It stood in total darkness, as he had expected.

Slowly and cautiously, moving from cover to cover, Thom crossed the remaining ground between himself and the orchard. Once he got in among the trees, he began looking around for Jinny. It wasn't a big orchard and he knew that if she was there she should be easy to find.

"Jinny," he whispered hoarsely into the darkness, trying to fight down the desperation he was feeling. He'd been hoping she would see him coming and come out from wherever it was she was hiding as soon as he got there. When there was no answer, he called out again, feeling his hopes rapidly sinking. She should be close by, within earshot. He wouldn't know where to begin to search if she wasn't here where she should be.

His stomach did a somersault as a frightened little voice came out of the gloom.

"Thom."

Turning in the direction he thought the voice had come from, Thom was startled to see Jinny drop down from one of the trees about a dozen or so paces away from him. She'd been hiding up in the branches. That was why he hadn't been able to see her.

As soon as she hit the ground, she darted across the space between them and threw herself against him, almost bowling him over as she did so. Wrapping her arms around him, she hugged him tightly to her. He could feel her slender body shaking against his as she sobbed out her pent-up fear.

"Oh, Thom! I was so scared. I thought you weren't coming back. Dad hasn't come and I saw sligs down at the house a while back. I think they've gone now. What are we going to do?"

Thom had been right to think she'd be distraught. The poor girl was almost frightened to death. He knew she must have waited and waited, wondering if he would ever come back for her, and wondering what she would do if he didn't.

"I told you I'd come back," said Thom, holding Jinny to him and swallowing his own emotions. He thought it ironic that he'd dreamt of doing this so often, of holding her in his arms, and now he was finally able to do so the circumstances were too tragic for him to gain any satisfaction from it. "What we gotta do," he continued, "is get out of here. Da said we gotta make our way to Kurandir."

"But what about my pa?" cried Jinny, almost hysterically.

"Shhhhhhh," soothed Thom. "Did you leave a note in the house like I said?"

"Y-yes."

"Well if he does come back here he'll know you got away. Okay? Jinny, we can't wait any longer. Your da wouldn't want you to wait here until you got caught. He'd want you to get yourself to somewhere safe. You know that."

"I guess. I don't know what to do, Thom. You'll have to work it out for both of us. I'm so scared. Those sligs looked horrible. I thought they were going to come up into the orchard."

"Don't worry," soothed Thom, stroking Jinny's back as he did so. Her clothes were as soaked as his were. They clung to her like a second skin. "We'll be okay."

Thom wished that he thought that was true. It was dark now and they were both soaked to the skin. He hadn't given a thought to what he would do once he found Jinny. All he had focused on all day was getting back to her and hoping she would be there waiting for him. Now he had achieved that goal, he realised he would have to focus on getting them both to safety. They were a long way from that at the moment.

"Are you sure the sligs have gone now?" he asked Jinny. "They didn't stay in the house?"

"No. I saw them leave. I don't think any stayed behind and I haven't seen any lights."

"Well, let's start off by seeing if we can get some dry clothes, and maybe some blankets."

It took them a while. They approached the house very cautiously, both unwilling to take the risk that Jinny was wrong. Once they were sure the sligs had left, the first thing they did was get into some dry clothes. Thom borrowed a jacket and some pants that belonged to Jinny's dad. Then they got some blankets and some weather jackets to provide them with cover until they found a dry spot well away from the house. Leaving the dwelling, they made their way west, steering away from any other farmhouses or villages in case there were sligs there sheltering from the weather. Their luck held and, after a while, the rain stopped and they were able to move along at a faster pace.

Although it was dark, Thom urged Jinny on. He knew they would travel much more safely at night than during the day, despite their fatigue. The plan he had formed was for them to travel as much as they could in the dark and to find somewhere secure and dry to rest up during the day. That meant they would need to be far away from Jinny's place before they stopped again.

Somehow they found the energy to keep going, but they were both desperately tired. They didn't talk much, and when they did, it was in whispers. The combination of their exhaustion and the worries each was harbouring about what might have befallen their parents was sufficient to keep them both occupied. Without anything having been said, they also sensed the need to travel quietly. As unlikely as it was, they didn't dare take the chance of waking some band of sligs that had decided to bunk down out in the middle of an open field.

When they finally stopped, it was almost morning. They bedded down under a little lean-to some farmer had built to provide cover for his horse. It was close enough to a grove of trees that they figured they should be able to get away fairly quickly if anything came their way. As much as Thom would have felt safer in among the trees, he knew there was more rain on its way. They needed to keep as dry as they could for as long as they could.

After they had eaten a little, he let Jinny sleep while he kept watch. The poor girl fell asleep within minutes. Thom longed for rest himself and found it a struggle to keep his eyelids from closing. He willed himself to stay awake, knowing they had come through too much to throw caution to the wind now.

When the sun finally rose, he saw the spot they had chosen was a good one. They were on the side of a gentle slope and could see anyone approaching from a long distance away, unless they came from out of the grove of trees that covered the top of the hill behind them. Thom knew the area well enough to know that the latter was unlikely.

He saw no sign of the sligs as the day progressed. The rain returned about mid-morning and kept up a constant drizzle throughout the rest of the day; not that he saw much of the second half of it. When Jinny finally woke around midday, he let her take over the lookout duties. As reluctant as he was to hand over that role, he knew that he had to get some rest as well. They would need to cover a lot of ground when night came and they both needed to be rested enough to do so. Although they still had a bit of food left, it wouldn't last them long. They needed to be in Kurandir before it ran out and that meant pressing on with as little delay as possible.

As Thom drifted off to sleep, his thoughts went out to his parents again. He knew they'd be worrying about him. His father would be fine, but his mother would worry herself sick until she saw him again. By his reckoning, if he and Jinny could keep making good time under the cover of darkness they should be in Kurandir the following night. That would be fine for him, but he knew poor Jinny was hoping her father would be there waiting for her. Thom didn't think that was likely to be the case.

His parents were the lucky ones. They'd had warning and been able to get out before the sligs had come. Thom knew that Jinny's dad wouldn't have had a chance. Brand's Ford had been caught totally unprepared. Jinny's dad was dead now, of that he was certain.

CHAPTER 15

"And what course do you recommend, Count Regulus?"

The moment the count had been dreading had arrived. The Queen of Algaria had listened attentively as the Guardian's assistant had recounted his message in the presence of the royal court. She had then sat impassively while her council of advisers had questioned the quickling, going over and over his message to ensure that nothing had been missed. Then, when he had finished and been dismissed, she had waited patiently while those same advisers had debated the matter before her. It was a procedure Regulus was very familiar with and one that had served the Algarian Queen well over the years.

As usual, the advisers were divided as to how the Algarians should respond to this alarming development. Regulus knew that the Queen had composed her circle of advisers with that very purpose in mind. He was aware that Elissa liked to ensure she was able to consider each of the many perspectives that might be brought to bear on an issue. The advisers she had chosen to surround herself with provided a well-balanced mixture from bold adventurers right through to conservative and cautious diplomats. It was rare that they formed a unanimous view on how to proceed.

Regulus also knew that the Queen would turn to him last of all. Once she had considered the views of all of the others, it was her custom to then turn to him for his opinion. It wasn't the weight of that responsibility that filled Regulus with dread on this occasion, he had already decided on the course of action he would recommend. What filled him with dread was that he knew his Queen so well. He knew that she would already have formed a similar view on this matter and that she sought his opinion only to confirm what she already knew they must do.

Turning his back to the others, Regulus lifted his eyes, locking on to those of his sovereign and seeing his own apprehension mirrored in her gaze. Taking a deep breath, he uttered the words he knew would come back to haunt him over the days that would follow. "We must retreat, my Queen."

"No." The cry went up from all around the room, all parties taking it up with a mixture of shock and indignation.

"Quiet." The Queen's strident voice silenced the clamour abruptly. "Let Regulus speak."

"We must retreat," Regulus repeated, turning to face his colleagues and pausing for a moment to ensure he had the attention of all in the room.

He was a tall man, as tall as anyone there, and his mien was an imposing one. His wavy black hair and closely trimmed beard framed a ruggedly handsome face that had turned the head of more than one of the ladies of the court over the years. Though his bearing ensured he stood out from his fellows, his attire was similar to that of his fellow advisers. His long maroon frock coat was bordered with gold twine in keeping with the fashion of the Algarian court. Only the star-shaped emerald that adorned its black velvet lapel marked him out from others as one of the Queen's inner circle of advisers. The high sheen of polish on the red leather boots that protruded from beneath his high waisted, tapered, black pants reflected the flickering torchlight that lit the royal audience chamber. All eyes turned to him now as he pronounced his view on the best course of action for Algaria in this fatal hour.

"We must retreat, but we must do so in an orderly fashion," he continued. As he spoke, his voice slowly rose. His words were rousing and inspiring, even to these advisers, many of whom had never lifted a weapon in defence of the realm. "When we take a stand, it must be only for brief periods. Just long enough to enable an orderly retreat and to allow the defences here at the heart of the realm to be bolstered. We cannot hope to stand against the sligs for long on such a wide front as we now face, not without the aid of a Guardian.

"It is only when that front has contracted sufficiently for our smaller numbers to have an even chance that we can then draw the line in the sand.

And stand then we will. And when we do, we will call upon the valour of the cream of the twelve great houses of the realm. Then, when the sligs have extended their lines of supply, and when they are far from the lands they know, then we will smite our foe and send them reeling back in confusion and dismay. That is my counsel."

And then, thought Regulus, as his colleagues burst into applause, swayed by his rousing speech, then if the Guardians have not yet come to our aid we will surely see what is to become of the Algarian people, whether we will survive this test, or whether we will pass from the history of Ilythia like so many peoples have done before us.

Having said what he had to, Regulus stood silently, turning once more to face his Queen and allowing the acclaim from his colleagues to slowly subside. Just as he had held the attention of the room while he spoke, all eyes turned now to the Queen. A hush fell over the room as it became apparent she too was waiting for the applause and murmurs to subside.

From her high-backed chair atop the dais that held the central position in the royal audience chamber, Queen Elissa looked every inch in command of her own emotions, regardless of the trepidation that was rippling through her council of advisers. Regulus knew that it was a practised look. Only her eyes betrayed her, and even then only to him. What the others saw was the commanding presence of the unchallenged ruler of the mighty kingdom of Algaria. The beautiful young woman atop the dais was the picture of a capable ruler of a powerful kingdom, from the glittering diadem atop her long golden hair right down to the jewel-bedecked white satin slippers that covered her feet. Only Regulus saw the barest hint of uncertainty, betrayed by the slight flicker of her eyes as she glanced his way. Only Regulus saw the vulnerability that hid behind the royal façade.

"Well spoken, Count Regulus," said the Queen, with the mere hint of a smile for her most trusted adviser. "And so it shall be. Only, we must look to our northern frontier as well. As unlikely as it might seem, we cannot run the risk of the sligs opening a second front with us under-prepared in that quarter." The nod of heads around the room showed that the Queen's decision was widely regarded as a wise one. Turning to the Marshall of the Realm, the only member of the council permitted to bear arms in the presence of the royal personage, Queen Elissa issued the direction that would now set Algaria on a course from which there would be no turning back. "Count Brassilius, Marshall of the Realm, you have heard my judgment. I leave it to you to oversee the retreat and the preparation of the necessary defences."

As the Queen rose from her throne, all turned to her and bowed, as was the custom of the Algarians. "This council is concluded," said the Queen as she swept out of the room. "Count Regulus, if you would join me in my sitting room."

Count Regulus nodded to the Queen and followed in her wake as she left the room supported by her attendants. Some of the other councillors took this as their cue to depart, no doubt anxious to be off to protect their own interests, particularly those with homes or businesses in the east of the realm where the brunt of the slig offensive would be first felt.

Some minutes later, when the Queen had dismissed her attendants and she and the Count were comfortably seated in a room closer to her own apartments, a room where they often sat and discussed the business of the realm, the Queen and her most favoured adviser were finally free to speak more openly of the situation the nation was now facing.

"So, Regulus, we must hazard all and hope that either the Guardians come to their senses or that the sligs run out of puff so far from their homes. It is a dangerous course we have set for the nation."

"Yes, my Queen," answered Regulus, his countenance now betraying the doubts he hadn't permitted the rest of the council of advisers to see. "I don't see any other way. We're in no position yet to meet this threat in the east. I might add that I think your counsel regarding the northern frontier a particularly judicious one. I doubt the finesse of the sligs to open a second front, but then who would have expected such a well-planned frontal assault as they're currently conducting?"

The Queen nodded as Regulus spoke, but the frown on her face betrayed her concern. "If only I hadn't listened to the Council of the Guardians when they promised us their aid in the autumn," she responded when he had finished. Elissa had dropped her mask of conviction and authority now she was alone with Regulus.

"Don't blame yourself, my Queen." Regulus' heart went out to his sovereign. She had reigned for barely five years since the untimely death of her father. Although she had a fine mind and a compassionate heart, she was still raw and inexperienced. Regulus knew that was why she depended so heavily on the council. Despite the fact that she often perceived the right path for her people, she hadn't the experience to quell the doubts that accompanied such heavy choices. Regulus knew that she had come to respect his own counsel more for the reassurance it gave her than for anything else.

"We all believed the Council would send us their aid. They have done thus for centuries. Don't chide yourself for not knowing that now, of all times, the Guardians would fail us. And don't despair, my Queen. They may yet come to our aid. Clearly, Kell and Tarak intend to do what they can for us once they are able."

"Yes, yes. I know you're right. Nevertheless, it has cost us dearly. Instead of spending the winter preparing for war, we did little more than dither. We could have done so much more for our eastern defences in that time. How many of my people will pay for that lapse with their lives? That is a heavy burden to bear, Regulus, a very heavy burden."

"I fear it won't be the last time you'll have to shoulder such a burden in the crisis ahead. That is the price you must pay for the role you play, my liege. I know it weighed down your father as well. Clearly, despite the length of his reign, he found it no easier in his later years than he did in his youth. For all that, as much as I would like it to be otherwise, it is not a burden that any can truly share with you. It is yours and yours alone. All I can suggest is that you make the choices you know are right. The gods will exact their own price in the end, no matter which way you turn."

Although Regulus said the words, his heart wished it were otherwise. His love for Elissa went far deeper than that of an adviser for his sovereign, as she well knew. He had courted her before the death of the king and she had returned his love freely in those halcyon days. On her ascension to the throne, Elissa had chosen to put aside her feelings for him and had asked him to do the same. She had said that as sovereign she had no right to selfishly pursue her own happiness. Her duty was to her people, not to herself. He had respected her decision and abided by it, outwardly at least.

Elissa had come to accept that he couldn't truly put aside the depth of feeling he held in his heart, even if he could maintain the appropriate public façade. Eventually, she had even confided that she couldn't do so any more than he could. Nonetheless, they had agreed, he more reluctantly than she, it would seem. Whatever they wanted their relationship to be, it could no longer be anything more than one of friendship; close friendship certainly, but no more than that.

Regulus hadn't pushed the issue. Although there was no reason why they couldn't marry, and there was never any question that if they did so she would still be the sovereign and not he, he hadn't wanted to add to the pressure she clearly felt as such a young leader. He no longer spoke of his love for her. He kept his feelings for the woman who was his Queen locked securely away, out of sight if not out of mind. The knowledge that Elissa knew how he really felt was all he had left to sustain him. It was enough. It had to be.

"Thank you." Elissa looked up at her friend with a wan smile. "You know I would rather that someone else had been born to this role than me. But you're right. That is not to be. It is my role and I must play it out as best I can. Only, I'd rather I was making decisions about taxes, or the law courts. I have no mind for military stratagems."

"You're wrong, Elissa. You have a fine mind and I have no doubt of your ability to apply it equally well to war as to finance or legislation. Trust in your judgement and continue as you have done until now. Listen to your advisers and weigh up their opinions. Then listen to your own heart. It hasn't led you wrong to date."

Elissa looked up with a start at his words. Regulus detected a moist sheen to her eyes as, after a brief pause, she spoke to him again, softly now and with a sense of suppressed emotions. "I wish that I *could* follow my heart, Regulus. I wish that so much sometimes my body aches."

~~~

Golkar looked up from his desk with a start. A being of power, another Guardian, in fact, was approaching Tu-atha. The spell of detection he had cast was designed to ensure he was alerted as soon as someone with the capacity to use magic passed within a league of his residence. He had just sensed that warning. A being of power, one of his colleagues by the strength and the nature of the feeling he had sensed, was approaching his house.

For a moment he considered whether it might be Tug returning with the girl. There was no mistaking the signature of a Guardian, however. It was definitely either Kell or Tarak. Golkar wondered what would bring either of them to him at this particular moment. He rarely received visits from his colleagues. If anything, he actively discouraged that level of personal interaction with the other two wizards.

Trying to suppress the worrying feeling that Sara might have somehow managed to elude Tug and his companions and, worse still, have gotten in contact with one of the other Guardians, Golkar closed the spellbook in front of him and rose from the table. Whatever it was about, this was unlikely to be a social call. He had best be armed for every eventuality.

Crossing his chamber, Golkar stopped in front of a finely wrought oaken cabinet. Reaching into his tunic he drew out a golden key that hung on a chain about his neck. The key slipped smoothly into the lock at the centre of the cabinet. Golkar felt his pulse quicken as he heard the mechanism turn when he slowly twisted his hand. Replacing the key within his tunic once more, he reached for the doors, pulling them open to reveal three shelves, on the uppermost of which sat a small ebony chest, the cupboard's only item. It still sat just where he had put it all those years ago.

Gently lifting the chest, Golkar turned and placed it on the table behind him. Pausing to consider the object for only a moment, the wizard cautiously opened its hinged top and gazed down at the gleaming object within. The long dagger that lay there, with its slightly curved blade and jewel-encrusted hilt, gleamed unnaturally in the soft candlelight.

With a wry grin, Golkar reached down and clasped his hand around the rough hilt of the dagger, feeling the precious stones that studded its length pressing into his palm and sensing the unnatural warmth of the object against his skin. Lifting the dagger from the box, he couldn't help but marvel at the object, knowing that the soft glow from the wicked blade was a portent of the awesome power of the thing. He had spent considerable time and effort in acquiring it and now, perhaps, it would finally be put to the acid test.

As far as Golkar could ascertain, there were only two things in the whole of Ilythia that had the capacity to overcome the invulnerability of the Guardians; two weapons the Guardians had reason to fear. One was the human female, Sara, so recently brought to their world. The other was this blade. 'DemonClaw' Tanis had called it, for he was its source. His diary had referred to it, just one brief mention was all there had been, but it had been enough to put Golkar on to its trail.

He had spent years searching for it once he'd become aware of it, knowing Tanis had hidden it away, but not knowing where, or if the mage had retrieved it and taken it with him when he had left Ilythia. Then, after a long and fruitless search, an obscure note in the diary, one he had not hitherto connected with the blade, had led him to its resting place. Of all places, Tanis had hidden it in the Hall of Embassy, in the Council Chambers high up on Ral Partha. A small panel, cunningly hidden under the large marble table right in front of the spot where Tanis' empty seat still stood had been its resting place for centuries.

Having found it, Golkar hadn't been sure what to do with it. And so he had locked it away, sensing, perhaps like Tanis, that one day it might be useful. Many were the times he had wondered why Tanis had acquired it, and for what purpose. And why did he hide it in the Hall of Embassy of all places? Had he intended to use it against his apprentices, or had he felt a need to protect himself from them?

And what was it that made this weapon so deadly, so much more so than any of the wondrous blades Tanis could have acquired here in Ilythia? As Golkar knew, the crystal shard that Tanis had bestowed on each of them generated a constant shield of protection no normal blade or weapon could penetrate, though spells were another matter altogether. The Guardians were each bound to the shard they had been given now, and, in turn, their shard was bound to them. It was that binding that guaranteed their longevity, just as it created the shield that protected them from all but the most powerful of spells.

But this blade, DemonClaw, forged, according to Tanis' notes, in the firepits of a world of demons, could slice through that shield almost as if it didn't exist, like a hot knife through butter. And how did Golkar know this was so? Because he had tested it on himself. For the first time in the history of Ilythia, he had drawn blood from a Guardian with a weapon, his blood. Oh, what a thrilling sight that had been! That was the first time he had felt some appreciation of the sligs' insatiable thirst for the blood of their enemies. And now he thirsted for more.

Gently, and carefully, Golkar eased the blade under his belt, feeling its warmth even through his thick clothing. Taking his wand from beside the closed spell book, Golkar turned and strode purposefully from the room, heading for the staircase. Once outside of the house, he took up his position, seated on a bench and leaning back casually in the sunlight against the stone wall of Tu-atha. There he awaited the arrival of his colleague, wondering which of them it might be, Kell or Tarak.

He had only been there a short while, perhaps a half an hour, when three horses emerged from the tree line and slowly approached the house. "Ho, Golkar," cried the lead rider with a wave of his hand as the horsemen drew to a halt a short distance from where he sat. "Greetings, my friend."

It was Tarak. With him were two rustics, *from the vale where Tarak played with his herbs no doubt*, thought Golkar derisively. He often wondered why someone with the awesome power the Guardians held would want to waste his time dabbling with plants.

"Greetings, Tarak," he replied, keeping his voice as casual as he could, despite the excitement he could feel building within him. "What brings you and your friends all this way? I thought you'd be busy gardening at this time of the year, pruning your roses or something like that."

"Ha," laughed Tarak, letting a grin split the serious look on his face. "Roses are pruned in late winter, after the last frost, as you probably know, Golkar. Now don't try and bait me about my work. I know you well enough to know what you're up to, so you're wasting your breath."

"Indeed. I guess you do at that. So, what does bring you all this way then?"

"Come now, Golkar," exclaimed Tarak, shifting in his saddle, whether nervously or uncomfortably Golkar wasn't sure. "I think you know that as well."

"I think you had better enlighten me," replied Golkar, still slumped casually against the wall of the house, unwilling to concede anything until he had to.

"Well, to get straight to the point after such a long ride, I hear you've been consorting with the sligs. And as if that wasn't outlandish enough, I also hear you've been plotting against Kell and myself, with the aid of some human from another world, it is said. What say you to all of this?" Having said what he'd come to say, Tarak fixed Golkar with a stare, clearly watching intently for a reaction to the allegations he had voiced.

Golkar smiled as he rose from where he had sat while Tarak had spoken, concentrating on doing nothing to betray the true mixture of emotions he was feeling as he did so. Although he was excited at the prospect of where this encounter might lead, he was in fact quite shaken by what Tarak had said. It was obvious now that Sara *had* escaped from Tug, Tarak was certainly aware of her existence at least, if not much more. He had also managed to find out about Golkar's dealings with the sligs. Golkar wondered if this meant Tug had been captured as well. He didn't think Sara would have known anything about the sligs that she could pass on to his colleagues, so that meant they must have obtained their information from Tug.

"I say I'm surprised to hear you would even entertain such absurdities," exclaimed Golkar with a laugh. "Who's been spreading this nonsense about me? And what madness would induce you to give credence to such a tale? Come now, is this some jest of yours?"

"This is no joking matter, but I'm sorry if I've offended you." Tarak was already beginning to show some sign of back-pedalling. Perhaps he didn't know as much as Golkar had feared he might. "You can understand that such serious allegations as these cannot be taken lightly. So you deny you've been plotting with the sligs? Why then have you not yet put an end to their raids on the Algarians, as you undertook to do at the last Council meeting? If you had done that, then there'd be no prospect of such a rumour being given any credence."

"So, am I to be condemned by my own colleagues, by my two fellows who I've worked with for the good of Ilythia for over half a millennia, simply because I've been tardy in carrying out my duties? Oh Tarak, that is too much." Golkar was in full flight now and had moved from bemusement to a show of righteous indignation. "I didn't expect that from you of all people, friend. Kell, I know, would only be too willing to countenance such nonsense. His rivalry with me eats at him like a canker. But I thought better of you."

"I didn't say I believed these allegations, Golkar. I have simply asked for your answer to them. To be truthful, I did find them hard to believe. That's why I've come here, to hear from your own lips your response to such spurious allegations."

Inwardly Golkar beamed. The fish had taken the hook. Now all he needed to do was reel him in and finish the job. "Well, now you've heard what I have to say. I demand you tell me who is spreading this poison about me. I have a right to know that."

"That will serve no purpose Golkar. I'll not betray my sources. But what of the second matter I raised? What do you know of this human that is alleged to have come here from another world?"

"Alleged by whom? I know nothing more about all this than what you've told me. Though I have to say that this is even more ridiculous than that nonsense about the sligs. You and I both know very well that it isn't possible to travel between worlds. If I remember correctly, even Tanis himself doubted whether that could be done. If this isn't simply more mischievous invention, then I daresay its source might be found in the bottom of a tankard of ale. Really, Tarak, I can't believe that you've come all this way to ask me to defend myself against alehouse gossip. What's really going on here?"

"I'm sorry I've questioned you so, Golkar," soothed Tarak, obviously intent on extricating himself from the awkward situation he had got himself into. "But these are serious charges and they can't be just lightly brushed aside. I didn't say I believed them, but they have been put about and they need to be dealt with. My feeling is that a special session of the Council may be called for. I'd like to see us all sit down to some plain talking about the whole matter, all three of us, that is. We might revisit the slig situation at the same time."

"You *have* taken this seriously, haven't you?" said Golkar. "Well, I too would like to get to the bottom of this. If someone is stirring dissension among us, we must deal with that, firmly. Come. Let me offer you and your companions a cool drink, as I would have done earlier if you hadn't jumped down my throat as soon as you arrived." As he said this Golkar allowed himself a smile and beckoned to Tarak to dismount and join him inside, approaching him and continuing to talk as he did so. "Then you can tell me who or what is behind all this mischief. It would seem someone thinks there is something to gain by setting the Guardians against each other."

Tarak began to dismount from his horse, not seeming to notice at first that his two companions made no move to join him. As his foot reached the ground, he happened to glance up at Nate. The vacant stare on his face both surprised him and alerted him to the fact that something was wrong. Sensing that Golkar had reached his side, Tarak spun around towards him. He had barely begun to turn when he felt a searing pain spear agonisingly into his torso. Looking down, he was dumbfounded to see a curved blade in the wizard's hand. Although it was dripping blood, Tarak found it hard to grasp what was happening. It had all been so quick and unexpected and the sensation of pain was so far out of his experience that his mind was struggling to decipher the strange sensations that were enveloping him. Then, as he looked up at Golkar's face in disbelief, he sensed a rapid movement on the periphery of his vision. The searing pain stabbed into his vitals again.

This time Golkar held the knife deep within his fellow Guardian, twisting it viciously as he did so. His other hand held the wounded wizard's shoulder in a vice-like grip, holding him firmly in place with his will as much as with his physical strength as Tarak's body threatened to sway towards him.

"You made one simple mistake, you fool," he snarled, his face only inches from the contorted features of his colleague. "You underestimated me." With that, Golkar wrenched the blade from the herb-master. With a soft groan, Tarak slumped to the ground at his feet.

Bending down, Golkar turned the head of his fallen enemy and quite calmly and deliberately drew his blade across the exposed throat, quickly jumping back as a spurt of blood gushed out from the terrible wound.

Golkar stood over the fallen wizard, gloating at the pitiful shape at his feet. As he watched, to his surprise it began to wither before his very eyes, slowly at first and then more quickly, contracting and curling up as it did so like an autumn leaf, only in this case in a matter of moments, not weeks.

And then it was done. Nothing remained of the former Guardian, or of the all-powerful crystal shard each of them always carried with them, than a small pile of detritus which quickly dispersed as a sudden breeze took it up and carried it away across the clearing. They were both gone. Just as the wizard and his shard had been linked in life, so they had shared the same fate. All that was left was a blackened patch of burnt grass at Golkar's feet.

Although his heaving chest and flushed face betrayed his emotional state, there was no one there to witness his triumph. Tarak's two companions still sat astride their own horses, staring vacantly into the distance, held by the spell of compulsion that Golkar had cast upon them as he had moved in to accomplish his task. For the moment they were blissfully unaware of the event that had just been played out only paces away from them.

Turning back again, he looked down once more at the blackened turf, the only remnant now of a once powerful foe, feeling for just one moment a tinge of sadness. He had no regrets at what he had done. On the contrary, he felt quite exhilarated by it. He couldn't help but wonder, however, at the ease with which he had despatched one of the Guardians of Ilythia.

END

OF

BOOK

ONE

Excerpt

from the conclusion to this story in:

CHRONICLES OF THE ILAROI: BOOK TWO

WHEN ALL THE LEAVES HAVE FALLEN

The Queen of Algaria wept silently as she stared out across the plain that spread from the walls of the city to the distant hills beyond. Though the battle was over, the signs of the carnage that had taken place only a few short hours earlier were still there for all to see. Other than an occasional sob or gasp from those around her, for several minutes, all were silent. The enormity of the situation could not help but weigh heavily on every observer.

"So many lives," she finally exclaimed in a hoarse whisper, struggling to keep her emotions in check as she spoke. "Such senseless slaughter, and for what purpose? This morning as I watched the ranks of our soldiers as they assembled I was so proud of their courage. I couldn't help but feel their vitality their vigour, their hope. Now . . . now it's like a forest floor in autumn covered in dead and decaying leaves. So many dead, from both sides. So many who will never return home again."

After a few moments of silence, she finally gave vent to the anger that was quickly displacing her grief.

"This is Golkar's doing," she exclaimed more loudly, turning her face away from her companions as she spoke to hide the tears welling up in her eyes. "What will he do when all of the leaves have fallen? What further horrors will he inflict on Ilythia then?"

ABOUT THE AUTHOR

Mark McCabe was born in Brisbane, Australia, later moved to Sydney and then to Canberra, the Australian capital city, where he completed a career in the Australian Government and Australian Capital Territory's public service agencies.

Upon retiring, Mark and his family moved to New Zealand and took up residence near Dunedin.

Mark holds a Bachelor of Arts majoring in Classics, Latin and English from the Australian National University.

Mark's favoured genres are fantasy (predominantly epic and high fantasy) and science fiction, although he does hope to write a series of crime novels at some stage in the future. He cites David Gemmell, Jack Vance and Ursula Le Guin as key inspirations and influences.

In his spare time, Mark is an amateur photographer and a keen student of the classics, with a particular focus on Rome as well as ancient myths and legends such as the Trojan Cycle.

Author website: https://markmccabeauthor.com